HAPPILY EVER BEFORE

BY

AIMEE PITTA

MELISSA PETERMAN

DEDICATION

For my amazing parents Rose and Tom who never stopped believing in me and for Lori, Andrea, Stephanie and Deanna my wonderful, crazy, supportive and always inspiring sisters who never let me give up. Without them I'm seriously nothing.

Aimee

For Pam and Dave Peterman who never flinched when I told them I wanted to be an actress and are my biggest fans. To John Brady for still making me laugh and always doing the dishes. To Riley Brady, you are the best thing your dad and I ever did and I'm sorry for telling you your Etch-A-Sketch was an I Pad.

Melissa

What you're about to read is the almost totally true story of two sisters. A modern day tale of love lost, love won, impatience, sacrifice, friendship, sex, loyalty, honesty, and at times, indecision, drunkenness, flatulence, and cookie dough. The names, places, and situations haven't been changed to protect the innocent, because these gals are far from innocent, but some things have been embellished for creative license, which we are legally required to say to ensure that our creative license won't be revoked.

Prologue

Once Upon A Time, and not a random far-away fairytale time, but 1991 to be exact, when hair was big and music was loud, there were two sisters, Grace and Clair. Sure there were other sisters living in Chicago, but these two, the Higgins sisters, are who we're concerned with. One was a dark haired Goth chick, with a penchant for Boone's Apple wine and guys who didn't respect her, and the other was a naive bookworm with a daddy complex who had just been dumped for the first time in her life. Clair was the younger of the two; the fair-haired sister. Every fairytale has one, but at this moment, Grace's light brown locks were dyed midnight black, giving Clair a role that wasn't exactly hers for the taking—hair wise that is. Clair's reaction to her father's surprising death when she was fourteen made her realize that life was out of control. Their father died while shoveling snow early one morning. Unfortunately, for Daddy Higgins, the snowplow failed to see him as he shoveled off the driveway and ran him down. Then to add insult to injury, it covered him with four feet of snow as it cleared the street. Later that day, while Clair and Grace where building a snowman, they found a little something that wasn't a corncob pipe or two eyes made out of coal. It was Daddy Higgins wearing a confused and, it goes without saying, frozen expression on his face. After that, he forever became their "Popsicle."

Clair decided shortly after to control everything she could control, so that she would be better prepared for any other nasty surprises along the way. She also came to the conclusion that snow was evil, snowplows were murderers, and that ice, even on the hottest Chicago day, was nobody's' friend. Now, the trouble with planning, and what Clair will learn, is that even the things we plan can't be controlled, but we're getting ahead of ourselves. Right now it's 1991 and Clair had planned the following: at twenty-seven years of age she was to marry Ralph Macchio, he of "Karate Kid" fame; become an Accountant; make Vice President at some important accounting firm that had five names, such as Friedlander, Smith, Wong, O'Brien, and Dakota; become Partner at said accounting firm; and have exactly two kids by the time she was thirty-five. Clair had done the math and she knew that if she was even one millisecond off her plan she would never be able to retire at sixty-five. And really isn't that what life was all about?

Now, Grace, she with the midnight black hair, had nothing planned. Well, apart from being a librarian, a chosen career because she reasoned that if she was on tour with her band Death Parade and they inexplicably got into some horrible fight and vowed never to play together again, she could find a job in whatever city she was in because—duh—every city had libraries! Logically, it made sense. What didn't make sense was whether or not Grace had given any thought to what it meant to be a librarian and if she'd even enjoy a career as one. As the first born, many would expect that because it has been psychologically proven, Grace would be the planner and Clair would be the wild child. To be honest, for a short period of time, a time we will refer to as BPP (Before Popsicle Passed), Grace had been known to plan out her fair share of activities and life goals and Clair did have a penchant for streaking and rebel rousing. Grace, with her midnight black hair, green eyes and pale complexion, was just as shocked as Clair when they found their Popsicle that random afternoon. At that moment, Grace also learned that life was uncontrollable and, therefore, decided she would never plan another thing for as long as she lived. Life, she learned, should be lived and planning every single second of your life meant that you weren't actually living it. Because she was in school studying to be a librarian at the time of the incident, she wasn't going to rock the boat. Her family, especially her mom, Diane, was in shock and so, for Grace, the routine of going to school was something of a relief. It meant she didn't have to think. The problem that Grace will eventually come to learn with not making any life plans is that you inevitably wake up extremely confused from your self-prescribed coma and wonder what the hell happened to your life. Oh, and APD (After Popsicle's Death), Grace decided that she'd never get attached to just one guy and sex was part of life and life was supposed to be fun, and... well, you get the picture, but that's neither here, nor there!

Here is where an inevitable pact was made in the basement of the Higgins' household on a bitterly cold Saturday night as they watched a Lifetime original movie marathon. "There" is the opening in the next chapter as the pact is set in motion nearly sixteen years later. But, because tales of what actually transpired will be told again, here is what you'll need to know for now:

There was a blizzard, there was the sister's aversion to snow, there was no parental supervision, but there was a case of Boone's Farm wine that Grace had accepted as payment for the Death

Parade's gig at Jason Freidman's Bar Mitzvah, and there was, as there always will be in some part of the world, a Lifetime original movie marathon. That night, after an excess of drinking and being moved beyond belief by the plights of McKeon, Bertinelli and Gilbert, the Holy Grail of Lifetime original movies, the sisters made a pact. The pact was simplicity at its best and in their drunken stupor they wrote it down and signed it for prosperity.

> *If your husband cheats on you with the babysitter, that slut Tori Spelling, then tries to kill you, I slovenly promise to kill him. If your son or daughter wants to be a cheerleader and if you kill the cheerleader who was better than your kid, I will appear as a character witness and tell them your hand slipped and I will help you bury the body because that's what Aunts do, and if you can't have a baby... I will steal you a Chinese baby or rent you my womb.*
>
>

Grace Higgins
Clair Higgins
February 2nd, 1991
>

It goes without saying that the word slovenly was meant to read as solemnly and that Aunts buy you toys and spoil you rotten—not bury bodies for you, but when one is drunk, forming a cognitive sentence and being politically correct is a most difficult task. Now you're officially ready for "There," but before you go, there are a few things you should know. Over the years, Grace and Clair remained close. They loved and respected each other as most sisters who don't appear on Dr. Phil or The Jerry Springer show do, but we would be lying if we didn't say they weren't just a tiny bit confused about their lives...

Chapter 1

The offices of The City of Chicago's 911 headquarters were, in a word, drab. They needed to be drab. They needed to be devoid of color, imagination, and inspiration, so that the 911 Operators could concentrate on the actual calls that came in. There was no downloading music, gossip, or web site surfing in this place. Saving lives was serious business and The City of Chicago respected that. Grace Higgins, who was now thirty-five years old, had survived a life thus far without planning. After a year of arduous training and test taking, she ended up as a 911 Operator. If you're wondering where she was prior to becoming a 911 Operator, you're not the only one. Grace has been wondering that ever since she inexplicably awoke from her self-prescribed coma at the ripe old age of thirty-three. Upon waking, she discovered that she hated being a librarian, that she had no idea why Death Parade had broken up, that at thirty-three she was the same age as Jesus when he died, and that Jesus had accomplished way more than she had at the same age. He walked on water, fed thousands of people off of one loaf of bread and seven fishes, and, well, he came back from the dead. And so, because of Jesus, Grace's letter of resignation still hangs in the break room at the Newberry Public Library. It simply states "Jesus Made Me Do It." Grace quit her job and embarked on a personal quest that has lasted over two years. After she woke up like Sleeping Beauty from the cold wet kiss of reality and before she became a 911 Operator, Grace had been many things to many people. She was a barber, massage therapist, barista, donut maker, bank teller, nanny, dog walker, cashier, postman, waitress, phone sex operator, house painter, cleaning lady, and a bike messenger—just to name a few. It goes without saying that Grace was searching for that missing piece in her life—a purpose. So, Grace became a 911 Operator when she discovered that it would take too long to become a doctor, a nurse, or a reflexologist, but her new chosen profession did give her a purpose—saving lives.

Tonight, the offices were slower than slow. It was only six o'clock and Grace was on 'til two a.m. Just about anything could happen during the next eight hours, but she hoped it would stay slow. A slow night may be boring, but it meant, for the most part, that their district was safe. Grace leaned into the phone, feeling guilty about being on a personal call, and whispered, "George, don't be such a whore! I know he's a fireman. I told you we've only spoken on the phone. I know it's been six months. I can't ask him out. I'm a chicken shit I guess. What if he says no? George, please, enough!" Her switchboard rang. "I have a call—no—I can't put them on hold! Do you even know where I work? No, that was a year ago. I have to go. Someone could have impaled themselves for God sakes! What? I'm a 911 Operator! Call me later." She quickly hung up and used her professional operator voice—not to be confused with her phone sex operator voice. It had taken Grace three months to break herself of the habit of falling into her low-pitched horny and available voice, which people who were in the midst of having a heart attack, didn't need to hear. "911, how can I help? Yes, yes, that's right, heavy machinery means just that, heavy machinery. I think it's okay for you to use your vacuum, but avoid driving your lawn mower, your car or, you know, anything else that you have to steer. You're welcome." Grace clicked off, leaned back in her chair and let the silence of the switchboard wash over her as she stared off into the empty space that is her life.

Clair, still fair-haired with a little help from her hairdresser, sat with her husband of two years, Henry, in their OBGYN'S office. Her plans were slightly off schedule. She was now thirty and she should have had her first child by the time she was twenty-eight. Even though she and Henry had gotten married six months after bumping into each other in Starbucks, it seemed getting knocked up took time. Clair had made V.P. at twenty-seven and she worked at a big accounting firm with five names: Cleary, Decker, Trees, Brady, and Verbouwens, but somehow meeting the one had proven to be a little more difficult to accomplish. Now, a more cynical person would say that Clair impulsively married Henry because that part of her life was off schedule in a big way. However, that wasn't the case at all. It was just plain and simple love at first sight. On the eve of her twenty-seventh birthday, after giving up on ever meeting and marrying Ralph Macchio, Clair mapped out a dating plan that would have ensured Napoleon's success at Waterloo. She was fastidious in her search. For an entire year, every weekend of her life—with the exception of birthdays and holidays— was filled with speed dating, Internet dating, and good old fashioned blind dating. She was relentless in her pursuit of her Prince Charming and like all good fairy-tales, she had to kiss a lot of wet, sloppy, soul sucking frogs along the way.

On one particularly hot Chicago day while leaving the museum after a truly horrendous blind date, Clair ran into the nearest Starbucks for an iced coffee, sans ice, to gather the strength she needed to recover. It was while standing in line in the Starbucks on the corner of 5th and 7th Ave. with all of the other heat challenged natives, trying to explain to the barista, who thankfully wasn't her sister, why she wanted an ice coffee with no ice, that Henry, who was standing in line behind Clair, stepped up to the counter. Within minutes, he expertly communicated her needs. Clair was immediately smitten with the crew cut and clean-shaven man before her. He had the most pleasant Irish face, sparkling grey eyes, and a winning smile. The fact that he was dressed in athletic shorts, a t-shirt that had more holes in it than a colander, and was wearing cleats did nothing to deter her. Needless to say, Henry scored that day in more ways than one! Well, actually, that's a lie. Clair was a cautious girl. Henry didn't score until at least four months later. Shortly after meeting him, Clair gave up Operation Soul Mate, and Henry gave up his on-again-off-again girlfriend, Sabrina, and they married two months after they consummated their relationship.

Right now, Clair was sitting in her OBGYN's office trying not to be nervous. She and Henry had tried for over a year to get pregnant the natural way and now after taking every test known to man to figure out why that wasn't happening, they were forced to wait an excruciating long time for those answers. Clair pulled her eyes from the receptionist and nervously smiled at her husband.

Henry squeezed her hand. "Listen sweetie, when we got married…"

Clair sighed. "When we got married we promised your parents that we'd produce grandchildren. And to quote your mother 'Never let Grace near them or alcohol while they still had the good sense God gave them.'"

Henry laughed. "Well, yes, we did promise that, but we also promised that we'd talk about whatever was bothering us."

Clair wasn't up for another round of baby fate chitchat. "We're all talked out."

Henry pressed forward. "No, we're not. We can adopt."

"Henry sweetie, you're working my last nerve. We've gone over this a million times. You did not marry Angelina Jolie. You married a selfish bitch. I know there are tons of babies who need good homes, but let her do it. I want my first child to be a part of us."

"And, if we can't do that, then what?"

Before Clair could answer him, the receptionist called their name and quickly ushered them into the Doctor's office. Clair took that as a bad sign. As they sat down Clair grabbed Henry's hand and squeezed it as hard as she could. Beth Peterman was one of the best OBGYN's in Chicago. She had gone to both Harvard and Yale Medical Schools and was a specialist in infertility. Beth smiled at Clair, but before she could even say hello...

"Just tell us the bad news and get it over with," Clair blurted.

Beth studied her patients. This was absolutely the worst part of her job. "You have an inhospitable womb. It's rare, but it does happen. Basically, your fluid is septic and attacks the sperm, which is essentially what birth control does."

Clair felt her stomach drop. "Are you kidding me? What do you mean inhospitable? I've done everything but put in wall-to-wall carpet to welcome a child into my womb!"

Beth had to smile at that. "I know this isn't easy to hear."

Clair held back tears. "What do you know? You have pictures of kids everywhere. Some of them, I'm sure, you gave birth too with your comfy welcoming womb."

Beth tried to find words of comfort. "You're right. I don't know how you feel. I just know how a lot of my patients feel when I have to speak to them about this."

A devastated Henry was at a loss. "How do we fix it?"

Beth hesitated. "We don't, we can't."

Clair could no longer hold back her tears. "There's no drug or operation or anything at all?"

"Physically, there's nothing we can do. But, there's always adoption, or you could try a surrogate. There are agencies that specialize in finding surrogates for couples. However, statistics show that they have a higher success rate if a family member, say a sister or a cousin was your surrogate."

Because Clair has an overly organized mind, while she sat stunned trying to process that her womb was inhospitable, her brain was searching for a solution. Then, tucked between memories of her senior prom and her SAT'S, ding, ding, ding! A Lifetime movie marathon, heavy drinking, Valerie Bertinelli, she would kill my husband- the pact. "Nancy McKeon!"

A confused Henry looked to his wife. "I didn't know we were related."

The whole ride home Clair kept mumbling incoherently, "She promised. Nancy McKeon would do it. We have a pact. You can't go back on a pact. It's way easier than killing Tori Spelling." If Henry hadn't been with her every moment since they left the doctor's he would have thought she had snuck off to the bar and was now drunk as a skunk! Once they pulled into their driveway Clair jumped out of the car and raced into the house. A bewildered Henry followed his wife past the country French living room furniture and up the stairs to their bedroom. It was there that Clair pulled out a long polished oak box from under their king sized bed. Clair stared at the box, her breath racing, then opened it to reveal mementos of her life that were carefully placed in hermetically sealed Ziploc bags. The bags were both color and numerically coded. Clair, an Accountant and the sister of a Librarian, always felt that the Dewey Decimal system was underrated. She carefully handpicked her way through her marriage license, senior prom corsage, and a variety of other items from her youth when she finally reached the red color-coded bag dated 1991. She slowly eased open the Ziploc top and pulled out a wine stained, badly written piece of notebook paper. Clair stared at it in wonder.

Henry peered over his wife's shoulder, "Clair, honey, you can't ask her to do that."

Clair, who was coping with everything she's just heard about her womb, answered, "why not? I have it in writing, we made a pact."

"I don't think a pact stained with wine is legally binding. I'm not a lawyer, but I'm pretty sure, so let's just sit down, talk about this, and take it one day at time." Henry pulled his wife into his arms.

It was after midnight now. The night had proven to be a slow one. Two of the other operators, Karen and Matt, got up to take a cigarette break when the phone rang. Grace waved them out the door. "911, how can I help you? Oh, hi Jack—how are you?" Grace immediately fixed her hair and put on lipstick using the back of a metal nameplate as a mirror. Fireman Jack was, well, a fireman. He belonged to Firehouse 93. He and Grace had never actually met. They first started speaking on the phone six months ago when he called to check in on a sweet little boy he had rescued from a submerged car. Once the kid was taken to the hospital, the firehouse couldn't get any follow-up information, so Jack took it upon himself to call the 911 operators to see if they had any new information. It turns out they did. And, so after that night, he and Grace spoke at least once a week, but usually more and always under the guise of checking up on the week's emergency calls.

Grace leaned in close to the switchboard and blushed, "well, I wouldn't know about that. Stop it Jack! You're making me blush. So, the kid with the rod in his head is going to be fine? You saved his life. No, you did! Oh, now you're blushing? Well, why don't you meet me for breakfast tomorrow and I'll make you blush again?" Grace panicked. "OH, MY GOD! I didn't mean that. I don't even eat breakfast. Breakfast is stupid. People say it's the most important meal of the day, but how can it be? You can't even have wine with it. What? Okay, I'll be quiet." Grace let out a giggle that she immediately regretted because she sounded like a mildly retarded dolphin, "Wednesday, two-fifteen at The Palace Grill. Sounds like fun. Um, sure, have a nice night." Grace hung up and did a little victory dance.

Karen walked in just as Grace was adding arm moves to her dance. Matt was close behind her. He had never seen her this excited about anything. "Did you win the lottery?"

Out of breath from dancing, Grace huffed, "I did it!"

Karen pushed past Matt. "You did not!" as she and a giddy Grace squealed and danced around excitedly.

Matt shook his head, "well, whatever it was, was it legal?"

"I asked out Fireman Jack!" Grace laughed. "He said yes. Oh yes he did! I laughed like a dolphin and he said, "yes.""

Grace walked in the door of her cluttered apartment at three a.m. She wasn't as tired as she usually was when she got home from work. She was completely energized and pumped. She had done one proactive thing today, she asked out a man. Not just a man; the kind that gets his own calendar— a fireman! She hadn't been out on a date with a nice guy, hell any guy, since she broke up with Ray. Ray was bad news. And, Ray was gone—along with her money, her car, her jewelry, and her entertainment center. It took Grace a long time to get over Ray. Well, it wasn't so much the getting over Ray that took so long as it was the restraining order, insurance claims, and the police reports that needed constant re-filing that made it hard to shake Ray from her system. Grace learned a lot from Ray, a lot about what not to do in a relationship. Like the song says. "Breaking up is hard to do," but it's much harder when it slowly dawns on you that the minute you started dating that particular individual, the person you really broke up with was yourself.

Grace took one look at the utter chaos that was her living space and her spirits were slightly dampened. She sailed past the barbershop chair, the messenger bike, the drop cloth and paintbrushes, and went into the kitchen. She sat at her tiny Formica table and then did what she did every night—made a cup of herbal tension tamer tea and ate a blueberry non-fat, non-sugar scone. It's hard for anyone to escape his/her past, but for Grace, who had odd remnants of her previous jobs scattered about her apartment, it was impossible. In her kitchen alone there were gourmet coffees, an über expensive coffeemaker, a collection of dog leashes that hung next to her cabinets, and a deep fryer from her donut days. All of these were reminders of her past as an utter failure. Grace needed a change. She always needed a change. Now, the fact that she had found her Popsicle on that random afternoon and it forever altered her life could very well be the reason why she constantly needed change. She desperately wanted to follow her bliss, but she had no idea what it was. She knew it wasn't being a 911 operator, but it was better than all her other jobs, so until she found her bliss she wasn't going to quit yet another job while she was on this seemingly unattainable quest. Her sister, Clair, had accounting and her Mother had art. The Higgins women didn't speak about their dreams. It's not that they didn't think the topic was worthy of conversation, but once you pass a certain age you're either following your bliss, or not, and no amount of conversation about what you hoped or dreamed to do with your life is going to change that. You were either living it or not—at least that's what Grace thought. But, unbeknownst to her, as she put her teacup in the sink, dust-busted the crumbs from her scone, and went to bed, a lot of what Grace thought was about to change.

Chapter 2

The next morning, Clair stood in front of her sister's apartment and paced. It was pretty early. Well, it was seven a.m., but that was early for Grace. Clair knew she was too early, but she hadn't been able to sleep the entire night. It felt like Christmas Eve when she was just too excited for Santa Claus to actually sleep. Clair tossed, turned, and paced the night away. She had tried to call her mom a few times to ask her what she thought, but she lacked the courage and kept hanging up the phone. Thankfully, her mother didn't have caller ID and most likely figured someone had a wrong number.

That morning, Henry's pacing and cajoling drove her right out of the house. She hadn't planned to come here. She had planned to go to Starbucks, but instead, here she was. Clair's stomach was in knots and she kept checking her handbag to make sure the hermetically sealed red color-coded Ziploc with the wine stained notebook paper was still there. Clair took out her key to Grace's, opened the door, walked quickly through the lobby and rode the elevator to her sister's floor. When the doors opened, Clair hesitated and then scooted out. She bit her lower lip as she strolled down the lime green carpet and past the art deco mirrors. Suddenly, there it was— Apartment 204. Clair was about to knock, but she knew her sister slept with earplugs, so she fingered the keys in her hand, sighed, and then unlocked the door and walked inside. Although she'd been in Grace's apartment at least a million times, every single time she opened the door, all that clutter completely surprised her. Now, in her sister's defense, Grace was not dirty; she was just disheveled like an old man who lived alone and had no one to tell him to tuck in his shirt or not to wear brown socks with black shoes. Clair stared down the hall past the aprons and massage table and fixated on her sister's closed bedroom door. With all of the courage she could muster, Clair steadfastly walked down that hallway, opened the door, saw Grace with her blackout curtains drawn shut, earplugs in, cooling gel sleep mask, and white hand softening gloves on and immediately lost every bit of courage she had. She felt extremely guilty, so she gingerly shut the bedroom door, tiptoed back down the hallway, moved the basket of dog toys and accordion files off the couch, and sat down. She looked around the apartment and sighed. She'd just sit here and wait for Grace to wake up. Clair allowed her body to sink into the cushions. Her eyes wandered about the apartment, which she thought was pretty nice if you got rid of all the clutter... BAM! She had a big idea. Not as big as the favor she was about to ask Grace, but an idea none-the-less. One of her errands for today was to take moving boxes to storage. Yes, frightening, but true, Clair actually had a storage unit for moving supplies. It was a color-coded, numerically numbered slice of heaven. The next thing she knew, she was in her car unloading boxes and calling Grace's landlord to inquire if her sister had a storage unit. For the record, Clair always had in her possession the name and number of every contact person her mother, sister, or husband might ever need in case of an emergency.

Now, as every woman knows, there are boundaries to sisterhood. You can borrow her new sweater if she already wore it more than once; you can't use her toothbrush— unless it's under duress; and you can never date her ex-boyfriend. When it comes to cleaning your sister's house and organizing her stuff, there is a fine line between being helpful and being intrusive. Clair, who had finally gotten all of the crap that Grace no longer used out of the hallway and into boxes, hoped she was erring on the side of helpful. It was a fascinating undertaking to clean her sister's house. First and foremost she had wanted to do this for a very long time. Clair believed that clutter begets clutter in all parts of your life. In her opinion, Grace lived in too much clutter. Clair felt that this physical clutter manifested as emotional clutter in Grace's love life, work life, and every part of her physical and spiritual being, which was why her older sister was such a loveable mess.

The second reason that Clair enjoyed the task at hand surprised her, but the reason was simple—it enabled her to get to know her sister again. Clair had forgotten that Grace was a puzzle freak until she stumbled upon her enormous collection. She uncovered her stash of Archie comics, old mixed tapes, and t-shirts, which would now be considered vintage, and her tenth grade diary. With each item she cleared, straightened, and boxed, Clair saw Grace for what she was—an amazingly kind, smart, and funny woman who thought much less of herself than she really should. And, that always made Clair sad. If her sister could only truly grasp how utterly spectacular she was, nothing else would really matter. Two and a half hours later, when the last box was packed, Clair found some teenagers playing basketball in the alley and paid them two hundred dollars to move everything into Grace's storage unit.

It was now eleven a.m. and Clair, who had stacked and organized her sister's storage unit, was exhausted and hungry. She ate one of Grace's non-fat, non-sugar blueberry scones and decided that the time had come. Clair once again mustered up some courage, walked down that hallway, admired her handy work along the way, opened the door and saw Grace with her blackout curtains drawn shut, ear plugs in, cooling gel sleep mask, and white hand softening gloves on and gently called to her, "Grace, Grace, Racy Gracie, come on sweetie, we need to talk." Clair nudged her leg then gently took out one of Grace's earplugs. "Racy Gracie."

Grace rolled toward her, "go away."

Waking her up was always a hassle— even when she hadn't worked nights. "Come on Gracie, we need to talk."

Grace tried to roll away, but Clair blocked her. "Clair Bear, leave me alone. I had an accidental poisoning, a suicide attempt, and a drive-thru…"

"Shooting? Where?"

"Not drive by, drive-thru. A kid climbed through the drive-thru window at McDonald's to rob the place and got trapped. They had to use the french-fry grease to get him out. Go away!"

"We need to talk. I have something to ask you—it's pretty important."

Grace pulled herself away. "Is mom okay, is anybody dead?"

"No one is dead, mom is fine, really."

Grace pulled the pillow over her head. "Then leave a note; I'll call you later, okay?"

Clair reasoned a note would make it easier. She wrote a short note, shoved it under Grace's sleep mask and left. Well, she thought, I guess I have time to reorganize her fridge. Clair walked down the clutter free hallway and into what was now a spacious living room when Grace came barreling through and almost knocked her down.

Grace struggled to take in her surroundings. "What the fuck?"

Clair was unsure what she was reacting to and in order to buy time she continued into the living room and sat in the chocolate brown leather club chair that faced a most spectacular view of the city. As Grace followed her, she looked around in wonder. Her mind was still filled with the early morning fuzzies and if she hadn't known better she would have thought she had stepped into an adult version of "The Little Princess," and that someone had come in the thick of night and given her the apartment of her dreams. Grace sat on the couch and for the first time in a really long time she was able to stretch out her long limbs. "Okay, obviously this isn't my apartment, so I'm hoping that note is for the person who lives here. What the fuck is going on?"

Clair decided to dive in headfirst. "Nervous energy and, you know, organizing calms me down. There was nothing left to organize at my place so I came here."

Grace's eyes narrowed, "to organize my life or my womb? Which, by the way, you technically didn't even ask. You put a note under my pillow and then nine months later I put a baby under yours? Are you drunk?"

Clair winced, "you told me to write a note."

"I thought you wanted to borrow my Donna Karan skirt. What were you thinking? I get you organizing my apartment because, well, you're a freak. But, why do you need me to have your kid? I'm just not getting this. I don't even know where all my stuff is."

"In your storage unit."

"I have a storage unit?"

Clair had to smile. "It's in the basement; the keys are hanging on the kitchen counter."

Grace was still shell-shocked. "How did you know I had a storage unit? Forget that. How in the hell did you get everything into it?"

"I called your landlord and I paid some kids two hundred bucks to move it all. Oh and I did a complete inventory it's on the kitchen table. You know, you could make some decent money selling that stuff on E-Bay."

"So, is it all in storage or did you toss some of it away like that time I went on tour with Death Parade and when I got back, all my beer can art magically threw itself out?"

Clair laughed. "You weren't on tour; you were less than twenty-five miles away. And, if I've said this once, I've said it a million times—tour means more than one gig! Hell, it means leaving the city you live in. You had one gig in your own home town."

Grace sighed, "You didn't answer the question."

"Nothing, and I stress this, nothing was thrown away—not even your pathetic collection of Flintstone jelly glasses."

"Well, good. It's my stuff and I should decide if it gets thrown out or not."

They sat there. They weren't really at a stalemate, but honestly, neither of them wanted to be the one to bring up the bigger and more important question that was looming over them, which was bigger and more important than either of them had ever imagined. Truth be told, they had each at some point gone over the whole donate an organ to your sister/mother scenario and had decided on their own that this was something they would be open to doing. In their minds all the bigger and more important questions that ever could be asked, up to and including, be my Maid of Honor, designated driver, and emergency contact had been asked. The womb thing was big. It was overwhelmingly mind boggling huge. There was a lot to consider. To lend your sister your womb pretty much meant that you lent her your body for at least two years. Who knew how long it would take to get pregnant, and then, well, you had to carry the child for at least nine to ten months and then depending on what type of delivery you had and all tons of other complicated shit, you just never knew when you would be able to call your body your own again.

Grace was still confused. "Why do you need me or anyone to have your kid?"

"The fluid in my womb is septic and attacks the sperm, which is what birth control does. Turns out I could have avoided that nightmare my whole life."

Grace felt horrible. Clair loved children. When they were growing up she was everyone's favorite babysitter, parents and kids alike. "Clair bear, I wish there was something I could do to help."

Clair whispered, "have my baby."

"Okay, let me rephrase that. I wish there was some way I could help that didn't include my uterus."

They sat in silence. Neither of them had imagined that they couldn't have kids. There was no rulebook to follow. No Miss Manner's Guide on how to ask your sister to lend you her womb. There was no proper way to do it, other than just doing it.

Clair got up to find her bag. "I know this isn't the same as borrowing a sweater, but I want to have a baby and this is the only way I'll ever be able to do that." She located her Kate Spade bag and pulled her hermetically sealed Ziploc out of it.

"Sweetie, I hate to break it to you, but you won't be having it, I will. I'll have the labor, the weight gain, and the flatulence. Can't you adopt?"

Clair blurted, "no," so angrily that she startled Grace. "I mean, we can, but I don't want to. I know it's completely selfish, but I want my first child to be a part of me and Henry and you and mom and dad."

Grace sighed. "Dad? Low blow, that's not fair."

Clair handed her the Ziploc. A confused Grace opened the bag and pulled out the wine stained notepaper. "OMIGOD. You kept this? I was nineteen, I had horrible judgment, and I had a spiral perm for Christ's sake! I also said I would kill Tori Spelling; do you want me to do that before or after I have your baby? Clair, this was not serious. We were just having fun. I was drunk, I mean really, really drunk. I didn't know what I was doing."

Clair leveled her with a teary eyed look, "Which is what most teenage mothers say when they find out they're pregnant and yet I can't have a baby. Just think about it."

Grace had to clean up her life before she even considered having her own kid, but having someone else's? That was huge. It wasn't just any old someone else, it was her sister, her baby sister. "Do you mind me asking? What does Henry think about this?"

"Henry thinks I'm wrong to ask you to do this for us."

Grace got defensive. "Why doesn't he think I'm good enough?"

"OMYGOD, no, I mean he thinks you're good enough, he thinks I'm being a selfish bitch in asking."

"I knew I liked him," Grace leaned back into the couch, "drunken pact or no drunken pact, I'm not making any promises, but I'm going to think about this, really think about this."

Clair squealed and pulled Grace into a big hug. "Did you tell Mom?"

Clair hugged her sister tighter. "Not yet. Not until you make your decision."

"If I say no, will you hate me and ignore me at family gatherings?"

Clair leaned next to her. "If you say no, then you say no. No harm, no foul." Clair put her feet on Grace's lap. "I won't hate you. I could never hate you. And, I won't ignore you at family picnics or weddings, unless well, you're drunk or you say 'no' to me and then go off and have someone else's baby."

Grace made a face. "P.S., your manipulation skills and passive aggressive techniques have really improved—bringing up Dad and the whole complete stranger having to have your kid, genius. Ah, Clairsan, the student surpasses the master."

"Let me know when to kick the emotional blackmail into high gear."

"Oh you haven't yet?"

Clair laughed. "Please, this is bush league; I learned from the best."

Grace nervously played with the silverware and menu as she waited for her friend George to show up. Once Clair had given her a tour of her own storage unit, took digital pictures of each and every item and thanked her for what felt like the millionth time for her promise to think about the bigger, more important question she had asked, and finally left, Grace called George. George was Grace's catch all. They had known each other for most of their adult lives — that is if you were considered an adult at fifteen. George was the one person Grace could really talk to about anything, well, anything-anything, like sex, politics, sexual politics, men, drugs, cosmetics, food, and anything she couldn't talk to her mother or sister about, which was either her mother or her sister or her mother and her sister. George was Grace's Switzerland. Grace liked to think she was George's Switzerland. While Grace was studying to be a librarian, George was studying communications and marketing. She was now a fabulously wealthy advertising executive. When George needed to unwind and really let off steam she called Grace, got a car service, fired up the Corporate Amex card, and off they went. Sometimes, it was a night on the town that ended at ten the next morning and sometimes it was a night on the town that ended at ten the next morning in an entirely different city. And, so, Grace was George's Vegas, and what happened when George was with Grace stayed exclusively between them. This little system of theirs fell into effect during spring break their senior year of high school when they took a class trip to California and got tattoos of dolphins on their asses.

While Grace waited for George, she stared at the pregnant woman coming her way and wondered if she could do it. Was she strong enough to lend out her womb? Could she handle all those hormones being out of whack, having to pee every five minutes, wearing maternity clothes, not seeing her feet for six months, and other things she couldn't possibly imagine? Then to add insult to injury, not reap the benefit of keeping the kid at the end of the whole ordeal? Would she even be able to hand the kid over? What would she feel like every time she saw the baby? Would she want to knock Clair over and steal the child? Grace had always imagined that she'd be married or at least with someone she loved when she had a child; that she'd be financially settled; have a career; and well, you know, have her shit together. She didn't expect to be a single thirty-five year old 911 Operator who was having a baby for her sister. That was nowhere near the realm of possibilities. Single, knocked up and abandoned; well, if she had stayed with Ray that definitely could have happened. She watched as the pregnant woman waddled out the door and immediately thought she couldn't go through with it. Grace loved her sister, she'd give her an organ in a heartbeat; well, she thought she would, it depended on what organ.

An Amazon of a woman dressed to perfection in a navy blue Donna Karan suit with a fabulous black leather Coach commuter bag and a knock out pair of Gucci kitten heels elegantly plopped herself down across from Grace. If anyone can elegantly plop, it's George. "You're up before noon, what the hell is going on?" she growled in her throaty, I've quit smoking for the second time this year, voice.

Grace laughed and handed her friend a menu. "More than even I care to admit. Order first, bitch second." George grabbed the menu and gave it a quick once-over as their waitress approached.

"What do you ladies want?"

George sighed, "a man who doesn't cheat, a boss who doesn't stab me in the back, and a stack of pancakes that won't go directly to my ass, but because I'm dealing in realities here—coffee, black; low fat cottage cheese; fruit, no berries; and that includes raspberries, blueberries, strawberries, boysenberries, gooseberries; a side of low fat turkey sausage; and one scrambled egg."

"Got it! And you?"

Grace gave the menu one more glance. "I'll take two eggs, fried, over easy, well done; low fat turkey piggy in a blanket; green tea; and a small cranberry juice—hold the ice."

"Got it! Syrup for your pancakes or honey?"

"Syrup."

The waitress grabbed a pot of coffee and filled George's cup before she left. George stared at Grace. "When did you order pancakes?"

"That's the blanket. Waitresses speak the same language." Grace started folding and unfolding her napkin.

"You were a waitress?"

"In between barber and massage therapist, but before dog walker and after bike messenger."

George grabbed Grace's hand and stopped the next round of napkin origami. "Ooh, yeah— Denny's. What's got your napkin in a twist?"

"Clair just found out she can't have kids. Her womb is inhospitable, which means that it's septic and attacks the sperm."

George took a long breath. "Kinda like my dating life; I'm septic and attack the right single men and, of course, sleep with the wrong single men. The married single men."

"Just because you say it like it exists doesn't actually mean it exists."

"Technically the married single man is a man who is separated from his wife and has no intention of going back to her and absolutely no intention of divorcing her either. It's a rare breed, but it does exist— mostly in France, I think. I should move to France." George narrowed her eyes and took a sip of water. "An inhospitable womb. Well, I guess that's what happens when you try to organize everything from your toilet paper to your vagina." George did feel bad though. "So, how do they fix it?"

"They don't. They can't." As the waitress refilled George's coffee, Grace leaned into the table and blurted, "she asked me to be the baby's mommy. You know, have her baby— be a surrogate."

George added milk to her coffee. "Borrow sugar, borrow milk, but borrow a uterus? There are boundaries Grace, boundaries!"

"She's my sister."

"I don't care if she's your conjoined twin. First rule of life— never lend family money or your uterus. Just let them hire a surrogate."

Grace thought the same thing, but now she just wasn't sure. "It takes too long to find a good one and with family there's a better chance the procedure will work."

The waitress dropped off their food. George picked through her fruit cup as the waitress turned to leave. "What's this?"

The waitress peered into the fruit cup. "I have no idea."

George huffed, "it's a gooseberry!" The waitress grabbed George's fork, cherry picked out all the gooseberries, and walked away with them. "You are not having Clair's baby. There is no way in hell you're doing this."

Grace, suddenly defensive, retorted, "I have no good reason not to. I mean really what am I doing with my life that is so damn important that I can't hatch an egg for my sister?"

George paused before biting into a piece of watermelon. "You're not just sitting on a nest for nine months. And, it's not going to be one of those Hollywood pregnancies where you don't gain any weight. And, it's not even one of those Heidi Klum pregnancies either where before your episiotomy is healed you're wearing angel wings and a push up bra on a runway. It will fuck your body up. My mother said she never felt right again." George paused for some coffee. "And, yes, right now your life quest is a bit sketchy, but you'll be sacrificing a lot of stuff—no drinking, no cheese, no more flat stomach, plus there's vomiting, all different kinds of swelling, hemorrhoids, heartburn, mood swings, and last, but not least, no sex and—No Fireman Jack! And, you won't even be able to drink to console yourself!"

"How do you know so much about pregnancy? You don't even like baby carrots!" Grace was a bit shell-shocked.

"Look, my mother always said knowledge gives you power. Anytime I get caught up in the heat of the moment and I don't have four safety nets in place I just think of that." George shook her head to make her point.

On the one hand, George was telling her everything she already knew. On the other hand, it's her little sister. She'd do anything for her, why should this be any different? "No Fireman Jack?"

George dramatically sighed. "No Fireman Jack. If your first date goes well, you could become a thing, but if you show up pregnant because you're carrying your sister's baby the only thing you'll become is the crazy girl he tells people about when they're playing 'pin the tail on the most worst date' game."

"I never thought of that."

"Well, sweetie, that's what I'm here for."

Grace took a bite of her pancake. "Really? Well, where were you when I woke up at thirty-three and realized that Jesus had not only died at that age, but walked on water, made it rain frogs, and came back from the dead! George, he came back from the dead and I hadn't even paid off my student loans. Where were you when Jesus made me quit my job and embark on a personal quest that has lasted over two years?"

"Cabo. You had that epiphany while drinking out of the same bottle of Tequila as me, remember?"

"Yeah? Oh, yeah. Well, why did you get the Target campaign out of that bottle and I became a dog walker, a barber, a massage therapist, an ESL teacher, a barista, a waitress, and a manicurist?"

George washed down her spoonful of cottage cheese with a sip of coffee. "Two very important reasons: I ate the worm and I hold my liquor better." George waited until Grace had a mouthful of pancakes to deliver her last piece of wisdom. "Three words for you, Gracie, You— Henry— Sperm!" George watched the color as it drained from Grace's face and knew her job was done.

Chapter 3

Clair sat. She sat in the living room. She sat in her bedroom. She sat in the kitchen. She sat on the back porch. The only time she didn't sit was when Henry entered the room, then she got up and sat in another room because she couldn't face him yet. What had she done? She asked Grace to have her baby. What the hell was she thinking? Grace had her own life to live; her own mistakes to make; her own pregnancy, at some point, to experience. She should say no. She had every right to say no. Clair was the freak, the half woman who couldn't have a child because her body hated her, and so, she decided to hate her body back by finishing off a box of Hot Pockets and a bowl of chocolate pudding. A nauseous Clair reasoned that maybe the whole inhospitable thing was because she had gone on the pill when she was sixteen, ate too much tuna, and drank an unhealthy amount of Tab while she was growing up. "Oh, God," she thought. "What if Grace had an inhospitable womb? With the kind of people she's let in to the place and all the alcohol she's drank, Grace's womb probably looked like a hotel room after Tommy Lee trashed it!"

"How you doing?"

Clair looked at her Husband, "I cannot believe I asked my sister to do this."

"That makes two of us."

"What was I thinking?"

Henry sat next to his wife. "You were thinking you needed to fix this fast, that you wanted a kid, and that Grace was the answer to your prayers."

Clair managed a small smile. "I need to talk to her."

Henry kissed his wife. "I know. Do you want me to go with you?"

"No thanks. I started this on my own and I have to end it on my own."

"Okay, but can we have dinner first? Someone ate all the Hot Pockets."

Children who shared the common bond of parentage also shared a certain amount of parental friction while growing up. If you found one of your parents dead while going through the growing pains of puberty, periods, and unruly body hair, the amount of parental friction escalated. Now, in this tale there is no evil stepmother or for that matter an evil stepfather. There is just Grace's and Clair's widowed mother, Diane, who never remarried after Daddy Higgins froze to death on that random afternoon. And so, in between the all too familiar mother-daughter wars of hair, clothing, drinking, belly rings, and tattoos, there was trust, patience, L'Oreal hair care products, and unconditional love that created an unspoken bond of survival. They knew there was nothing the three of them couldn't face as long as they faced it together. Thus far, they had survived a death, an abusive boyfriend, a semi nervous breakdown, a dye job gone badly, near bankruptcy, and the dread that fell upon them every winter when the first snow of the season sprinkled onto their lives. Now, as curveballs go, Diane was not expecting this one. She had retired two years ago from her professorial duties at The Art Institute of Chicago and effortlessly segued into the Head Curator position at the Institute's museum. Her first exhibit, Cézanne to Picasso, was a smashing success and paved the way for a leisurely life of wine-tasting, art, literature, foreign movies, and if she was lucky, a little bit of grandmother-hood— a hood that in the last ten minutes became more complicated than she had ever imagined. And, as she sat across from her daughter, who stared at a pile of medical brochures and in vitro pamphlets, she was completely flummoxed.

Grace was flummoxed as well. She promised Clair that they wouldn't tell their mom about the biggest and most important question she had ever been asked until she had made a decision, but in order to make that decision, she needed her mother. As she sat in her mom's kitchen with all of this information swimming around her head, she felt sick to her stomach. Maybe the morning sickness for the pregnancy she hadn't planned had somehow already started? "Oh, my GOD! Did you read all the shit you have to do? There's a psychologist evaluation to make sure you're not a whack job and there are rules, like they prefer a surrogate to have already had a kid, so they know she can successfully carry a baby to term. And, do you know how much this costs? I knew having a kid was expensive, but this is ridiculous!"

Diane put on a pot of tea. "It's a lot to take in."

"How can she ask me to do this? It's a huge commitment. I'm talking HUGE!"

Diane set the mugs on the table, leaned against the counter, and waited for the teakettle to whistle. "Gracie, sweetie, I don't know what to tell you."

"Would you do it?"

The kettle whistled, and Diane pulled the cherry red teapot off the stove and poured water in the mugs. "Wow! I just don't know. I'm an only child. I didn't have to share much of anything growing up. I'd like to think I'd say yes, but I can be pretty selfish. And let's be honest, you know me, I don't have what it takes to subject myself to all those shots and psychological evaluations and then nine months of the actual pregnancy. And then the whole labor thing— I'd probably say no."

Grace picked a tea bag from the basket and unwrapped it. "One minute I feel that way and then ten minutes later I'm like it's Clair, this is something I have to do for her." She pushed her chair away from the table. "How the hell am I supposed to figure this out? What the fuck is the right decision? And what if I decide to do this and something goes horribly wrong? I'm thirty-five years old, what if I miscarry? Or, what if I have the same problem as Clair, or if I end up carrying twins or the baby has Down's syndrome, or some horrible genetic disease?"

Diane poured some milk into her tea and sighed. "Calm down. Before you can even go there you have to decide what you want to do." She put her mug down and grabbed a tin of Mrs. Fields cookies off the counter. "At the very least, this will force you to examine some things in your life. You don't give yourself enough credit. You're one of the smartest women I know, plus you've got balls. I mean, not many women can admit that they're in an abusive relationship, let alone get out of it, and then deal with the financial fall-out when the scumbag cleans out their bank account."

Grace grabbed the tin from her mother and peered inside. She pulled out a double chocolate chip cookie and dipped it in her tea. "Yeah, well, I didn't do it alone. I had you and Clair. What if I say 'no' and it pushes her over the edge—again?"

"Now you're not giving your sister enough credit."

"Yeah, well, it didn't take much to push her off her rocker the last time."

"I was not pushed off my rocker." Clair stood in the doorway of the kitchen. "I was under a lot of pressure working two full time jobs, going to school for my MBA, and volunteering at the women's shelter. The doctor said that I was suffering from exhaustion. I repeat, there was no rocker falling here, it was not a nervous breakdown."

Grace jumped. "Jesus, you shouldn't sneak up on people especially when they're talking about you. And, you can call it whatever you want, exhaustion, retreat at a health spa, but we all know when a superstar shaves her head and is whisked off to rehab, no one thinks she's exhausted, they think she fell off her rocker!"

"I got highlights!" Clair sat down next to Grace and foraged in the tin of cookies. "I'll make you a deal. If I allow you to refer to your weekend gig in a Volkswagen van as being on tour, you let me refer to my episode as exhaustion."

Grace stole the last double chocolate chip cookie out from under Clair's nose. "Deal."

Clair grabbed the cookie back and quickly bit into it. "You told Mom? You can never keep a friggin' secret."

"I can, too."

Clair gave her the stink eye. "Johnny Desmond, The Bangles concert, the crock pot incident, and the Dodge Polar breakdown!"

"He got you drunk, you lied and were driving without a license, it exploded— and I stress it exploded! And, you were stranded in the middle of the night in the middle of nowhere and you called to ask me to pick you up! What was I supposed to tell Mom? That Avon was calling and I had to go pick up my Cherry Cola lip-gloss because they no longer delivered? You know, for someone who prides herself on planning out every detail of her life you sure missed a few."

Clair gave her the finger. "Well, you, as per usual jumped the gun because I'm taking it back!" She then picked a packet of apple spice tea from the basket and sniffed it.

Grace was relieved, shocked, and oddly pissed. "You already asked me the biggest and most important question I have ever been asked. You can't pretend like it never happened!"

"Yes, I can!"

"No, you can't! That's like eating a whole pie and then saying you never ate it."

"I'm not asking you to have my baby."

"Why? Is my womb suddenly not good enough for you?"

Diane sighed. "Okay, stop it! Your womb is a fine, upstanding womb. Clair, what is this all about?"

"I shouldn't have asked in the first place; it was completely selfish of me."

"Now you're trying to convince me to not have your baby, so I'll have your baby?"

"That makes no sense. I'm taking it back because it was wrong to ask. I totally overstepped my bounds."

Grace softened. "Lord knows I've overstepped my bounds over the years. Although, not directly onto your womb." Grace picked at the cookie tin. "Now, here's the thing. What if I can't have your kid?"

Clair stared at her. "It doesn't matter, I'm taking it back."

Diane cleared her throat. "Well, you know there was a woman in Italy who gave birth to her daughter's child when she was seventy. I just want you to know there's no way in hell I'm doing that. I love you, but that's absolutely insane. But I will go to Italy and help you find that old lady."

Grace sighed. "Let me take all the tests and find out if I can actually do this, then I'll make a decision." Clair jumped out of her chair and pulled Grace into a hug.

Diane smiled, she was relieved that her daughters had reached a happy medium, but worried that it depended on Grace passing a psychological evaluation.

Decisions big and small were made in just about every moment of a person's waking life. Now, if you're a member of the Higgins clan and happened to decide on a bitter cold morning many years ago that you didn't need to get up and help your Dad shovel the snow, well, decisions big and small are always, and this can't be stressed enough, always second-guessed. With that in mind, a fearful Grace waited to be analyzed—within an inch of her life. In the past three weeks, she'd been tested for stress; body fat; heart rates—sleeping, waking, and exercising, to be exact; and she'd been poked and prodded in places one normally would have thought was illegal for a person, gynecologist or not, to do to another human being. She'd met with a reproductive endocrinologist and an embryologist— all for the sake of trying to decide if she can psychically have her sister's baby.

Grace looked around the sleek and modern office. She got up to examine the certificates on the wall and was both relieved and intimidated that Dr. Yael Bedouwin graduated from both Harvard and Yale. When Dr. Yael Bedouin walked into the office Grace was stunned. She had expected someone like Dr. Ruth Westheimer, an intense short woman of Jewish decent. What she got was a tall Egyptian woman who was a cross between Halle Berry and Iman. "Ms. Higgins?" inquired the mocha skinned Goddess with a slight French accent as she dropped the files on her desk and sat.

"Uh, yeah, that's me." Grace hoped that was the right answer.

"Thank God. My assistant is rather new. Last week she mixed up the files of two patients. It took me half a session to figure out that the young woman sitting in front of me with the eating disorder was really a young man with a transgender issue. They were both thin and boyish and, well, you can understand my confusion."

"Completely." Grace figured she'd stick to one-word answers. It felt safer.

Dr. Yael opened the manila file on her desk and perused it, shut the file and smiled. "Well, I'm very pleased with the results of your MMPI personality test."

"Thanks, I think." Damn, three words thought Grace, keep it to one she told herself.

"There's really no one to thank except you. You're a well-adjusted, socially acceptable, and intelligent individual."

"Are you looking at the right test?"

"Are you Grace Heloise Higgins?" Grace nodded and as she watched her elegantly sit back in her chair, she decided that Dr. Yael was a Nubian Goddess. "That name is printed in bold letters at the top of this test, so yes, it's you."

"Really? Well, that's a relief." Grace sighed.

"You were concerned?" chuckled the Nubian Goddess. She leaned forward and when she did, Grace smelled a hint of musk and sandalwood.

"Well, I've made some questionable decisions in my life."

"We've all made questionable decisions in our lives, Grace, the proof is in how we handled the fallout from those decisions."

For some reason, the first thing that popped into Grace's mind was Fireman Jack. Grace had successfully rescheduled their first date three times, but now she had to go through with it. She both dreaded and looked forwarded to their Friday morning breakfast.

"What are you thinking of right now?"

"Fireman Jack."

"Who is Fireman Jack?"

Grace blushed. "Just a guy that I'm hoping will no longer be just a guy anymore."

Dr. Yael smiled. "I see. Does he know?"

"About my pending seat on the Jerry Springer Show if I agree to have my sister's baby? Or that I hope we turn into a thing?"

"Both."

"Uh, no, we haven't even had our first date yet."

"I see. Well, his reaction to the Jerry Springer Show reveal will definitely clue you in about whether or not he should move past just a guy to *the guy*."

"I suppose."

"Well, there's no supposing about it. Everything about his reaction will tell you that. So, make sure that you're listening, really listening to everything he says— especially his body language. The old says one thing, but does another is tied into the body language. It lets you know how he truly feels."

"Listen, if he doesn't run screaming from the room, I'll see that as a plus."

Dr. Yael laughed again. "You know, a true test for any man is pretty simple; just bring him around a dog or a child and if he doesn't get bitten or peed on by either, chances are he's a good man."

"Does it count if the kid is in utero?" Grace looked around the office and sighed.

Dr. Yael leaned back in her chair. "There is no physical reason why you can't have your sister's baby. From these tests, I fail to see any psychological setbacks, but that doesn't mean there won't be any. What are you feeling?"

"I'm completely freaked out. If I agree to this, I'm giving Clair full control over my body. That's a bit too sisterly for me."

"I can't disagree with you, but what's the real issue?"

"I don't want to get fat—I'm kidding, kinda. Uh, don't you mean issues? There are so many issues that my issues have issues! " Grace stared at her.

"No one is going to make you do this. It's a big decision with a lot of ramifications. Now, from my side of the table you are a hundred percent capable to handle this. Obviously, from your side of the table you're stuck. Why?"

"I never really thought about having kids. Now I'm supposed to have one for my sister? It's her kid for all intent and purpose, but I have to carry it. I have to forego cheese, alcohol—not that I need alcohol, skinny jeans, high heels, sushi, dating, sex, my Audrey

Hepburn ankles, sleeping on my stomach, hot tubs, drinking alcohol and eating sushi in hot tubs, roller coasters—I don't even like 'em, but what if I felt like going to Six Flags one day?"

"Slow down! Not all of those things are really scaring you except maybe the alcohol and sushi. You did mention those twice. What's the real problem?"

"Well, among other things, sex." Grace looked at her toes. "Not that I'm fornicating like a bunny. I've basically stopped having sex because I realized it clouded my decisions when it came to men, but come on, there's a difference between not having sex because you don't want to and not having sex because you can't—that's just torture!"

"Well, you don't need to give it up. You can have sex while you're pregnant."

Grace sarcastically drolled, "really? Me pregnant, my boyfriend, for arguments sake let's say Fireman Jack, making out on the couch, we get all hot and heavy and then BAM! He's going to have sex with an enormous—I've seen pictures of my mother, so I know what's gonna happen to my ass—pregnant woman who's not carrying his child?"

Dr. Yael smiled. "A lot of men find pregnant women sexy, but I see your point."

Grace sighed. "It's backwards. You're supposed to fall in love, get married, have kids and live happily ever after. This way it's all jumbled up, it's happily ever before!"

"But, you'd be giving Clair her happily ever after."

"Yeah, well I taught her how to skateboard, how to drink, how to wear a mini skirt, and most important, how to dance. I helped her study and nursed her back to health. Why is it my job to make sure all her dreams get fulfilled? What about my dreams? What about my life?"

"I don't know. Why don't you tell me about them?"

Grace grabbed a tissue. "Oh, who am I kidding? I don't have any dreams. I never had any fucking dreams. My goal was to avoid ever making another decision as long as I lived."

Dr. Yael pulled a couple of cans of Coke out of the mini fridge and offered one to a surprised Grace. "You do know by not making any decisions, you made decisions."

"No shit. And, by deciding to stay in bed I killed my father."

"I thought a snow plow killed your father."

Grace was surprised. "How did you know that? Same difference though."

Dr. Yael opened Grace's file. "Here it is, Question number 453. You answered, and I quote, 'death is to me like a snowplow running over my father', end quote. That's why I get the big bucks. I read between the lines. How does your staying in bed equate to a snowplow killing your father?"

An irritated Grace stated, "if I had gotten up to help him, he'd still be alive."

"Or you'd be dead or you'd both be dead."

Grace didn't want to dwell on it. Instead, she popped open her can of soda and took a sip. "What's with the soda?"

"It throws my patients off and calms them down."

"Caffeine calms them down?"

"The action of doing something familiar in the middle of an awkward situation calms them down. They may leave here jacked up on caffeine, but that's not my problem, is it?" Dr. Yael tried to get Grace to focus. "So why the fear of making this decision?"

"Holding the fate of someone's happiness in my uterus seems precarious at best."

Dr. Yael watched as Grace fidgeted uncomfortably on the couch. "Okay, so how about this. Come up with a pros and cons list. Bring it to your next session and we'll get down to the nitty gritty."

"The nitty gritty? You learn that in Harvard or Yale? That's gonna be fun isn't it?"

"Well, it depends on how you classify fun. If I recall, there was something about a tour with a heavy metal band in here." She pointed to Grace's file.

"Death Parade." Grace got wistful. "I haven't done anything important since then. How can I have a kid if I haven't even lived my life?"

"But, you don't get to keep the kid."

"But, that doesn't change much does it?"

Dr. Yael studied her patient and sighed, "I suppose not."

Chapter 4

Earlier it was noted that in this tale there was no evil stepmother or, for that matter, evil stepfather and there isn't, but there is a somewhat opinionated, domineering, witty, corporate shark who happens to be Henry's mother, as well as the primary shareholder of the family's mayonnaise empire. Patricia Erickson was married to her second husband, Henry, Sr., an athletic, handsome, and amiable man. Many things have been said about Patricia: loving mother, loving wife, dog lover, philanthropist, cutthroat bitch, and a morally challenged, price-gouging whore. And, really, with credentials like that, how could you not love her? Patricia sat in all her glory in the middle of the Union League Club of Chicago and studied them. Something, as far as she could tell, was rotten in Denmark.

Henry tried to remain calm and relaxed. His dad, with his thick head of silver hair and early spring tan, always looked calm. He envied that. "So how's retirement?"

Patricia took a sip of her Long Island Iced Tea and looked for the waiter. Monday's were slow lunch days, so where on earth was her Cobb salad? "Just being the Chairman of the Board, dealing with big picture stuff, and not running the day-to-day operations frankly, sucks. I miss the intrigue."

Henry, Sr. smirked, "it's mayonnaise dear, you're not creating alternative fuel options that the government is trying to protect from our enemies."

Patricia snapped, "considering the shape our country is in, mayonnaise may be our future—especially since the United States doesn't have many friends these days."

Henry, Sr. laughed. "You're going to get the Middle East to declare peace, cure the aids epidemic in Africa, and stop genocide with mayonnaise?"

"A good egg salad sandwich can heal a lot of things." Patricia narrowed her eyes at Henry, Sr., a sure sign that her retirement wasn't agreeing with either of them, and honed in on her son. "Okay, spill it. You practically threatened us to come to lunch; what the hell is going on?"

Henry grabbed Clair's hand "Oh—, well—, that—, you see— it's like this. We, uh, that would be Clair and I, well, uh, we can't have kids."

Patricia did not expect this. "What's wrong? Did you check your plumbing?"

"Yes, we checked the plumbing."

Henry, Sr. gave his son a sad nod. "I'm so sorry."

Patricia studied Clair. "Did you get a second opinion?"

Clair started to nervously organize the sugar packets. "And, a third, and, a fourth—we're thinking of having a surrogate."

Patricia did not like the sound of that. "That's quite a risk don't you think?"

Henry started to speak, but Clair cut him off. "My womb can't nurture an embryo, but my eggs are good enough to plant into another woman's uterus, so we thought we'd have Grace carry our baby to term."

To say the bottom just fell out of Patricia's world is to understate how she really felt. "No, no! There is no way a grandchild of mine is going to spend nine months in that roach motel!"

Clair was dumbfounded and Henry was appalled at his mother's behavior. "Grace is a sweetheart."

Henry, Sr. leaned in and whispered, "forgive me Clair, but Grace is a whore and a murderer."

"She got drunk at our wedding, everyone was drunk at our wedding—it was Vegas! If I recall, you and Mom went skinny dipping and ended up in jail." Henry huffed.

"Yes, dear, but your father and I didn't dirty dance with your ninety-five year old Uncle Harrison who turned up dead two days later."

Clair couldn't believe what was just said. "He was sleeping with his caretaker, a thirty year old ex-stripper. Did it not occur to you that maybe she was the problem?"

Patricia scoffed. "Bambi came from a good family—old money."

Through gritted teeth Henry retorted, "how are crumpled dollar bills in her G-string old money?"

Patricia took another swig of her drink and sighed. "I hardly see your point."

"If Grace agrees to do this huge favor for us you are going to treat her with love and respect or you're never going to see your grandchild. Do you understand?"

Patricia did not like her son's tone. "Oh, so now you're threatening me."

"Do you understand the terms of the threat?"

Patricia both admired and despised her son right now. "Perfectly, dear." She smiled at the waiter when he brought her salad, nodded sweetly at what was now her disappointment of a daughter-in-law, and vowed that the subject was far from closed. This was the Erickson family bloodline and she'd be damned if anyone screwed it up. And, by anyone, she meant Grace.

Clair stared at her grilled Mahi-Mahi sandwich. "Unless we adopt or hire a complete stranger to have our baby, Grace is our best alternative."

"Honey," said Patricia between bites of tiny cubes of lettuce and avocado, "Grace is no one's best alternative. I mean no disrespect, but really, Grace? Grace who hasn't held down the same job for longer than six months? Grace who lives in squalor? Grace who hangs out with a woman named George and wakes up drunk in foreign countries? That, *Grace,* is your best alternative?"

Clair was pissed. "Yes, Patricia. *That* Grace! The one who kept my family from falling apart after my dad died, saves lives as a 911 Operator, took care of me when I was too sick to take care of myself, and yes, hangs out with a woman named George and occasionally wakes up drunk in foreign countries, which in my opinion is better than being a bitter-country-club-lunching-Long-Island-Ice-Tea-swilling-bitch!" And, with that said, Clair stormed out. "And Patricia, for the record, a Long Island Ice Tea is *not* the epitome of class unless you're a twenty-two year old sorority girl!"

Her mother-in-law, the Long-Island-Ice-Tea-swilling-bitch, finished the rest of her drink and laughed. "Henry, go after your wife. If I've told you once, I've told you a thousand times that girl's a keeper!"

Henry, Sr. chuckled as his son left the table. "A bitter-country-club-lunching-Long-Island-Ice-Tea-swilling-bitch. The very words I've been searching for, for the past forty years!" Patricia kicked her Husband hard, yet discreetly, as only an Erickson could do.

Henry found Clair as she paced outside by the valet. The club was quiet today. The usual crowd of ladies who lunch, husbands, wives, and the soon-to-be mistresses weren't in attendance. Henry hated *the club*. It was fine as clubs go, but it wasn't his style. From the moment he recognized, at the age of five, that his parents held this place in such high esteem it annoyed the living shit out of him. "You okay?"

"Sometimes your mother, well she just..."

Henry pulled her into his arms. "I get it, she's my mother, remember?"

Clair relaxed into his arms. "I'm sorry I snapped like that, but really how the hell can she say stuff like that about Grace while I'm in the room? We're not going to be like them as parents are we? I refuse to raise my child to think they're better than seventy-five percent of the human population. She's insane. Truly insane and drunk, she's drunk too!"

"Honey, she thinks she's better than ninety-five percent of the population. And, she's never drunk. To be truly drunk she'd have to loosen up and be open to change. And, for the record, the only time I'd ever seen her drunk was at our wedding and even then, well, I thought she was faking."

Clair pulled away and Henry followed his wife as she strolled past the cars and onto the club grounds. "How did you come from them?"

"My father's side—normal people; they always blew a hole in my mother's hypocrisy. That's why she loves them and you—she loves you Clair. She's just testing you."

"For what? For Malaria, or allergies, or to see if my bitch levels are elevated? I don't want to be the type of parents who test their kids. If we do this at the end of nine months we're going to be parents. We have to make sure we're on the same page when it comes to child rearing."

Henry grabbed his wife's hand. It sometimes surprised him just how much he loved her. As they passed the stone fountain in the middle of the club's driveway he used his Grandfather Al's stern lecturing voice. "You're right. And, I strongly believe there will be no running with scissors, glue sniffing, or nose picking and definitely no tattoos, belly rings, or piercing of any kind. They must color within the lines and call me father. I will not stand for dad, daddy or the dreaded pops."

Clair punched him. "Idiot."

"And, no name calling." Henry pulled his wife behind one of the oak trees, kissed her, and started fiddling with the buttons on her starched white shirt.

"This conversation is far from over." Clair whispered as she pulled Henry further from view and started undoing his belt buckle.

Chapter 5

Big decisions are hard. Big decisions that involve your uterus are even harder. To make such a decision you must be armed with a few things: your best friend, a never ending flow of alcohol, a pen or number two pencil, some paper, fried calamari, spinach and artichoke heart dip, and a booth in Piazza Bella, a fabulous Italian restaurant deep in the heart of Chicago's Roscoe Village. At this moment, Grace was in such a booth. To her right sat George with an almost empty bottle of red wine; to her left was her own almost empty bottle of white wine and with all of these tools available, big decisions should be as easy as one, two, three. Unless one, two, three referred to how many bottles of wine you drank and how quickly you tossed them back. Grace leaned into the table and poured herself another glass of wine. "Ooh, I should put down being the mother of my own niece or nephew as a pro. No, no as a con."

George picked up a breadstick and pretended to smoke it. "Face it. There are no pros to being artificially impreganated, damn that's hard to say."

"Yes thherre are!" Grace picked up the smudged cocktail napkin, "There's helwping Clair be an aunt, a grandmamama, a daddy, oops, not Clairrrr, but you know people, and there's something about a perm, I'd have a perm. I looked good in a perm, didn't I?"

"Not perm, it's sssperm, you wrote it on the wrong side."

Grace put her head down on the table. "I'd have sppperm in my hair. I don't want sppperm in my hair, but, I looked good in a perm right?"

George bit her breadstick. "You looked awwwful. You were on the sweam team— your hair was fried like a wooonton. Woonton, woonton, wontonwontonwontonwonton. That's fun, you try it."

Grace pushed herself off the table. "Wontonwontonwonton— I don't get it." She tried to sit up straight. "I looked good in a perm, I did."

"Okawy, you looked good in a perm. No, I can't. You looked like a dead French poodle."

"Least I didn't put Sun-Innnnn in my hair and turned it orange!"

George laughed. "We were quite the pair, the dead poodle and the orange haired Amazonian." They shared a look, giggled, and then fell into uncontrollable laughter.

Grace munched happily away on a handful of fried calamari. "We should get tattoos. I could get a stork for the other side of my ass."

"What other side?" asked George. Grace got up, looked around the bar, and dropped trough to reveal her dolphin. "Oh, that other side, but what if you say no? You'd have a stork on your ass forever."

Grace pulled her pants back up. "You could get one too."

"Why? I'm never having somebody else's kid; fuck!" George spilled her wine.

"Kid fuck? Is that slang for dating a bachelor boy who doesn't want to get married or is that for dating a single married man?"

They got quiet for a few seconds. Not because they wanted to share some sort of deep thought moment, but because they'd lost track of the conversation. It took a second, but George picked up the missing thread. "I'm nevereverever having my owwwn kid, I can't even find a nice guy to date." George decided to lie down.

Grace could only see the top of her friends' bent knees. "Georgie if we wanted to be in a good solid relationship we'd be in it. It has nothing to do with getting a stork on your ass."

George hit her head on the table. "Oww, you've got a point."

Grace struggled to sit up. "So, are you in?"

George pulled her drunken ass out of the booth. "You've gotta be in it, to win it! But, first I've gotta pee!"

"There's got to be a morning after..." and like the lyrics written and sung by Maureen McGovern for the movie, "The Poseidon Adventure," the morning after wasn't very good. Grace woke up on the living room floor in George's sleek penthouse. After a night out with her friend and champion drinker she was used to having her whole body ache, but this time there was an unmistakable throbbing in her ass. She rolled over and tried to get a handle on the time. She couldn't tell if the Tiffany clock on the mantle was saying it was eight o'clock in the morning or maybe twenty to one in the afternoon or twenty to one in the morning or maybe eight o'clock at night? All she could gather right now was that her tongue was fuzzy, her ass killed, and George was snoring like a bulldog on her Shabby Chic sectional. Grace picked herself off the floor, stumbled past the couch to the kitchen, opened the fridge and poured a glass of orange juice, and became fascinated at how George was laying on the couch. She was on her stomach, Grace knew George hated sleeping on her stomach, she was bare assed, George only did one thing bare assed, no, wait, that's a thong! Grace was relieved, but the thing that really caught her eye was that her lower body was propped with a pillow.

Grace tiptoed to get a better look and gasped as it hit her. She stared at the stork tattoo on her friend's bare butt when Grace's glass of orange juice slipped out of her hand and splashed down on George's ass. George ricocheted off the couch and landed the most obscene, yet oddly menacing, "Crouching Tiger Hidden Dragon" pose anyone who has watched porn has ever seen. Apparently, Grace was wrong—George wasn't wearing a thong.

"You have a stork on your ass!"

George struggled to keep her balance. "Why is my ass burning?"

Grace ran into the kitchen to grab a paper towel. "I spilled O.J. on your ass."

"How in the fuck? Did you? What the hell?" George started jumping around the apartment while Grace chased her with a paper towel. "It hurts, it hurts, it hurts!"

"Stand still!"

George allowed Grace to do something she never expected anyone to do for her until she was at least eight-five years old—wipe her ass. "It hurts."

"Okay, okay, oooh, lay back down, oooh." Grace led George back to the couch. "It's a little red. Okay, a lot of red." George could still feel the burn as Grace tried not to panic. "Maybe we should call 911?"

George freaked out. "You are 911!"

Grace had dealt with burn victims before, but this really wasn't a burn. She had dealt with skin irritations and allergic reactions before, so maybe if she combined the two protocols... "Are you allergic to oranges?" she asked as she rushed to the bathroom.

"I'm allergic to assholes who dump orange juice on my ass five hours after I've gotten a tattoo!" George buried her head into the couch cushions and screamed.

Grace came back with an armful of supplies, got a glass of water, had George take some Motrin, and then she set about dressing the wounds. As she washed the red inflamed area with the cool wet washcloth, she noticed the craftsmanship that had gone into the creation of the stork tattoo and was impressed. She hoped hers looked just as good. While she wrapped her friend's left buttock in a sterile bandage and harnessed it with adhesive tape, George had an epiphany. "This has got to stop. I'm too old for this shit!"

Grace patted down the last bit of tape. "For tattoos and OJ on your ass?"

"Well, for starters yeah." George closed her eyes. "I drink too much when I'm with you, when I'm alone, when I have a shitty day, when I have a great day, when I'm happy, when I'm sad. I drink too much! And, it's not fun anymore. I have the inflamed stork on my ass to prove it."

Grace knew there was some truth in that, but she didn't want to admit it. "Yeah, but you know we're just having fun."

George let the reality of her life sink in. "I need to do something about this."

Grace watched as George accepted a harsh truth. "You mean like AA?"

George winced. "Ugh, AA meetings. Grace, they're in church basements and YMCA's and people wear bad shoes and drink shitty coffee. I'm going to have to start smoking again 'cause they all smoke and then I'm going to have to get the nicotine patch." Grace made room next to George on the Shabby Chic sectional and stared up at the ceiling with her. George sighed. "Will you go with me?"

"Yeah, I have lots of shitty shoes." Grace affectionately tugged George's hair. "And, you know what I'll do better than that? I'll quit drinking with you."

"Really? You'd do that for me?"

"Of course, that's what friends do."

George was certain most friends didn't do that, only exceptional friends like Grace. "Thanks. Uh, but even though you're quitting drinking with me if you decide to have Clair's baby, I'm not getting knocked up too, but, I'll take you to a fat farm after if you want."

Grace laughed. "If we're not drinking or smoking and I'm getting knocked up we may need more than the promise of a fat farm to get us through this."

"Well, what if it's a fat farm in Bali with half nude male models waiting on us hand and foot?"

Grace grinned. "You're getting warmer."

Chapter 6

Clair nursed a cup of coffee as she waited for her mother and Grace to arrive. She hated the color orange and yet here she sat in a restaurant named Orange, whose décor was completely orange based. She didn't know anyone or anything other than a pumpkin or an orange that looked good in orange. Yet, here she sat debating the color orange because she was too nervous to allow herself to wonder why Grace wanted to have brunch on a Thursday. Who had brunch on a Thursday?

Grace entered the restaurant a few steps behind her mom. Even though she was branded with a stork a whole four days ago, her ass still ached. She had forgotten the pros and cons of getting a tattoo on your ass. Pro: very fleshy and cushiony, so less pain than say, your leg. Con: very fleshly and cushiony, hence, why the big guy upstairs made it the place you sat on, so more pain than say, your leg. Ever since her session with Dr. Yael, the Nubian Goddess, Grace has been into the pros and cons list. She was astonished that you could use such a list in every area of your life—from laundry to sex and back again. She found it fascinating. Grace spied Clair sitting under a portrait of an orange. She knew it wasn't a still life because her mother made her memorize the difference between a still life and a portrait when she was sixteen. A still life gave the artist more leeway in the arrangement of design elements within a composition. Portraits are often simple headshots and are not very elaborate. Grace found it disturbing that she had enormous amounts of useless information in her head. As she cautiously sat down, she wondered how her mother would classify the stork on her ass; was it a still life or a portrait?

Clair read the menu. Grace read the menu. Diane tried to read her daughter's mind, but couldn't tell if Grace had made a decision yet. However, she kept shifting uncomfortably in her seat, so that had to account for something. She didn't care what decision Grace made, she just wanted to be ready once the decision had been made. The waitress came over and as the girls placed their orders, Diane thought that maybe Grace's choice of breakfast food would clue them in to which way she was leaning. She smiled to herself. She wasn't sure what she expected—that pancakes meant yes, I'll be your surrogate and, perhaps, an omelette meant no? Diane decided she had had enough. "What the hell is going on?"

Grace and Clair were both startled. The waitress sensing some sort of mother-daughter confrontation hurried to place their order. Grace laughed. "Well, you sure scared the shit out of her!"

"Oh, well I didn't mean too. Grace what's going on?"

"Yeah," chimed in Clair, "what's the deal?"

Grace took a sip of her water and carefully chose her words. "I had another session with NG." Diane had no idea who her daughter was talking about and looked to Clair for help.

"Grace calls the psychologist that the surrogacy program referred her to as the Nubian Goddess, NG for short."

Diane clucked her tongue, "to her face?"

"Why, is it offensive? Should I just call her the goddess?"

Clair snapped, "Jesus, Mary and Joseph, Grace, just tell us why we're here."

"Hmm, someone got up on the wrong side of the bed."

"Grace," implored Diane in her frustrated mother tone, "stop torturing us."

"Okay, okay, the NG had me create a pros and cons list, you know, on the whole being a surrogate for Clair and Henry thing, which wasn't as hard as I thought it was going to be, but, well, I have no idea what you expect out of this."

Clair wasn't sure what she meant. "You mean besides a baby?"

Grace rattled off her concerns. "How is it going to work? Do you expect complete control over my body if the procedure is successful? Obviously, you'll be paying the medical expenses, but what about maternity clothes? My feet are going to swell, so I'll need new shoes. What if it doesn't take the first time; how many times are you willing to try and really, how many times am I willing to try? Do you expect me to pump breast milk, so you can feed the baby or will we let my breasts dry up? What happens if I have to go on bed rest? I am thirty-five, so it could happen and if it does, who will live with me, how will I pay my bills, who will do my grocery shopping? And, what if I don't like your OBGYN, will you find one that I like?"

Clair looked at her Mother and then grabbed a waiter as he walked by. "I need a Bloody Mary, now!" The waiter hesitated, saw the desperation in Clair's eyes, and took off.

Diane called after him, "Make that three. And make them strong."

After six Bloody Marys and one round of surrogacy roulette, the Higgins' trio was still figuring out the logistics to baby-gate. Clair was exhausted. "I think the best thing would be for us to let your breasts dry up."

Grace tucked into her French toast. "But, breast milk is the best thing for a newborn."

"I know, but it would be too hard on you. You'd be pumping milk for a baby that isn't yours. And, really, the kid is going to be my kid, so I should feed him or her."

"Yeah, but breast feeding is not only the best thing for the child, but it's also the best weight loss remedy there is. So, I could pump and then you could use what I pump. It's a shame they don't have wet nurses anymore."

Clair poured herself another Bloody Mary. "That is gross! We'll send you to a health spa."

"George says she'll go to a fat farm with me." Grace suddenly felt guilty. "Don't tell her I drank, okay? I promised her I'd go on the wagon with her, but since I'm not taking her to an AA meeting until Saturday…"

Diane was happy George was finally going to clean up her act. "The wagon? That's great. I hope it sticks."

"You're not the only one," said Grace. "Okay, so breast feeding is officially off the table. If you don't want your baby to have the benefits of breast milk, fine by me. What do you think Mom?"

Diane contemplated the oddness of their conversation. "I never expected to be here. You know, with my daughters discussing the boundaries of carrying one another's child, its uncharted territory."

Clair smiled. "We're nothing if not borderline original. I'm sure there's a Lifetime original movie about this very subject that we missed."

"I'm so Mary Louise Parker."

"Mary Louise Parker?" Clair made a face.

"She's the new Melissa Gilbert," said Grace.

Clair thought about it. "I could live with that." She turned to her Mom and was about to say something when she noticed her staring at someone across the restaurant. She kicked Grace under the table. Grace followed her gaze. That someone, was a man— tall, well built, in his late sixties, early seventies, handsome, but didn't know it, and extremely comfortable in his own skin. Now, if this were one of those Lifetime original movies, he would be a long lost relative like a rich uncle, a deadbeat brother, or Patricia's first husband and he would start a torrid love affair with Diane and cause strife in the family. But, because this isn't one of those stories, the truth was he was just a man. A man who ignited a much extinguished longing in the heart of the beautiful, independent, and always charming Diane Higgins.

"He's cute," whispered Grace.

"Totally," said Clair.

"Really? You think so? I guess he's okay," a red-faced Diane said.

Grace studied the man as he sat with friends. "He doesn't look like he's romantically involved with any of them. Do you know him?"

Diane was immediately flustered. "He's just a guy who comes into the museum occasionally."

Clair grinned. "How occasionally?"

"I don't know. It's not like I look for him."

"Fridays, she's always dressed up on Fridays. You've noticed that, right?" a knowing Clair declared.

Grace laughed. "Or Wednesdays. She made a point to reapply her lipstick after we had lunch last week. I bet that's when he comes in." Grace egged her sister on. "I bet his name is something regal like Pendleton, yeah, Foster Pendleton."

Clair cracked up. "No, he's a guys' guy. He's wearing jeans with a jacket. His name is Chuck. Oh, no wait, it's Anthony Daniels, but his friends call him Tony."

"It's Salvatore Piceno, but he goes by Sal," blurted Diane. "I looked up his membership status. He's single, a widow, a retired lawyer, and he volunteers with the ACLU, as well as at The Sisters of Mercy Mission downtown where he counsels homeless families and helps rehabilitate them."

"Geez, how much information do you have to give to become a member of the Museum?" giggled Clair, "Are you an undercover FBI profiler?"

"Faye in membership knows him. Now, can we please drop the subject?" implored their Mother.

"So, you haven't spoken to him? Are you going to?" queried Grace.

Diane sighed. "Just leave it alone, okay? It's a harmless flirtation."

"Really? Do you bat your eyelashes at him?"

"Grace Heloise Higgins," threatened Diane, "drop the subject or else!"

"You're going to send me to my room? Or, will you punish me and make me go to bed every night without watching TV?"

Diane sighed. "If we can change our history, so you can say you went on tour with Death Parade and Clair suffered from exhaustion, can't we just call this a harmless crush and let it go?"

"That could be arranged." said Clair, "but only if you talk to him."

"Yeah," replied Grace.

"Fine, when you make a decision about your womb, I'll talk to him. Okay?"

"Deal," said Grace.

"Deal," said Clair.

Diane sighed. "Can we get back to more important things like what happens if Grace has to go on bed rest? For the record, she's not moving in with me. She is the most difficult sick person I've ever met—well, next to your father." They took a moment to pause on the memory of their beloved Popsicle.

"I'm not difficult," retorted Grace.

"No, you're a bitch. There's a difference," laughed Clair.

"I don't like burnt toast, who likes burnt toast?" Grace scowled at her sister. "I'd be a little nicer if I were you; this womb is no way near being yours yet."

Diane rolled her eyes, then turned to get their waitress and noticed that Sal was looking at her. She got nervous and immediately spilled a glass of water. Her daughters jumped, "oh, shit Mom," and swung into action to clean up her mess as Diane turned bright red and hung her head in embarrassment.

Chapter 7

More than anything in the world Grace hated clothes—not that she had some desire to be a nudist and walk around naked all the time, but clothes were annoying. When you are five-eleven in stocking feet, finding something that fits, which means it was long enough and didn't cling in all the wrong places, was like trying to find a needle in a haystack. "No way! You look like a reject from outer space." Grace stood in front of Clair and George in an outfit.

George reacted badly. "Did you get that from Judy Jetson's closet?" She pushed Grace out of the way. "Sit down. Give us control of your closet, okay? You were never really good at this."

Grace did what she was told. "Yeah, well try to find a happy medium between slut and school teacher."

"Who you calling a slut?"

George giggled, "you wish Clair Bear," then dug deep into Grace's closet. Somewhere between the bell-bottoms and clam diggers she found a pair of black Marc Jacobs tights.

Clair looked through Grace's dresser and sighed. "Please let me organize this room, please—getting dressed would be so much easier." She stopped talking when she hit pay dirt with a cute Lerario Beatriz jersey dress.

Grace stared at her. "You already reorganized my house without my permission and asked for the use of my womb—don't you think you're pushing it?"

George, who was now on the bottom of Grace's closet, said, "well, she's got a point."

"Who's got a point?" Clair and Grace bellowed at the same time.

George crawled out with dust bunnies clinging to her arms and legs, and a pair of black ballet flats under her arm. "You both do. Grace, you should have Clair reorganize your bedroom. You were just saying the other day how much easier everything is to find." Clair gave Grace a triumphant smile as George continued. "Now, we all know Clair gets an enormous amount of pleasure out of reorganizing ,which is equal, at least in my book, to the amount of pleasure she'd get from Grace carrying her child, so yes, you could say that Clair was pushing it." Grace then shot Clair a triumphant look.

"Well, you're hardly impartial. You told Grace, and I quote, 'first rule of life: never lend family money or your uterus.'"

George gave Grace the stink-eye. "I stand by that, but you actually have a solid relationship. Now, if you want to keep it that way, I suggest getting a lawyer."

"Henry and I discussed this very thing last night. We should definitely get a lawyer and we're paying you."

George threw Grace the outfit they wanted her to wear. As Grace changed into it, she sighed, "come on, that's ridiculous." Grace stood before them in her Lerario Beatriz jersey dress over her

Marc Jacobs black tights. "Does this say breakfast?" George smiled approvingly.

Clair grinned, "it's the perfect two in the morning breakfast date outfit."

"Oh, shit, what about my hair? I haven't gotten it cut in months."

"No problem. I made an appointment for you with Cherie; wash and blow dry, my treat, for four o'clock," smiled George.

Grace gave George a hug. She turned to Clair. "There is no way you're paying me if I have your baby."

"Then there's no way you're having my baby."

George high-fived Clair, "that's my girl."

Chapter 8

Grace walked into The Palace Grill a bit uncertain about how she expected to find Jack. She hadn't even asked him what he looked like—better to keep the dream of the hot fireman who looked like George Clooney alive. At least she knew she'd be safe here. The place was big with cops from the 911 Center, which was right across the street. Grace smiled at Betty, who was working behind the counter tonight, and grabbed a booth in a more secluded area of the diner. She realized that beside Betty, Shari the other waitress, two policewomen, and a prostitute, she was the only woman in the place who wasn't in uniform, so she'd leave the finding up to Jack.

"Coffee?" asked Shari.

"Nah, I'd love some orange juice though," said Grace.

"Juice? Sure, anything else?"

"Nope, I'm waiting for someone."

As Shari left to get Grace's juice, a tall Greek God scooted into the booth. "Hey."

Grace smiled. This was too good to be true. "Hey."

"Been waiting long?" The guy asked.

"No."

"Good, good. You hungry? I'm starved," the guy said.

When the sound of his voice finally caught up with the warm, honey resonance Grace associated with Jack, she was confused. "Uh, who are you?"

"Jack," he said.

Grace studied him. "No, you're not. Who are you?" Grace had seen too many episodes of "Law and Order" not to know this could be some type of set up.

The guy smiled. "You're good." He looked around the diner, zeroed in on a cute, clean-cut man who appeared to be Italian and said, "she's good," gesturing to Grace. The man smiled and made his way over to their booth with a bouquet of flowers.

"I hope you like lilies," he said, as the guy got out of the booth.

"I'm Rich. This is Jack. If he turns out to be a big disappointment, which he will, give me a call." He pulled his card from his wallet and handed it to Grace.

"You're a cop?"

"Detective," he smiled, slapped Jack on the back, and left.

As Jack sat down, an annoyed Grace snapped, "what was *that*?"

Jack, feeling a bit sheepish, sighed. "Well, Rich is my go-to guy."

Grace was incredulous. "You have him check your dates before you meet them?"

"No." Jack looked at Grace's big green eyes and suddenly couldn't lie. "Well, just the blind dates. You see it's like this, most blind dates seem too good to be true. You get the set-up from your friends that she's great, she's this, she's that, and she pulls small children out of life threatening situations on the weekends and then you meet her, and this—is the lazy eye they forgot to tell you about;

that—is the baggage from the ex of five years ago; and she doesn't pull small children out of life threatening situations on the weekends because she's going to garage sales hunting for the limited editions of Beanie Babies she's missing. So, when I decided I was looking for a keeper I came up with this little system. You would not believe how many women I haven't met because of that guy."

Grace stared at him as Shari delivered her orange juice. "Really?"

Jack grinned. "Really. Can I get some coffee?"

"Sure." Shari plopped down two menus and walked away.

"So, I take it you do the same thing for Rich?"

"Yeah, but I don't get laid as much. Apparently, I'm not that cute."

"You're a dog," Grace growled, but she was too intrigued to really be upset.

"No, I'm not. We've been speaking for six months. If I was a dog, I would've slept with you and broken up with you by now." Jack grinned. "You're staying, right?"

Grace didn't know what to make of a guy who used a boy toy as his own personal natural selection when it came to the women he dated. It was like a reverse "Suddenly Last Summer" and the last thing she wanted was to end up, well, dead. "You're a bit too sure of yourself."

"...And you're better than I ever imagined," Jack flashed her another smile. "So, you hungry? I'm starved!"

To reiterate, and to make sure that we haven't gotten off track, this tale is about two sisters, the biggest most important question you can ever be asked, and how that question and subsequent answer informs every aspect of their lives. This is not a tale about princes, charming or otherwise. There is no white horse, no castle, no amazingly true of heart kiss that will wake anybody from a coma. Now, as far as dates go, this one was going well. They had gotten over the awkwardness of bait and Rich switch and successfully traded stats. Jack is the youngest of five—the other four are his sisters: Donna, Debra, Tina, and Toni. Yes, he's Italian and he's the only single one left in his family. Because Grace and Jack only spoke while both of them were at work, so many of their calls were interrupted by actual life threatening emergencies, which gave them the patience that they needed to take things at a slower than normal pace.

For Grace, who was still recovering from Ray, this was a good thing. And for Jack, who had a tendency to bed women too quickly—before he had actually figured out who that woman was and where she stood when it came to the key levels of life emotionally, spiritually, intellectually—and would then find himself in many awkward situations, one of which notably got him engaged, married, and divorced within ten months, the slow boat to a relationship was a great thing. He just had no idea how slow the boat with Grace was about to get!

Jack had recently decided, between her hot chocolate and his black and white shake, that his instincts about Grace were right. She was a terrific woman and he definitely wanted to get to know her better. As he cut up his pancakes, he smiled. "So, let's deal with the basics—Archie or Reggie?"

Grace took a bite out her waffle and thought as she chewed, "Jughead. He was cute, sweet, funny, and everyone liked him."

Jack laughed. "Didn't see that coming."

Grace grinned, "I have a few surprises—baseball or basketball?"

"I'm a guy; put up a scoreboard and I'll watch two old ladies pummel each other."

Grace leaned into the booth seat. "Well, there goes bingo night. Okay, so Stewart, Leno, or Letterman?"

Jack shoveled in the last of his pancakes and eggs, then took a big sip of his shake. "Actually, Stewart, Colbert, Letterman, Maher, O'Brien, Kimmel, and well, Leno is...not for me."

Grace blurted, "I think we can move forward to a second date," and immediately felt self-consciousness. Jack grinned. Grace blushed. "I mean if you want too."

Jack noticed a wave of concern washed over Grace's face. "What? Is there a reason we shouldn't?"

Grace hesitated. "Well..." The biggest most important question she had ever been asked was something that loomed pretty prominently over this moment.

"Well? You're married, divorced, recently separated, just finished a year experimenting with lesbianism, which, by the way, I'm totally fine with, just found out your Visa's been revoked and are about to go to prison to serve back-to-back jail sentences for identity fraud, just declared bankruptcy, what?"

Grace went for it. "My sister wants to rent my womb."

Jack was confused. "Your room?"

"She wants me to have her baby because she can't, you know, have it herself."

Jack put down his shake, stood up, wasn't sure why he was standing up, and then sat down. "Wow!"

"You ready to run for the hills? You can probably catch a cab." Grace and Jack shared a look. Not many people get to this point in a relationship. Usually, if you're a surrogate you've already had a kid and/or you're married and you just like being pregnant, but don't want another kid of your own. And, if you do get to the pregnancy part of a relationship it's usually not before you've slept with the guy you're dating.

"Wow."

"Uh, you said that already."

Jack gave a weak smile. "I know, I just can't think of anything else to say."

"That pretty much was my reaction."

"This must be tough for your sister and her husband. They don't want to adopt?"

"No. I mean if they have to, but first they want to try this. I sorta promised her when we were kids."

Jack didn't think he could be shocked again, but he was. "Man, I was just figuring out that you shouldn't eat paste when I was a kid."

"Let me rephrase, not kids—teenagers."

"Still, that's some promise."

Grace bit down on her bottom lip as an awkward silence kicked in and tossed her directly into non-stop chatter mode. "Well, she wants me to have her baby because Lindsay Wagner couldn't have a baby and she adopted Nancy McKeon's baby, but then she wanted it back. And after Melissa Gilbert was running from her abusive husband and Valerie Bertinelli was a nun in love with a priest and we finished a whole bottle of apple wine and two boxes of Twinkies…I mean, I was drunk, I was nineteen, I was high on sugar, and moved by the plights of McKeon, Bertinelli, and Gilbert—the holy grail of

Lifetime movies. I'm putty around them. I dare you to find me a woman who isn't. And, my sister—she's tricky—she took advantage of me. I didn't know what I was doing when I double-pinky-sweared-blood-sister-oathed and signed that damn contract!"

Jack took Grace's hand to calm her down, "I don't think the contract is legal."

"I know, but then I never thought she'd ask me to have her baby either. What would you do?"

He shifted in his seat, still holding onto her hand. "Me? This isn't me. I can't answer that."

Grace liked the fact that Jack was holding her hand. It felt nice, comfortable, and very sexy. His hands were strong and safe. "But if it was you?"

"Then it would be a medical break-through."

Grace laughed. "Seriously, what would you do?"

Jack shook his head. He looked around the diner, not sure for what, and then sighed. "To be honest, I don't know. My sisters would step in front of a bullet for each other, but this isn't fair because I know no one would ever ask this of me." He played with Grace's hand, he liked how if felt in his. "I look at it this way, there are times when a choice shows up out of the blue, from nowhere, and you're like where the hell did that come from? But, it came to you for a reason. The universe brought it to you because it knew you could handle it. And, maybe you're the only person who can do this particular thing at this particular time. When you love someone you sometimes have to sacrifice a little bit in order to show them how much you love them, but that's me and I'm not the one who's going to have to give up ten months of my life or, may I say, a spectacular body, to have someone else's kid. So, you need to look into your heart and figure out who is in there and why."

Grace stared at him. The NG was right. His answer did hold the key to what type of man he was and just might have answered once and for all what type of woman she was.

Chapter 9

Grace and Jack parted company about twenty minutes after the end of that conversation. He had offered to take her home, but Grace knew she wasn't ready for that. Like Jack, she had a tendency to sleep too quickly with the person she was dating and the results had been disastrous. This time she was going to respect herself and him for as long as she could hold out. The date had ended nicely. No weirdness based on the "womb for rent" conversation. He said he'd call, Grace knew he would. For the first time in her life, she felt like she had found someone who got her. Grace now stood in front of her sister's house. She liked it the minute Clair and Henry had shown it to her. They excitedly pointed out the backyard, which would be great for a tree house; the pool where they expected Grace, the ex-lifeguard, to teach their kids to swim; and the master bedroom that had a bay window and library nook, which is where they planned to put the baby's basinet for the first year.

Overwhelmed, Grace sat on the steps. Grace was at a crossroads—again. First, there was the great become a librarian debacle—after the Frozen Popsicle Affair, then the endless journey of self-discovery and dead end jobs after the Jesus died at thirty-three and did more than me epiphany, and now here she was on the corner of yes, the biggest most important question in our life does involve your womb, but you can say no. In the past, Grace waited out the decision making process until the bitter end and usually there was only one choice left. This time, she couldn't do that. Her pros and cons list was done. The cons were selfish physical annoyances: hormone shots, swollen feet, bad back, bad gas, gaining weight, etc. The pros were more substantial: the ultimate act of sharing, giving the gift of life, sacrificing herself for someone else. All of those years at St. Crawley's were finally kicking in. Grace thought about what the NG said and what Jack had said. She went through all these steps numerous times and always came up with the same answer. She just had to tell Clair.

Of course, we all know Grace is going to ring the doorbell or Clair is going to conveniently walk out the front door and sit down next to her sister at this very moment because this is THE moment, but because we pride ourselves on being somewhat original, we must admit that we tried to come up with something better than the truth, but sometimes a tale—fairy or fractured—is like life and the people in them do the obvious. Grace stood up and walked to the front door and knocked. She didn't want to ring the doorbell because it would startle Clair, who would jump out of bed and wake Henry. By knocking, Clair, who had the hearing of a Doberman Pincher, would eventually hear it and calmly get up without waking Henry, who slept with earplugs. Grace knocked again and when the lights in the hall went on, she sat back down on the porch steps.

Clair, in her perfectly matching pajamas and robe, answered the door and saw Grace sitting on the steps. She knew it was the moment. She calmly took a breath, walked out, and sat next to her sister. "You okay?"

Grace leaned into Clair. "I'm fine. I just had a date with a really great guy who might actually transition from just a guy to maybe *the* guy."

Clair was thrilled for her and sad for herself. Obviously, becoming pregnant with her kid didn't fit in to Grace's plan. "That's great. So, what's up?"

"Oh, the usual stuff, gas prices, meeting my possible Mr. Right, and my uterus. Pick a subject Oprah."

Clair closed her eyes. "Meeting your possible Mr. Right."

Grace looked up at the night sky. It was beautiful out. A clear night; big moon; not cold, not hot; and you could see the stars. "He's great. I mean, I knew that just from talking to him for like six months, but even in person he's like totally great, which wasn't what I was expecting. I was expecting gives good phone, but you know, gives bad one-to-one interpersonal skills thingy plus a hook nose, a lazy eye, and maybe a limp."

"So, he disappointed you? That's wonderful."

"I guess, but then there's the whole biggest, most important question I've ever been asked thingy. You know, the old, will I have your baby? So, the timing sucks, but then, you're my sister and he's a just a guy who might transition to not being just a guy, but he could still mess up and be just a guy. And, if I ask you to wait for me to see where the relationship is going, well that could take years and I could keep coming up with excuses like we just started dating or he broke my heart and I need time to recover. And, if I ask him to wait, you know, for ten months that's a little more reasonable, but who's going to hang around a fat, hormonal, human rollercoaster?"

Clair put her arm around Grace. "I don't know."

"I hate to say it, but I'm in no place to have a baby right now. I've had about forty jobs in the past two years. I have no idea what I want to do with my life. I finally weigh what my driver's license says. I'm at my goal weight. It's like Hawaii. I keep planning to go there, but I never got the chance. Now, I'm actually there and damn, I look good in Hawaii. Besides, I'm not sure if I want to have kids of my own let alone yours and if I do want to have kids of my own, what happens if after I have your kid I can't have my own kid? Plus, I'm thirty five years old, I'm a 911 Operator, I'm a slob, chaos follows me everywhere, and in spite of all that, I'm gonna be on an episode of Jerry Springer because I'm about to let my sister and her husband knock me up!"

While Grace took a well-needed breath, Clair took a moment to understand what she just said and when she did, she excitedly pushed her off the porch. "Get out! Are you serious? You sure, really sure, that you want to do this?"

"Well, not if you're gonna hurt me."

Clair helped her up. "Are you sure, really sure? You know we're going to pay you and we're going to go to a lawyer and do this like completely one hundred percent legal, so we don't screw up our relationship."

Grace was shaking. "I'm scared shitless, but someone told me to look into my heart to see who's in there and why and you're in my heart. We've always been there for each other. I can't turn my back on you now."

"There is no way I'm ever going to be able to thank you."

Grace smiled, "I know, but you can try," and pulled a Tiffany catalog from her jacket. "I marked a few things. The sapphire on page fifty-seven goes great with my eyes. Oh, and the diamond necklace on page eighty is not my taste. I wanted to let you know that in case you were thinking diamonds."

Clair started to cry. "We're going to have a baby."

Grace started to cry. "With each other, which is so wrong and so right in so many ways." Grace pulled Clair into a hug.

"His parents freaked when we told them we were considering a surrogate and that surrogate was you."

Grace smiled. "Having a child really is the gift that keeps on giving—especially if it annoys the Queen of Mayonnaise." And so, this is how we got from here, to there, to now... The Higgins Sisters were about to enter a phase in their lives that would confuse, delight, frustrate, and scare them more than they ever imagined.

Chapter 10

NOW, that's where the Higgins Sisters were. Every single second of every day was consumed in the "now" of trying to get Grace knocked up—it wasn't easy. Like most couples struggling to have a child it never is, but Grace called it fun and more specifically fun to the third power! In this case, the third power wasn't The Father, The Son, or The Holy Ghost. It wasn't even lions, and tigers, and bears, oh my! It was more like The Lawyer, The Psychiatrist, and The Fertility Specialist. So, where would you expect to find two gals hot on getting one of them pregnant by her husband? Well, today they were with The Lawyer. Grace sat with Clair and Henry as The Lawyer, a tall, balding jovial man explained the surrogacy laws of the state of Illinois. He smiled at them a little too much. Clair thought he was just trying to be kind. She was barren. People tended to be nicer to women who wanted to have kids, but couldn't.

The Lawyer rambled on, "So, Illinois law provides for gestational surrogacy where the surrogate mother is not biologically related to the child she is carrying, but does not address traditional surrogacy in which the surrogate mother is the biological contributor of the egg. Now, because Grace is biologically related to the egg, but isn't the contributor of the egg, we need to cover a few bases. The first being, according to Illinois law, a parent and child relationship may be established voluntarily by consent of the parties when the surrogate mother certifies she is not the biological mother and the husband of the surrogate mother must also certify that he is not the biological father, but because Grace is single that shouldn't be a problem. Have you been sexually active in the past five months? Could you be pregnant and not know it? Will that pose a problem in anyway?"

Grace felt all the heat in her body rise to her face. Clair, Henry, and The Lawyer were staring at her. Grace hadn't been sexually active in a long time and saying it out loud wasn't easy, but she supposed it should be easier than saying she was a whore—not that she was. Okay, maybe in her younger days she was promiscuous, but she was never a whore. Grace smiled weakly, "Um, no."

Grace thought The Lawyer smiled just a bit condescendingly. "Great," he said. "Then the biological mother must certify that she donated the egg, the biological father must certify that he donated the sperm, and then a licensed physician must certify in writing that all of the above is true." He leaned back and put his pen down. "Okay, so these papers are what you're going to sign today. Do you have any questions?"

Henry hated going to a lawyer's office. As a kid, with every corporate takeover or some will or trust fund codicil, he was dragged by his parents to the family lawyer where he sat through hours of verbal gymnastics only to get to the part where he had to sign on the dotted line. He vowed he'd never make his kid go through that and now he can't even have a kid unless he goes through it again. Henry sighed. "Uh, this is kinda morbid, but what happens if one of use dies before the baby is born?" Grace and Clair both gasped.

The Lawyer, who was very matter of fact, stated, "actually, that's a very good question. If the surrogate's life is in danger for any reason you must decide if everything should be done to save the surrogate or the baby. If Clair dies, Henry, of course, gets the child; if Henry dies, Clair gets the child, and if you both die, then I'm assuming Grace, being your only sister, would get the child."

"Not necessarily." Clair was shocked that those words came out of her mouth.

"What the fuck?" said Grace. "Who would get the kid?"

Clair hesitated. "I don't know. I need time to figure it out."

"Really Clair, how much? An hour? A month? A week? How much time do you need to figure out if I can care for the child that I gave birth to? Oh, and if it comes down to saving me or the kid how much time would you need to figure that out?" Grace dramatically paused, "buzz, times up, you picked the baby."

Clair's look gave it all way. Grace stood up. The Lawyer looked at Henry then at the women. "Uh, you know there are a lot of variables that must come into play before any of this could happen."

"No shit," said Grace. "And one of them is that I still agree to this asinine plan."

So, where would you expect to find two gals who were arguing over the ramifications about getting one of them pregnant by her husband? Well, they decided to continue their argument with The Psychiatrist or as Grace calls her, The Nubian Goddess.

"Let me get this straight," sighed Dr. Yael. "You want Grace to have your baby, you're willing to sacrifice Grace if something goes wrong to protect the baby, and yet you don't want Grace to raise the child if you and Henry happen to pass away?"

Clair, who was feeling ganged up on, rolled her eyes. "I didn't say that."

"Yes, you did," growled Grace. "Your look said it all."

Clair knew Grace was right, her look did say it all and it said sacrifice Grace. "Come on Grace, if it was me I'd tell Henry to do everything it takes to save us both, but if push came to shove, save the baby."

Dr. Yael tried to steer the conversation a bit. "Really in all likelihood neither of you will be dying before the baby is born."

Grace pouted. "But the fact that she's willing to be so cavalier with my life is pretty disturbing. By the way, you're no longer in charge of my living will. You'd probably pull the plug if I sprained my ankle."

Clair was shocked. "I'm not being cavalier with your life and I would do everything in my power to save you, but if the choice was between you and the baby..."

"You'd save the baby because you'd love it more." Grace pouted.

"You're nuts! If the choice were between you and the baby I would save whoever would have the best quality of life. End. Of. Story! Would you really want to be saved if you couldn't live your life the way it was before?"

"That would depend. If my quality of life got worse and I was brain dead or was going to need someone to help me pee and had to use a pencil to press buttons on some big machine so I could talk, well, then no. Let's face it, I'm no Stephen Hawking and my life wouldn't be about quantum psychics and the string theory. But, if for some reason my life would be better than the way it was like I won the 'go away from the white light' lottery and my prize was a million dollars and I could eat all I want and never gain weight and was given the power to transport myself everywhere I wanted to go, then yeah, I think I'd want you to save me!"

Clair deadpanned. "Duly noted."

Grace dryly asked. "Why can't I raise the kid if you and Henry die?"

"Because I'm never dying," stated Clair.

"Well," added Dr. Yael, "Immortality aside, I think Grace asks a valid question."

Clair fidgeted. "If I die and Henry dies and you raised the baby then you'd be the mother and that makes me uncomfortable."

Dr. Yael sighed. "Uncomfortable because you'd be dead?"

"No. Well, yes that too, but Grace is the baby's mommy."

"No. I'm not. You and Henry are the baby's parents. I'm just UPS."

"But, for ten months it's you who has the baby's heart next to hers, it's you who is literally and figuratively tied to the baby, and who is bonding with the baby for approximately the first seven thousand, two hundred hours of its life. That makes you the baby's mommy and if I'm dead, what's gonna stop you from having the kid call you mommy and forgetting all about me—the egg donor?"

For the first time since her sister's long ago breakdown, Clair had finally beaten Grace in the crazy department. "Okay, first—you did the math on how long the kid will be in my womb? That's sick! I'm never going to forget you, believe me, I tried. Remember in tenth grade when I told everyone you were an exchange student from Russia?" Grace turned to the NG. "She was going through a horrific bushy eyebrow period, no doubt trying for the Brooke Shields look, didn't work." Grace stared at Clair. "I would never have your child call me 'mom,' Auntie Mommy maybe, but never mom. And, being your sister is supposed to be a good thing. I'm the only one besides our mother who can fill the kid in on every single detail of your life. No stone will go unturned. Not only will this kid be able to conjure up an image of you at any age—especially the costume wearing fad you were into at twelve—but...," Grace, now visibly upset, caught her breath, "...if you're dead, what about me? I'm going to need this child to help me get over losing you and, well, don't I deserve to have a part of you?"

Clair felt bad and softly said, "it just scares me." She then tried to deflect her selfishness. "Uh, Aunt Mommy? No friggin' way!"

"That's not yours to decide. You're dead. Besides, that's between me and the kid," argued Grace.

"Oh, really?" said Clair.

"Really!" a defiant Grace retorted.

"Okay, no, I'm putting that in my will too and you're so not the godmother."

Grace was completely shocked. "What?"

"Listen, if I live..."

"If you live, oh now it's if you live?"

Clair rolled her eyes. "I'm just not comfortable with you having a title with the word mom, mother, mommy, or whatever idiotic variation you come up with."

Dr. Yael attempted to smooth things over. "Grace, Clair does have a valid point. Feelings of insecurity, even of inadequacy, are bound to come up for any traditional mom, but this bond you have as sisters, and will now have as co-mothers, is bound to intensify those feelings."

Grace sighed. "I get it. I get it. So, I'm the guardian, but not the godmother?"

Clair sighed. "Yes."

"Fine, but just for the record, when you're dead, and you will die one day, and I don't care if you're one hundred and two when you croak, I will outlive you and that kid is calling me Aunt Mommy whether you like it or not!"

Clair rolled her eyes again. "Fine."

Now that they had stopped arguing over the ramifications about getting one of them pregnant by her husband and everyone had signed on the dotted line, Grace and Clair went to their OBGYN Beth, who was also a Fertility Specialist or as Grace calls her "The Frigidaire" because she's always trying to get them to freeze their eggs. "Okay," said The Frigidaire, "are you ready?" Henry looked at Clair who looked at Grace who suddenly felt not so ready after all. Frigidaire knew how scared they were and tried to be as jovial as possible. "We've got the eggs, we got the sperm, we've got the uterus."

Before she could give herself a chance to chicken out, Grace jumped up. "Let's do this!"

Within ten minutes. Grace found herself in a white gown, legs spread eagle and staring up at the mosaic tiled ceiling in the examination room. Now, there are many things that go through your mind while you're waiting for someone to insert a foreign object filled with your brother-in-law's sperm into your cervix. First, there's the "eeew, gross, it's my brother-in law's sperm" factor; then there's the fear of peeing out said egg and sperm before they have a chance to acquaint themselves; then there's gee, am I on a hidden camera show? Not to mention the fact that, well, you're bare assed; you're cold; where the hell is the doctor; and last, but not least, you're day dreaming about the two hour nap you get after the procedure is done because you're not supposed to move and how you're going to ask your sister to stop for frozen yogurt on the way home. Obviously, Grace had a lot going on!

Grace was trying to unscramble the letters on the tiled ceiling, which was one big Scrabble board, when Frigidaire made it through the door. "Great, isn't it? Makes the wait bearable, plus I'm addicted to Scrabble." Just then, the nurse came in with the foreign object, Grace averted eyes. Frigidaire put on some gloves and picked up the foreign object. "Try to relax, try to keep your cervix relaxed, okay?"

Grace wondered how one went about keeping their cervix relaxed? She supposed she could just take deep breaths or maybe they should just give her drugs that were strong enough to relax her for the rest of her life. "Okay, we're done."

Grace looked at Frigidaire. "That's it?"

"Yep. Stay off your feet for at least two hours and I'll see you on Friday, so we can shoot you full of hormones."

"Uh, okay. So, how long till we know?"

"About two weeks," Frigidaire smiled. Grace didn't move, she was unsure if she could truly get up. Frigidaire laughed. "The sperm and the egg aren't going to fall out of you and no, they won't come out when you pee. I promise."

Frigidaire left to let Grace get changed. Wow, in two weeks she thought, I'll know if I am someone's Auntie Mommy.

They drove home in silence. Well, except for when Grace asked for frozen yogurt and, of course, they stopped. When they finally got

Grace home, Clair put her on the couch, made sure she had the clicker, snacks, a couple of bottles of water, and the phone close by, so that she would never have to get off the couch. Well, except to, you know pee, but because they were assured she couldn't pee out anything of importance, they were okay with that.

And, that's how the Higgins Sisters made the inevitable jump from now to now what?

Chapter 11

NOW WHAT? Grace didn't do well with now what. When she was a child, pre Daddy Popsicle, she was the one who would ask without ever pausing for a breath, "are we there yet, are we there yet, are we there yet?" She was impatient and bored easily. Once she learned a task and then mastered it, she had the inexplicable need to move on. Ever since her mother potty trained her at twenty months, Grace was always ready for the next big challenge. The trouble was that post Daddy Popsicle Higgins she never truly challenged herself again—unless it was to a game of solitaire. What's a girl to do? Well, this girl went back to work. It was three a.m. and Grace was exhausted. She wondered if that meant she was pregnant. The baby books Clair had given her to read each stated that being tired was a symptom of pregnancy, but Grace figured it was because the night held, thus far, a sewer explosion, three false alarms, a pretty bad highway crash, and yet, with all that to distract her, Grace couldn't shake the *Jeopardy* theme song that was playing in her head. Two weeks was a long time to wait to figure out if you were knocked up or if you had to go through the entire procedure another time. Grace and Clair, with the help of NG, had negotiated the three-strike rule. If she wasn't preggers after the third in vitro attempt, the deal was off.

Grace watched her coworkers as they sat off in the corner chatting and decided that because she and Jack had had three official dates, three a.m. wasn't too late or too early to call. Jack was in Los Angeles for the next week because his cousin was getting married and he was the best man, and it was only midnight there... Well, you get the idea. These are the thoughts that raced through the mind of a hormone induced, practically knocked up 911 Operator. Grace tapped the fingers of her right hand on the desk as she waited for Jack to pick up.

Jack hadn't expected his cell phone to ring. He wasn't even sure why he had brought his cell phone into the bathroom to begin with, but he made sure he washed his hands before he picked up the call. "Grace?"

"Yeah, is it too late?"

"For you? Never." Jack immediately hated his answer.

Grace smiled, "well, if it is or I've caught you in the middle of doing something you're not supposed to do, like robbing a bank, having sex with a stripper, or you know, standing in line at an ultra-trendy LA bar with a bunch of supermodels, let me know and I'll call you back."

Jack laughed. "No such luck. I'm in my pajamas in my cousin's sorry excuse for a guest room where I'm surrounded by his high-school track trophies and will sleep on Bart Simpson sheets. Right now I'm watching Stephen Colbert and trying to convince myself that if I grab that last slice of pizza I will lose my boyish figure forever."

"Lay off the pizza. I like your boyish figure A LOT!" Grace said in her best come hither voice, which truthfully sounded more like Bea Arthur than Kathleen Turner.

"Oh, you do? Well, how much is a lot?"

"Enough to want to jump your bones, but not enough for phone sex."

Jack was mildly disappointed about the phone sex, but reasoned that because they hadn't actually slept together yet, he really couldn't expect her to put out long distance. "This jumping of the bones that you speak of—will this happen any time soon?"

Grace laughed. "Get your ass back from la-la land and find out."

"If I could get on a plane tonight, I would."

"So, how are the best man duties going? Throw that wicked bachelor party yet?"

Jack chuckled, "not exactly. We're having dinner tomorrow night at Ruth Chris' Steak House, then we're going to the Buena Vista Cigar Club, and if we're not too tired, we may take in some sort of burlesque show in Hollywood."

"Wow, that's pretty hot stuff."

"Jimmy's a pretty tame guy."

Grace grinned. "Well, tame is good— especially good for me. I can just wipe all those images of sexy bulimic blondes throwing their bodies at you from my mind."

Jack loved how funny Grace was. "Well, now just because Jimmy is tame…"

"Hey, hey, pretend if you have too. At three a.m., a girl needs peace of mind."

"How do I know some random stockbroker jock isn't shaking his booty for you while I'm gone?"

"Trust me. The only person who has violated me this week is my OBGYN."

Jack liked being in bed and hearing the sound of Grace's voice in his ear. "Oh, yeah, how did that go?"

Grace made herself comfortable on the couch in the office. "Hard to say, won't know for a few weeks, but now that the lawyer, the psychologist, and the fertility specialist are through with me for a while I feel a bit used and whorish. And, you?"

"Well, I wish you would make me feel used and whorish!" He gave his pillow a good whack before lying back. "You're doing a very noble thing."

"Am I?" Grace bit her bottom lip. "Or am I just trying to score brownie points to get into heaven while I avoid, once again, figuring out what I want to do with my life?"

"You've got to shut off that brain of yours and relax."

"You're right, you're right." The switchboard lit up and Grace's co-workers looked at her. "Shit, I've gotta run. Bye."

Jack sighed. "So soon?"

Grace raced to the switchboard. "Yep, call me tomorrow after your wicked night on the town."

"Will do, will do. Night." Jack hung up. His heart was in a very precarious place right now. And, so, to elevate his pain he went down stairs to get that last slice of pizza.

The call turned out to be one of those this isn't an emergency dealios and more of a, "if I take Tylenol PM with Benadryl is that okay," questions. Grace decided to spend the rest of her time coming up with a recipe for the remaining food in her fridge. This was a game Grace loved. She was usually pretty successful except for that one time when she only had a bottle of beer, an apple, and a box of baking soda. Not even Bobby Flay could make something edible out of that. Grace loved to cook. It filled her two basic requirements— instant gratification and instant gratification. She was never bored when she cooked. The next big challenge was washing the dishes; a task Grace enjoyed so much she rarely used her dishwasher and the other challenge was fitting all the food she had cooked in her fridge. It was just a huge refrigerator puzzle of fun and cooking completely engaged her. With the shopping, the prep time, the actual cooking, and the cleanup, it kept her busy for hours on end. All in all, cooking was a win-win situation.

Grace went through what she knew she had in the fridge— butter, the usual condiments, bell peppers, carrots, mushrooms, left over brown rice from Ben Pao's Chinese Restaurant, an egg, two pieces of raisin bread, half a container of low fat milk, and a bar of semi-sweet dark chocolate. This would be a relatively easy meal to make and there were a few variations she could try. Fried egg sandwich with grilled veggies, veggie omelet, egg fried rice, and if she wanted she could dip the raisin bread into the milk, make it really soggy, melt the chocolate, pour it on the bread and make a poor man's bread pudding. Grace was suddenly very hungry when her cell phone rang. "I want a drink."

"Well, you can't have a drink. Where are you?"

"Home. I had some stupid business thing and we ended up at a bar. I drank club soda all night and now I'm jonesing for a drink. Maybe just a glass of wine?"

"You've been clean for three weeks. Why would you screw it up?"

George sighed. "Because I can. Isn't that what I do?"

"Did you call your sponsor?"

"Grace, how long have you known me? Am I the type of person who is going to confess my deep dark fears to a virtual stranger and then call said stranger whenever I get the urge to drink? No. This is just like the time I taught myself how to build a boat. I have to do it my way, on my terms."

"For the record, you didn't build a boat, you built a toy sailboat."

"Semantics."

Grace laughed. "I'm off in forty five minutes, meet me at my place."

"Do you have any milk? I went to Swirlz's Cupcakes and bought a dozen."

"Yummy, see you in an hour."

"Can I stay all day, eat crap, and watch old movies?" George sounded like she didn't want to be left alone.

"Of course you can, stay strong. Later." As soon as Grace hung up with George, her sister called. "Why aren't you asleep?"

"I can't sleep and you're the only one I know who is up at this hour. I think you should move in with us."

Grace nearly dropped her phone. "Excuse me?"

"It just makes sense. Then I could be part of every stage."

"Huh? It's your kid; you're part of every stage."

"No, you'll, you know, have private moments with the baby. When you go to sleep at night or you eat something spicy and it kicks." Clair tried not to cry. "I'm never going to know what it feels like to have my baby inside my body. I don't have to stop drinking, or eating cheese, or be careful of artificial sweeteners, or stop running. It's just not... I can't help... fuck it."

"Whoa." Grace tried to take it all in. "Okay, first of all, I'm not moving in with you. There's just no way that's even a possibility. Now, what happened?"

Clair can no longer hold back her tears, "I got my period."

"Oh, wow." Grace had no idea what else to say.

"Of course, good old inhospitable Clair lived up to her reputation!"

"Well, somebody's got too. I'm tired of living down mine."

"I'm scared," Clair sniffled on the other end of the phone.

"You're scared? Sweetie, try being me."

"I did—that's what got us in this mess in the first place!"

Grace felt like an idiot. "You're right. Sorry. Hey, how about if I'm actually knocked up, you give up everything with me? We'll have sleepovers, so you can feel the baby at night. This way you'll be a part of almost every single second."

Clair sniffled on the other end of the phone. "I can live with that."

"Get some sleep okay?" Grace hung up and looked down at her stomach, "wow," she thought, "and I'm the one getting the hormone shots."

Chapter 12

After figuring out, addressing, and finalizing the—you're having my baby— financial situation, they found themselves back with The Frigidaire who informed them that the first round of in vitro didn't take. Now, in an odd turn of events, Grace was disappointed, Clair was relieved, and Henry thought it was his fault. Eventually, Grace got over her disappointment, her surprise at her disappointment, was shot up with a second and third set of hormones, and a few weeks later found herself in a white gown, legs spread eagle and staring, yet again, at the mosaic tiled ceiling in the examination room. Clair surmised that her feelings of relief stemmed from the fact that she wasn't really part of the process. So, this time when the nurse came in with the foreign object and Grace averted eyes and Frigidaire put on some gloves then picked up the foreign object and said, "try to relax, try to keep your cervix relaxed; okay?" Clair was holding Grace's hand.

Three weeks later it was confirmed that Grace was officially knocked up. And, so, the Higgins Sisters officially moved from now to now what to you don't say and onto the big—you're having my baby—game board that was about to consume their lives.

"You don't say?" That was the first thing Patricia said when she heard the good news. The second thing she said was, "so you're still going through with this?"

At least Henry, Sr. offered his congratulations. That is before pouring himself a stiff drink. "Grandpa? Does the kid have to call me grandpa?"

Henry knew they weren't thrilled by the idea of Grace carrying their child, but even for them this was a bit extreme. "Is something wrong?"

Patricia sighed, "other than that woman giving birth to our grandchild, what could be wrong?"

Clair had had enough of the Grace bashing. "Grace is making a huge sacrifice for us. She didn't have to do this. We could've hired a stranger or adopted, but no. She stepped up because she loves me, loves us. Now, you either accept that or you don't, but let me tell you this—one more rude comment at all about my sister and you will never, I repeat, never see this child!"

Henry, Sr. watched his daughter-in-law trembling in front of him and felt like a fool. He walked over to Clair and put his arm around her. "Now, let me get this straight, it's your egg, his sperm, and your sister is basically the Easy Bake Oven my grandchild is being cooked in?"

Clair traded a confused look with Henry. "Uh, yeah."

He guided Clair out onto the porch that overlooked the pool and tennis courts. "So, I was thinking we should come up with a few alternatives. Maybe the kid could call me Papa Henry?" he asked, as they disappeared into the vast back yard.

Henry didn't look at his mother. He knew that would be a huge mistake. Instead, as he concentrated on his imperfect rendition of

"Twinkle, Twinkle Little Star," Patricia sat down beside him, took his hand in hers and declared, "I will seriously hire a guy named Big Moe to break every one of your fingers if you ever touch this piano again!"

Henry laughed, "I thought it was your dream to have a concert pianist in the family?"

"Honey, I dreamt of a lot of things, but I learned to give up the unrealistic ones. Apparently, you're not meant to be a concert pianist and your father wasn't cut out for the boardroom. You adjust."

"Well, if you adjust, why are you having such a hard time with the baby thing?" Henry could've sworn he'd seen a pained expression wash across his mother's face, but she got up too quickly for him to tell for sure.

Patricia grappled for a way to articulate what she was thinking. "I, well, here's the thing, what if something goes wrong? I don't want to rain on anyone's parade, but something could go wrong. Can you handle that, can Clair, can Grace? And, I know you've said you've covered all the bases legally and financially, but have you really? What is Grace going to do after all of this? I know it's your kid, she knows it's your kid, but this is a huge responsibility and at the end of the day you and Clair have a child. Grace, who God willing won't need a C-section, has forty pounds of baby weight, breasts overflowing with milk, and no kid. Is that fair?"

Henry was at a loss for words. "You like Grace." Patricia ignored him. "You do. You don't think she killed Uncle Harry at all!"

Patricia sighed. "Tell anyone and I will kill you in your sleep. I wish I had a sister that was willing to sacrifice her entire life for me. My sister tried to strangle me in my sleep!"

"Uh, she short sheeted your bed when you were at sleep-a-way camp."

"Same thing Henry. That girl has been searching for something since the day we met her. And this, well, she needs something of her own when this is all over; we should buy her an apartment or a condo."

Henry, Sr. and Clair walked in on that last sentence. "Buy who what?"

"Grace, an apartment. It's the least we can do. She's giving our grandchild a home for ten months. Besides, she's not in a very good neighborhood and if she's not moving in with you, well, our grandchild has an image to uphold."

Henry, Sr. went to the phone. "That's a splendid idea, I'm calling Carl."

Clair looked at her just as confused as her husband and felt like she'd just been played.

"You don't say?" squealed Diane, then immediately burst into tears, laughed, kissed her son-in-law, hugged one daughter, and patted the other's belly. "I'm gonna be a grandma, how cool is that?"

"Not as cool as the fact that I'm carrying my own niece or nephew!"

Clair touched Grace's belly. "It doesn't seem real yet."

Henry pulled out a gift-wrapped box and handed it to Diane. "A little token."

"You didn't have to get me a gift." Diane opened the box, which held a Zagat's restaurant guide for Chicago and a book entitled <u>Going Out Without Freaking Out: Doing It Right From The First Hello.</u> "What the hell is this?"

Grace took her mother's hand. "Now, I know how excited you are about this whole grandma thing, but first, well, it's time for you to make good on a certain promise."

"Oh, no, no, no!" Diane shook her entire body to get her point across. "And, I actually encouraged my daughter to continue dating you. You're off the list Henry."

Her son-in-law shook his head. "Now, a promise is a promise."

"Yeah, Mom," sighed Grace, "you told us we must never break our promises."

"So, next Thursday?" asked Clair. Diane so didn't like the sound of this. "You said he stops by every Thursday." Clair added, "Henry went through Zagat's and ear marked some nice places."

"Yeah, ones that say I'm a nice respectable woman, but I still have needs!" Grace cracked.

"Oh, just leave," growled Diane.

Clair and Grace answered in unison, "leave? You want us to leave?"

"Wow," Clair turned to her sister. "We just gave her the best news of her life and she's kicking us out."

Henry marveled at their close bond and blurted. "I hope we're having a girl."

Clair impulsively kissed him. "I hope we have a healthy child."

Grace looked around the room. "I hope my water doesn't break while I'm buying groceries, but what I really hope is that Grandma Diane gets lucky!"

"Out! Now!" Diane shouted as the rest of them erupted in laughter.

"You don't say," was also the first thing that George said. Because they were at Margie's Candies, George ordered them a round of black and white milkshakes, a turtle sundae, and toasted to her friend's upcoming motherhood. "So, you're knocked up?"

"Yep." Grace tried to smile, "and scared shitless."

"Well, I'm sober. Officially for two months, so join the club."

The waitress who delivered their order had a can of whipped cream attached to the side of her uniform. George eyed it, "Leave the can, it's gonna be a long night!" The waitress laughed and was about to walk away when George grabbed her arm. "Seriously, leave the can." Unnerved, she did as she was told.

"Tough day?" asked Grace.

George took a sip of her shake, then grabbed her spoon, covered it in whip cream and then dug into the sundae. "The thing is I knew this was going to be hard. More so because I'm a social drinker or, if you will, a social drunk not a closet drunk, so the days aren't as rough as they could be. For the past eight weeks, I've moved all my dinners and drinks to lunches because my clients are less inclined to drink at lunch, thank God, but it's the twenty pounds I've put on and the break-up stuff that is doing me in."

"Huh? Broke up, with whom?" Grace was digging into the turtle sundae. "We talk every day and you leave out a guy? Who were you dating?"

"Alcohol," George said in between mouthfuls of sundae. "Like with Ray, it's the stuff they leave behind or in your case the stuff they take that is the hardest to get over. I miss the fun of choosing the right bottle of wine at dinner, the smooth taste of cognac after a steak dinner, and the way a guy smells after a couple of bottles of beer and a game of basketball—all tangy with a hint of salt, mmm, like a human margarita—yummy!" George got a far-a-way look in her eyes.

"Okay, Rachael Ray, I get it. When did you date a guy who played basketball?"

"A girl can dream can't she?" sighed George. "I'm okay half the time then the other half everything I do, everything I see reminds me of alcohol and that I'm not drinking it."

"Just masturbate and get it over with."

George chocked on her mouthful of the sundae, "what!"

Grace laughed. "Well that's what you do if you'd just broken up with a guy right? It would be either great break up sex or masturbation. It'll relax you the way alcohol did."

"You think if I masturbate it's going to make my sobriety easier?"

"Masturbation makes life easier. 'Nuff said. I read that a woman should have an orgasm a day; it keeps the stress away."

A laughing George sucked down her shake, "you're serious about this?"

"Damn straight sister!" said Grace as she finished off her sundae. "You'll be glowing, more relaxed, and, you know, satisfied. Plus, it's enjoyable and let's face it, you haven't been laid in a while; hell, I haven't been laid in the while and I'm pregnant!" Grace stopped chewing for a moment. "You know a girl can always use a new vibrator. There's this thing called the Water Dancer that I've been meaning to pick up. We should go shopping on the way home."

George shot a stream of whipped cream into her mouth. "Masturbation—who knew it was the key to life?"

"Men," deadpanned Grace.

Chapter 13

Now, it should be noted that Grace and Clair didn't tell people who weren't family members about the pregnancy until she was three months pregnant; suffice it to say, she waited to tell Jack. She wanted to do it in person, but because Jack had traded shifts with his fellow firehouse buddies, so he could attend his cousins wedding, he ended up working every night and weekend during the past four weeks. Therefore, Jack and Grace spent a lot of time on the phone, more so than they had even during those first six months of phone dating. The conversations were longer because they weren't being interrupted by life threatening work emergencies and covered a myriad of topics. Jack told Grace about his brief, but disastrous first marriage to a woman who is now living in Westchester County, New York and sells Mary Kay, that he's allergic to peanuts, loves Hong Kong action movies, broke his arm when he was ten, his nose when he was sixteen, and his leg four years ago. Jack also disclosed that he wants kids and wants to be in a lifelong committed relationship, but he doesn't necessarily think marriage is the only way to accomplish that and last, but not least, he believes in God, but not in the institution of religion, per se. Grace was grateful that he wasn't an atheist. She had found over the years that it was best to avoid people who didn't believe in a universal higher power whether it was Buddha, or God, or even Hare Krishna, because those people had no checks and balances to keep them from becoming morally bankrupt and she knew about morally bankrupt. After all, she had dated Ray.

And, so, all of their trading of personal information leads us to exactly where Grace and Jack are right now—thoroughly besotted with each other as they stand in the middle of an art gallery gazing at a painting of the letter E. Grace, realizing there was no good time to tell the man you're dating that you're knocked up with your sister's kid, took Jack's hand and finally blurted those special words, "I'm pregnant."

Jack, like everyone else said, "You don't say?" But, he said it in such a way that you would think he was being told some elaborate magic trick about where babies came from. In addition, Jack immediately got Grace a chair and made her sit down. Once she did, he bombarded her with questions, such as "how do you feel? Do you need anything?" And, for the first time Grace felt a twinge of sadness that the child she was carrying didn't belong to her or maybe even to her and Jack. Of course, the moment Grace had that thought she internally freaked out, but thankfully the Howard Miller Grandfather clock that just struck five saved her. "Oops, George, I have to go," said Grace.

Jack smiled, and then in the middle of the Heaven Art Gallery in Wicker Park, he pulled her into a hot kiss in front of the letter M, "congratulations!"

A half-hour later, Grace was sitting with George at an AA meeting in the Wicker Park Alano Club, which was for women only. George knew that if she were going to be serious about staying sober, not having any men in her meetings would make life a bit easier. Besides, she had her brand new rabbit vibrator to help her avoid the temptation of switching from alcohol to men—not that she actually needed to switch because for the past five years she only hooked up when she was drunk. When she drank she got horny. Drunk, horny, and pathetic. Her dad would be so proud. George felt the sweat beading on the back on her neck. Man, she thought, this place is hot. She took a deep breath and when the group leader asked if anyone had been sober for thirty days or more George squeezed Grace's hand and then went to the front of the room.

George took a deep breath and nervously started lacing and unlacing her fingers. "My name is George and I've been sober for forty days." After the usual applause and hellos George swayed back and forth. Normally, when she stood in front of such a large group she was doing a presentation and the focus was on the campaign. This time, it was about her and she was never really comfortable when the spotlight was on her. George cleared her throat and looked at Grace who smiled encouragingly. "It's been pretty hard to restrain from drinking. I have a very social job and I'm usually meeting clients for drinks three to four times a week, but this week when I was sitting at the hotel bar with one of my biggest clients, for the first time, I didn't panic. I didn't think, oh, 'if I order a juice he's going to know I'm in recovery or he's going to think I'm a prude or even, well, if she's no longer drinking then clearly she's no longer talented.' I just ordered a club soda and nothing happened. We had a great meeting, plus he bought the new pitch. It was an amazing feeling that lasted until today when I had my usual Sunday night 'oh, shit work starts tomorrow' panic attack and really wanted a drink, but I came here instead." The room clapped as George got her forty-day chip and walked back to her seat. Grace got up, hugged her friend, and suddenly fainted in her arms.

Nobody panic! We can't promise you a harm free tale. For the most part pregnancy isn't all sweetness and light because women who are pregnant are sitting ducks for diabetes, hemorrhoids, swollen feet, and the hormones that rage within their bodies that cause various mood swings. Plus, there's anemia, ectopic pregnancy, placenta previa, hyperemesis gravid arum, eclampsia, and good old abruptio placenta. All-in-all, pretty life-threatening stuff. However, fainting while pregnant is a fairly common occurrence. Grace, now sitting in the emergency room behind a white curtain with George, was being told just this as the Doctor left with the blood he had drawn. Suddenly, she heard the unmistakable shriek of Patricia, the Queen of Mayonnaise. "Where is she? Of course we're family, that woman is carrying my grandchild."

Grace looked at George, "who did you call?"

George went into over-drive. "You're pregnant, it's not your kid, you fainted in my arms, and so, I covered all the bases. I called your sister, the mother of the child you're carrying. She wasn't home and I couldn't reach her on her cell and, so I called your Mom, the in-laws from hell, and uh, Jack."

"Why in the hell would you call Jack? How did you call Jack?"

"I used your cell phone while they were examining you. No worries, he didn't answer, so I hung up."

"Now he thinks I hung up on him? Great."

As George realized that she might have called too many people, Clair poked her head in, "hey, you okay?" her trying not to panic sister asked.

"I'm fine. According to the doctor, fainting is a pretty common thing for pregnant women."

"They took blood to make sure she's not anemic, but if she is, she may need an additional iron supplement," George smiled weakly, "uh, do you want me to go?"

Clair pulled the curtain shut. "Oh, God no; if you go out there now, Patricia may pounce and I couldn't do that to you."

George sighed. "Oh good, she scares me."

"Join the club," Diane said as she pushed herself into the small space, "hey baby." She kissed her daughters then gave George a big hug. "Congrats on your forty days of sobriety." George beamed while Diane studied her daughters' faces. "What's the deal? What's going on?"

Grace sighed. "The doctor thinks I may be anemic, but that's it. The baby is fine. They made sure of that as soon as I came in."

Patricia pushed her way in. "What the hell is she doing here? I'm at least related to you!" She looked around. "There aren't any sick people here are there?"

Grace rolled her eyes. "Hello Patricia, how are you? George brought me in."

"Oh, thanks George. Nice to see you're not drunk and waking up in some foreign country," a twitchy Patricia said.

George squeezed Grace's hand. "Well, it's nice to see you're not drunk and waking up in jail." With that, George pushed her way past Patricia and out the other side of the curtain to freedom.

"I don't think I can stay here much longer, all the germs and such," Patricia looked at Clair, then Diane, and then Grace, "did you tell her?"

"Now is not the time," Clair stated rather firmly.

Patricia ignored her daughter-in-law. "We're buying Grace an apartment in a better neighborhood. There's no way a grandchild of mine is living in squalor."

Clair turned to Grace and mouthed, "I'm sorry."

"Squalor? Last time I checked, the baby was living inside of me."

"Yes dear, we all know how pregnancy works. The baby is living inside of you and you are living in squalor; hence, we're buying you something in a better neighborhood," Patricia looked around again, "some place sterile."

"More sterile than a hospital?" an incredulous Diane asked.

"More people get sick and die while in the hospital than succumb to household accidents," snapped a clearly hospital hating Patricia.

Grace gave Patricia the stink eye. "Let's get one thing straight. You have absolutely no say in any situation involving me and this child."

Patricia, feeling the germs closing in, tugged her coat closer around her body. "Now dear, I understand you're upset, but for God's sake we're one of Chicago's finest families and there is no way you can continue living as you do. It's bad enough we're in this embarrassing situation to begin with."

"Patricia, you're aggravating my daughters." Diana gently led Patricia out of the curtained off cubicle. "Oh, and another thing, I will not have you using that annoying condescending faux term of endearment with my daughters, myself, or any other member of my family."

Clair rolled her eyes, "I'm so sorry."

The Doctor finally came in. "You're good to go Ms. Higgins. I spoke to your OBGYN and we went over the blood tests. You seem to be developing anemia. I'm giving you a prescription for an additional iron supplement and she wants you to call the office tomorrow and make an appointment for this week."

"Really, that's it? Nothing wrong with her, nothing wrong with the baby?"

The Doctor patted Clair on the arm. "She's fine, the baby's fine, all good. I promise. You and your partner have nothing to worry about." He handed the prescription off to Grace then left.

Clair started laughing. "Please, you're so not my type."

Grace tried to keep a straight face. "Oh, please, I'm everyone's type."

Chapter 14

After the commotion at the hospital, Grace was relieved to be home and more important, to be alone. This was one of those moments, she thought as she stretched out on the couch, one of those private moments that Clair got so worked up about. It was strange to think that here she was alone and yet she really wasn't alone at all. Grace patted her stomach. "Listen kid, I'm your Auntie. I know odd, eh? I will do my best to protect you from that motley crew you're gonna call family, but no matter what they say or do, they love you." Grace closed her eyes. The moment she did, she relived her kiss with Jack. She smiled and then panicked. She hated not being in control. Thinking about one person all the time and maybe falling for them when you knew that at some point, along with not having control of your emotions, that you weren't going to have control of your bladder was disconcerting at best. She patted her stomach again. "I know we're sharing just about everything right now, food, organs, but uh, I hope we're not sharing brain cells because I'd hate to pass on the neurotic inner workings of this mess of a mind to you. Now that's the gift that keeps on giving."

Grace was drifting off to sleep when there was a knock on the door. She thought, "if this was anyone she was even remotely related too, she was going to pitch an all out fit." She pulled herself off the couch and opened the door. It took Grace a full minute before she realized that it was Ray standing in front of her. She felt a shiver go down her spine and stepped out into the hall. "How did you get into the building? What are you doing here?"

Ray smiled. He always had a great smile. He looked good. "My key," he rocked back and forth on the balls of his feet, "can we can talk?"

Grace pulled her door shut. "No."

"Come on, Gracie, just a talk for old time sake. What harm can come of it?"

"Hmm, oh, I don't know, you'll clean out my bank account, steal my appliances, and put me into debt for the rest of my natural born life?"

"Hey, I said I was sorry."

Grace rolled her eyes. "Ray, if you've got something to say, say it; if not then get the hell out of here."

He stared at her. For one brief second he seemed vulnerable. "Gracie, Gracie, Gracie—after all these years?"

Suddenly, the buzzer rang in Grace's apartment and she hit the button knowing that even if a Jehovah Witness showed up in the next five minutes it was better than standing here with Ray. "I've had a really bad day. I'm tired and I don't want to do this right now. Actually, I don't ever want to do this or anything else with you, so just cut bait and leave!"

Ray pulled an envelope out of his pocket and handed it to Grace. "That's everything plus interest. I'm getting my life together.

I'm in sales now—legitimately—and I'm doing well. My therapist says the only way I can move on with my life is if I made amends with everyone I wronged."

Grace hesitated and then took the envelope. "Well, uh, good for you."

"I'm sorry Gracie. I'm sorry that you think so little of me that we have to have this conversation in the hall. You were the best thing I had in my life and I'm going to do everything in my power to win you back."

"Oh God, no! No winning me back, not now, not ever. It's over, has been for a long time—OVER!" Grace opened her door and backed into her apartment.

"I deserve a second chance, we deserve a second chance," Ray pleaded.

Grace trembled. She wasn't sure if it was because she was afraid of Ray or afraid Ray still had a hold over her. "No second chances Ray, no way, no how." They simply looked at each other. Grace took in his slightly crooked nose, the three freckles below his lip on the right side of his mouth, and the tiny scar he had above his left eyebrow. She sighed. There was just so much to love and hate about this guy.

Ray leaned in and kissed her gently on the lips. "You love me Gracie, you always will."

It was a very nice kiss as far as kisses went. It scared Grace that she thought this, that she thought anything at all tender and sweet about him. She cleared her throat, "give me the key. Give me the key, Ray."

"Give her the key Ray." Startled, they both turned to find Patricia standing there. "And get the hell out of here before I knock your sorry ass from here to Kingdom come!"

He pulled the key from his pocket and handed it to Grace. "This isn't done." Ray backed away from Patricia who was closing in on him like a Doberman. "We're not done Gracie, we'll never be done." As he walked away, a shaken Grace backed into her apartment. Patricia followed. They said nothing. Grace put the envelope Ray had given her on her kitchen table and poured Patricia a glass of wine.

"A small sip won't hurt," Patricia said. Relieved, Grace poured herself a small sip and knocked it back. Patricia looked around the apartment. "It really isn't as bad as I thought." Grace nodded. She had somehow lost her power to speak. "But, really dea..," Patricia, remembering what Diane had said, stopped herself. "A better neighborhood wouldn't kill you. Do you really want your sycophant ex-boyfriend disrupting your life?"

Grace didn't want to admit it, but Patricia had a point. Moving to a new place that didn't have any memories of Ray associated with it would be nice. Owning something had always been her dream. Everyone she knew owned something. Even with the money she just got from Ray, it would take her years to afford a mortgage on her own.

Patricia could tell by the way Grace was staring off into space that visions of king sized beds, entertainment centers, and anything else that was in the godforsaken Pottery Barn catalog were dancing in her head. Patricia plied on the pressure. "Think of it as a signing bonus. You signed on to have my grandchild; I buy you an apartment or a condo. The big executives do it all the time, and this way after the baby's born you'll have a little nest egg of your own." Patricia smiled. There was a knock. Grace couldn't, or perhaps wouldn't, answer the door, so Patricia strode over in her Giorgio Armani suit and Manolo Blahniks ready to do battle. With a flourish of pride and determination she opened it and declared, "leave!"

"Uh, who are you?" asked Jack.

Patricia took in the tall good-looking man in front of her. "Who are you?"

"I believe I asked you first."

Patricia smiled. "I'm Grace's sister's mother-in-law and the grandmother of the child she's carrying. Who are you?"

"Oh, you're the mayonnaise queen."

Patricia choked back a laugh. "Yes, I am. And again, young man, who are you?"

"Jack, I'm Grace's boyfriend."

Patricia looked at Grace then back at Jack. "I see. Well, since you don't have a key how did you get in the building?"

"Some twitchy little guy let me in."

"Really?" She said pointedly. "What has this neighborhood turned into?" Patricia gave Grace a peck on the cheek and made her way out the door. "Next Friday. What time should I pick you up?"

Grace, who was staring at the envelope in her hand, finally spoke, "how's noon?"

Patricia smiled. "Great! Nice to meet you Jack."

Jack shook her hand. "Nice to meet you Patricia." He shut the door behind her. "She doesn't seem so bad."

Grace sighed. "No, she isn't."

"You okay? What's that?"

Grace put the envelope down. "Nothing, uh, what are you doing here?"

"You called, but you didn't leave a message." Jack moved closer to Grace. "I was thinking that maybe you were thinking what I was thinking."

Grace liked the way her body felt when Jack was close to her. She tried to figure out if she felt like this with Ray. She took a deep breath. He smelled like green apples. "Uh, what were you thinking?" He kissed her. Grace kissed him back, "I was thinking dinner."

Jack laughed. "Well, I'm hungry, I could do dinner."

Grace smiled. "So, I hear you're my boyfriend."

"You got a problem with that?" Jack asked, as he kissed her again. Grace shook her head no and grabbed her jacket. Once they were in the hall, Jack took Grace's hand, "do me a favor, okay? Don't break my heart."

Grace was suddenly covered in goose bumps. "Okay." She whispered.

As Jack and Grace lay side by side on her couch, she remembered why she had bought it in the first place. It perfectly fit two bodies. Grace flashed to being nine months pregnant and hoped that Jack would still be around and that they'd both fit on the couch. Jack had his right arm around Grace and patted her belly with his left. "Are you sure you had enough protein? Maybe you need a glass of milk or orange juice with calcium?"

Grace, who felt both safe and dangerous in his arms, rolled over and kissed him. "I'm good. We're both good." Grace kissed him again, this time more forcefully and Jack immediately forgot what he was thinking, which included things like what was the score of the game, did I get this week's issue of Maxim, and do I have a cavity?

As the passion built, shirts were taken off; lips, hair, and limbs were tangled, skin touched skin and as Grace reached to help Jack undo his pants, "Oh, God, no!"

Grace froze. "Huh? How? Aren't...am I missing something?"

Jack, embarrassed, sat up. "Uh, no—It's just, we can't, you know, do that."

"Why the hell not?"

"You're pregnant." Jack pushed a lock of hair out of Grace's eyes. "I don't want to hurt the baby."

"Trust me the baby is not the one being hurt right now. And where you're going and the kid is, well, it's hermetically sealed, so not gonna get hurt—I promise."

"I know, but still it's not even my kid and I don't know, it's rude."

"Rude?"

"Yeah, rude to you know be poking at someone else's kid."

Grace grabbed her shirt and sat up. "Uh, are you serious?"

Jack, who really wanted Grace right now, sighed. "I think I am."

"That is the most ridiculous yet sweetest thing I've ever heard. Are you going to be okay with us dating and me being pregnant with another man's child?"

"I don't think so." Grace's face fell. "No, no." Jack tried to find a way to say what he really meant. "You're pregnant with another man's child, but it's not like it's another man's child, you know? That's not to say that this whole pregnancy thing isn't going to be a problem, but not like a problem for our relationship, which we don't even really know what that is yet, but the pregnancy stuff and the relationship stuff won't always see eye-to-eye. So, as long as we're honest with each other and don't let things fester, we should be able to manage this."

Grace felt her stomach drop just a bit. "Honest, eh? Are we talking I hate you in the color orange honest; or the I didn't call you tonight, George did because I fainted and she had to take me to the emergency room honest; or are we talking soul bearing, life changing, that twitchy little guy you passed on your way up tonight was Ray, who came by to make amends, gave me back all the money he stole—at least I think he did I haven't checked the envelope yet—declared his love, said he wants a second chance, and uh, he kissed me, honest?" Grace waited for Jack to process everything she had just blurted out.

Jack felt an ache the size of a watermelon in his gut. "Are you okay? Is the baby okay?"

Grace loved the look of concern that washed across his face. "I'm just a bit anemic, but it's controllable and no one is, you know, in danger."

Jack swung his long limbs over the side of the couch. "I was thinking more the I hate you in the color orange honest." He tried to get his bearings, but this moment of unbridled honestly threw him off his game. "I'm assuming that because you're here with me you're not that into reconciliation or am I some sort of test market, so you can figure out if you like Coke better than Pepsi?"

"Oh, I definitely like Coke better than Pepsi," purred Grace.

"Good," sighed Jack. "Who's Coke, I'm coke, right?"

"You're totally Coke. All coke, all the time," Grace said as she leaned in for a kiss.

Jack kissed her back. "You're not gonna turn around and suddenly like Pepsi more are you? 'Cause you know, Coke and Pepsi are really different."

Grace had never made a guy jealous in her life and it felt good. Not because it made him feel bad, but because, well, he liked her that much. "Trust me, I like coke. So, again I ask, now what?" She leaned into his body and went in for the kill.

Jack struggled, but slowed her down. "We're still not..."

She laughed. "Going to be rude and poke another man's unborn child?"

Jack pulled Grace to him. "We can do other stuff—that's just as fun."

"Oh really?" said Grace, as she burrowed against his body.

"Really," said Jack, as he lightly bit her bottom lip.

Now, if this was a movie we'd fade to black as Jack shimmied down her body. If it were a soap opera or even a Lifetime original movie, we'd see them go at it from tasteful and discreet angles, but this, well, this is neither one of those and it sure ain't porn, so here it goes... They're adults. They had fun. That's all you're getting. We're leaving it up to your imagination. Now go take a cold shower or you know, rent one of *those movies!*

"You're shitting me, right?" Clair stared at Grace.

"Do you think she planned it?" Grace was sitting with her eyes closed in the massage chair at the nail salon.

"I don't know. I agree it was all very convenient, but tracking him down and paying him to show up out of the blue with an envelope filled with money would be giving her too much credit."

George breezed in from her massage. "Buy in my hood."

"She should buy close to me."

George pushed her hair out of her face and nestled into the empty massage chair next to Grace. "Why? Because she's going to be Auntie Mommy?"

"She did not just say that!" glared Clair.

Grace and George laughed. "I'm not buying anything. I only agreed to it because I was under mental duress." Grace leaned back into the massage chair.

"Mental duress? You have got to stop watching *Court TV*."

George picked out a nail color and handed it to her manicurist. "The lady's right, big executives and athletes do it all the time."

Clair agreed, although not so much with the ginger spice nail color George had picked out. "It's an investment in your future. Real estate is only going to make you money."

"You want me to bilk your in-laws?"

"You're not bilking anyone. You're providing a service." Clair, whose red crimson toes were finally done, pulled them out from under the dryer. "You've busted your ass at shitty jobs your entire life. You're the first one to do something for someone else and face it, Grace, if you weren't such an easy touch, you wouldn't have stayed with Ray for as long as you did. Fucking go for it! Oops, I don't want to curse in front of the baby."

George laughed, "Yeah, because in between all of Grace's organs and the fact that he's under water, he can hear you plain as day."

"He?" asked Clair.

"You're having a boy." George matter-of-factly stated. "Trust me, I'm never wrong."

Grace pulled her toes out of the nail dryer. "She's never been right."

"What about Marianna Evans?"

"You said she was having a girl."

"She had a girl." George defended.

"Yeah, after she had two boys."

George closed her eyes, "I didn't say I predicted when they were having it, just that they were having it."

Clair grinned. "Buy the apartment."

"Really?"

George exhaled loudly. "Really. We're going to Margie's Candies after this. I'm jonesing for some sugar. And yes, I know I'm not supposed to substitute sugar for alcohol, but too frickin' bad. Besides, Grace and I are going to the fat farm after the baby comes, so I'll work this all off or pay someone to suck it out of me."

Grace suddenly sat up. "Okay, I'm going to do this. I'm officially a whore. I'm knocked up by my sister's husband with my sister's eggs and living off his parents."

Clair laughed. "I'm so proud!"

Chapter 15

And so, the Higgins Sister's pregnancy rolled on. The fainting scares were just that, but for some reason Grace's morning sickness got worse. It wasn't pretty. Vomiting never is unless you're a bulimic super model. Grace did not, with a capital DID NOT, like morning sickness. She hadn't thrown up so much in her entire life, which led her to believe that she was carrying some sort of alien spawn or demon seed and no amount of discussions about the improbabilities of that could convince her otherwise. The other thing was the tiredness. She could barely stay up past ten p.m. Needless to say, that made her job pretty difficult. So, all in all, Grace was not enjoying this stage of the pregnancy.

Clair, on the other hand, was having a ball. She and Henry were shopping for baby furniture, toys, books, clothes, and well, not throwing up at all. Whenever Clair told anyone they were expecting they always remarked how wonderful she looked and that she had a real pregnancy glow about her. Sometimes, because Clair liked to believe for a little while that she did have a real pregnancy glow about her, she didn't tell the person the Grace part. These people didn't know her, they weren't a part of her everyday life, and with them she could pretend she was a whole woman, a woman who was actually going to give birth to her own child.

As for the rest of them…

Diane was skating under the radar hoping to avoid the "asking out of Sal Piceno" deed; George was now seventy days sober; and Henry, well, Henry was another story. Like most fathers-to-be, Henry was a pendulum of emotions. He was filled with excitement, he couldn't wait to hold his child in his arms, and he was filled with fear. He never held a baby before. What if he dropped the baby? Excitement—he couldn't wait to teach his kid how to read or ride a bicycle and fear—what if the kid hated the sight of him? These scenarios played out in Henry's mind all day long and all night long too. He couldn't sleep anymore. He was tossing and turning so much that once Clair was asleep, he'd get up, go into his office, and buy stuff for the baby. That's when the trouble began.

"Crackers?" Grace opened the door a bit disheveled from a full on bout of the grossness that is morning sickness to find Henry standing with a box of saltine crackers.

"They say they help with morning sickness."

"Who are they? Are they the same people who say that four out of five dentists recommend Crest? 'Cause I still got cavities." Grace smiled at her brother-in-law. "Uh, do you want to come in?"

"Am I interrupting anything?"

"Uh, no, just the vomiting, which seems to have subsided for now." Henry entered the apartment. He brought with him a huge bag of stuff. "Uh, any bagels in there?"

"Do you want bagels? I can get you bagels." Henry offered.

Grace smiled. "No, I was just teasing. Are you okay?"

Henry was nervous; he'd never been in this situation before. And let's face it, only about ten percent of the population is ever in the "my sister-in-law is knocked up with my kid" position, so who could blame him? "You should sit down. Don't you think you should sit down?"

Grace had never seen him like this before. "Uh, sure, I can sit down if you want."

"Great, great." Henry waited until Grace sat. "So, I did some research and, well, there are a few things you need to have, you know, while you're pregnant."

Grace laughed. "Really? Things I need to have? Like a box of saltines?"

Henry reached in and pulled a pair of fuzzy pink Ugg slippers from the bag. "Okay, so you're feet are gonna swell and your shoes are going start to hurt and they say that slippers are the best things in the world to live in at home and they should, you know, be a size larger." Henry dug back into the bag. This time he pulled out a container of Kiehl's foot lotion. "Not only will they swell, but well, they'll ache and this should help relieve tension and stuff."

Grace was amused by his sincerity. "Wow, well thanks."

He then pulled out a bellyband. "Now, while these aren't designed to give support for your back, according to the research I've done they do offer some, but they're also great if you wear it with your regular jeans for while. You just leave them unbuttoned with the band over them." Henry handed it to Grace then pulled out an iPad. "Okay this is for what they call placenta brain. You're going to become scatter brained and forgetful. There's nothing to be worried about, but you should be prepared. You can write down all your appointments, lunch dates, birthdays, and test dates—it's really handy."

"Wow! Clair will be thrilled to know that doctors recommend something she's been doing her whole life. Uh, don't you have to get to work?"

Henry, who was now totally consumed with his big bag o'surprises, pulled out a fan and a rather nice over-sized red-striped Gap sweater. "Your natural thermometer will be a bit out of whack because, well, you have all those extra hormones running rampant through your body. And, so, you'll be hot when everyone else is cold and cold while they sweat. So, these should help with that."

"You really did your research. I'm impressed."

Henry clearly wasn't done yet. He pulled out massage oil. "To help with your back pain in the last trimester;" a support bra, "I think, well, you understand what this is, but it helps as they, you know, get bigger and I, uh, guessed at the size, and here's the receipt, so you can exchange it." A packet of maternity underwear. "Well, that's just, you know what that is, again I guessed at the size and, uh, have the receipt." A box of Kotex panty liners. "In the third trimester when the, uh, baby's head is pushing on your bladder, besides, uh, you know, bladder leakage pregnancy comes with all other sorts of, uh, um, discharges and stuff, so you should be prepared." Grace was now concerned by Henry's behavior. She was also completely overwhelmed by all the things that were about to happen to her body. She hadn't gotten through the first chapter of <u>What To Expect While You're Expecting</u> because every time she opened it she fell asleep. She stared at Henry and honestly couldn't figure out if he had crossed the line or not. Henry, on the other hand, checked his watch,

"I have about twenty minutes before I've got to be at the office. How about I get you that bagel? What do you want?"

Grace snapped out it. "Uh, thanks, um bagel? Rye, cream cheese, tomato—no onion, no capers."

"Great!" With that, Henry was out the door and Grace was left with a coffee table display of the ten things she has to have while pregnant and, well, the need to vomit yet again!

Chapter 16

"I'm not doing it." Diane could be very stubborn when she wanted to be.

"Yes, you are." Clair pursed her lips and held her ground.

Diane pulled away from the curb and merged into traffic. "It's the stupidest thing I've ever agreed to do and now that I've reflected on it, I'm not doing it."

"Do we need to get *you* a surrogate?" Clair wryly asked.

"Oh shut up." Diane groaned.

Clair watched as her mother slowed down at the red light. "Seriously, mom, this is the first guy you've showed an interest in since dad. You need to go for it."

"Honey, I know you have this image of me as this born again virgin since your Father died, but that is not the case. He's been gone a really long time." Diane caught Clair's look of surprise. "Sweetie, how late do you think a curator has to work? I mean what did you think I was doing on all those business trips?"

"Well, well," clucked Clair, "the apple doesn't fall far from the tree. And, by apple I mean Grace and by tree, I mean you; my Mother, the whore!"

"I wasn't a whore, but I did have fun."

"Well, goody for you. You're still asking him out."

"No, I'm not." Diane checked for a parking space.

"Mom, you're pretty spectacular, smart, funny, and from what I've just learned, easy, so you're a catch. Why the hell wouldn't you ask this guy out? What is the deal?" asked Clair.

"I'm parallel parking honey and you know how much I hate parallel parking."

Clair patiently waited for her mom to park. She even waited until she had put money into the parking meter, but she drew the line at her mom applying lipstick before entering the building that her in-laws may be buying an apartment in for her sister. "What gives Hester Prynne?"

Diane shook her head. "It's different."

"Okay, I'm biting—different than having anonymous sex in foreign hotel rooms or different than say, a root canal?"

Diane playfully smacked Clair on top her head, "I didn't have anonymous sex in foreign hotel rooms!" She stopped Clair from walking into the building's lobby. "Did you ever feel like if you did this one certain thing your entire life would change?"

"Uh, who asked her sister to have her kid?"

Grace came up behind them…"and who said yes? What are we talking about?"

"How mom was a whore after dad and she thinks if she asks out Piceno her whole life is gonna change."

Grace took this in. "Good change or bad change?"

Clair turned to her mother. "Trust me, after the whole quality of life conversation we've had, don't go down this road with her."

Diane gave her kids the once over. "You're not going to let me off the hook are you?"

"Nope," they answered in unison.

Grace took her mom's hand. "Okay, let's go see this apartment your knocked up, kept woman of a daughter is going to buy on her sister's in-law's dime. People, we are so living the American dream!"

When they got up to the apartment, Grace was surprised that Henry was there. She hadn't seen her brother-in-law since the ten things you need while you're pregnant incident. Henry smiled when he saw Clair and Grace. "How are my two favorite ladies doing?"

Grace immediately felt weird. "Good, good, wow this place is great."

Henry took Clair's hand. "You should check out the master bath, it has a Jacuzzi, but you can't use that until after you've had the baby. Oh, I forgot, I got you something."

Grace was frightened that her brother-in-law was going to pull out a breast pump or, worse yet, more panty liners for all her yucky discharges. "I should check out the bathroom."

"Come on, wait until you see what he got," said Clair.

Henry pulled out the latest and greatest camera phone/video recorder. "This way you can record the stuff we don't see. We have one, you have one, got one for my parents and your mom." He handed them out.

"You shouldn't have," said a relieved Grace, "this is great."

Diane noticed Grace's reaction and pulled her away. "Can you show me how to use it after we take a little tour?" Once they moved out of the living room and into the master bedroom, Diane pounced. "What gives?"

"Gives? Don't say gives. Henry keeps giving me things."

Diane stuck her head into the walk-in closet. "Whoa!" She and Grace admired the huge custom closet and observed a moment of silence. Grace sighed. "My clothes aren't worthy of this closet. They get kicked out of places like this—usually with me in them!"

Diane nudged her. "What things?"

"The ten things I must have while pregnant: slippers, fan, a sweater..."

"That's sweet." Her mom smiled.

"Massage oil, panty liners, a pregnancy bra, and panties. He guessed at the sizes. I'm sorry, but that's a little bit odd."

Diane stifled a giggle. "He's just trying to feel part of the pregnancy. Does Clair know?"

"I didn't tell her. Who wants to have *that* conversation? I was hoping she knew, but then I was a bit afraid if she sanctioned it."

Before they could finish, Patricia and Henry, Sr. strolled in. "So?" asked Patricia, "what do you think? Come on, out of all the ones we've seen, this is the best isn't it?"

Grace smiled. "Don't you think it's a little much? I'm just one person."

Henry, Sr. patted her on the arm. "You're one person now, Grace, but you're not always going to be one person."

"You do know that Henry and Clair will be taking the baby home once it's born, right?"

Henry, Sr. smiled. "Of course we do, but why not build yourself a field of dreams? If you build it, they will come, Grace, they will come." He sighed and then strolled off into the master bath.

Diane and Grace looked at Patricia who shrugged. "He was on the golf course all day. The sun fried whatever brain he had left. Now come on de..." Patricia caught herself. "It's a great place. It's big, but not so ostentatious that it isn't cozy. And, did you see the kitchen? I know you love to cook, Grace, and this kitchen is state of the art. Come on, let me show you."

Chapter 17

Normal wasn't feeling so normal anymore. Change was happening so quickly that Grace barely had time to catch her breath. She was now four months and two weeks pregnant, the soon to be owner of a swank apartment on S. Michigan Drive, and dating a really great guy. So, of course, Grace was freaked out. And, when she was freaked out she was usually in the NG's office.

"Grace, don't you think it's a little late for that?"

Grace stared at NG. "I'm pregnant, I'm in this, I'm doing this, but I'm also freaking out—aren't I allowed to freak out?"

Dr. Yael smiled. "Of course; every expectant mom freaks out at least ten times a day."

"It's just…I forgot that all this stuff happens. I mean, I knew there was morning sickness, swollen feet, yucky discharges, but then… oh my God, I'm having my sister's baby!" Grace, in the midst of a panic attack, put her head between her legs.

Dr. Yael poured Grace a glass of water; she even put in a slice of lemon that she had cut up while eating her lunch. "When you freak out, you freak out."

Grace bellowed from between her legs. "You got a problem with that?" Dr. Yael handed her a glass of water. "Unless there's vodka in it, it's so not what I need right now."

In a very soothing voice Dr. Yael asked, "what do you need right now?"

Grace got up and started pacing. "I don't know. Maybe to not be pregnant with my sister's baby, to finally stop vomiting, and not having ordinary every day smells—smells that I used to love like peanut butter and French roast coffee—turn on me like a rabid dog. It would also be helpful if my brother-in-law didn't show up every morning to monitor my progress and give me inappropriate gifts like support bras and panty liners and maybe, just maybe, if my sister didn't call me every ten minutes to see if the baby and I, a baby that's like not bigger than a frickin' zygote yet, had any intense bonding moments. And, I'd really love it if the guy I was dating was much less concerned about whether or not I was eating right for the baby and much more concerned with having sex that didn't avoid the one area sex shouldn't avoid! Oh, I almost forgot, and if the guy who ripped out my heart and ripped off my bank account would stop calling all the time— that would be just swell!" Exhausted, Grace sat down. She looked at the NG, who was rapidly writing on a pad and suddenly felt foolish. "Uh, are you having me committed?"

Dr. Yael smiled, "I'm writing you a prescription."

"I can't take anything."

"A half a glass of wine, a pregnancy yoga class, and a weekly massage. These should help keep you, well, not entirely stress free, but a little less stressed."

Grace sighed. "Uh, can I have that wine now?"

Dr. Yael laughed. "We don't keep alcohol on the premises."

"I find that hard to believe." Grace suddenly had a need to lie down. "What should I do about Henry?" she asked as she stretched out on the couch.

"How bad has it gotten?"

"Well, the inappropriate gifts have stopped, but for the past two weeks he's been at my door at nine every morning with breakfast and healthy treats. Today, he came by with Reid, the personal trainer he hired for me."

"Have you spoken to Clair about it?"

Grace closed her eyes. "I didn't want to cause any problems and, well, I also liked the attention. Not in a, you know, bad way, but just well...man I'm just whacked aren't I? One second I'm ranting and raving that I want my brother-in-law to leave me alone and the next I'm saying that I like the attention 'cause I never had a guy take care of me before. Ray was so not the caretaker type and with Jack, we've only been dating a few months and there's no need for him to take care of me. It's not his kid."

"Are you disappointed about that?" asked Dr. Yael.

"No, I mean yes; I mean, what if I'm falling in love with him?"

"Is that such a bad thing?"

"Last time it was a horror show. I'm hormonal. What if it's just my hormones and I really don't love him, but I'm pregnant and alone, not really, but you know what I mean, and I'm just convincing myself that I love him."

She stared at her. "So, you think you're in love?"

Grace popped up off the couch. "Oh God, not love, oooh, no! I'm in intense like. You know, where you want to see him all the time and you get excited when you hear his voice and stuff. Not love, sooo not love!"

"Does he know? Does he feel the same way?"

"Well, he keeps calling and we keep dating and he told me not to break his heart, but really how am I supposed to know? I don't read minds. Maybe he's just some weird guy who likes to date single pregnant women."

"Or, maybe you're in a genuine adult relationship with a good guy who is falling in love with you."

"Oh, well, when you put it like that, I really need a drink!"

She laughed again. "How does Ray figure into all this? Do you have any residual feelings for him? Is that maybe why you can't tell if you're falling in love with Jack or just hormonal?"

"I feel guilty. I know, right? He breaks my heart, cleans out my bank account, and I feel like I let him down. What's with that?"

"After your dad died, how many of your significant relationships were based on saving the guy you were with?"

Grace spat out, "every single fucking one! Am I textbook case or what?"

"We're all textbook cases Grace." She took in Grace's pained expression. "You're not the reason he died, forgive yourself."

"Yeah? And how do I do that? Eat a box of popsicles and be done with it?"

"Maybe your unwillingness to let yourself fall in love with Jack has something to do with the fact that he doesn't need to be saved." She said as she handed Grace her prescriptions and walked her to the door.

"Couldn't I just deal with the super of my building and the guy directly above me who plays the piano at three a.m.? Cause he's not very good. Last night he attempted Mozart's "Prague Symphony Number Thirty Eight" and, well, I'm no music critic, but I've heard a cat in heat who sounded better than that."

Chapter 18

Clair didn't feel normal at all and her hormones were raging because she had gotten her period again, which was one huge slap in the face. As if her period, if periods could speak, was saying "you're half a woman, you can't have a kid, you're defective." Once the novelty of the pregnancy wore off, Clair had to face the harsh realities and because of this she was pissed at everybody and everything. It was as if her inhospitable womb decided to encroach on every area of her life and she had no idea how to keep it at bay. Clair sat with a bowl of uneaten Raisin Bran and a glass of orange juice. She kept staring at the Visa statement. With just one glance she felt like defective merchandise—a jilted wife and an irrational shrew. She tried to calm herself down, but she couldn't get there; that is until Henry walked into the kitchen. Then for reasons she had no insight into, an icy calm fell over her. Poor, unsuspecting Henry kissed his wife, got himself a glass of orange juice, and sat down. When he did, Clair slid the statement over for his perusal. Henry, having no idea what he was getting into, looked it over.

"A support bra?" Clair said through clenched teeth. "Maternity panties? A four hundred dollar oscillating fan?"

Henry, a bit clueless, grinned. "It's for the baby."

Clair had an overwhelming urge to hit something and that something was Henry. "For the baby? Really? Last time I checked the kid was residing inside my sister. Don't you think a four hundred dollar oscillating fan is a bit extravagant for a kid who is still swimming in amniotic fluid? What are you doing, huh, Henry? What exactly are you doing?"

Henry finally connected the —oh shit I made my wife angry— dots and cleared his throat, "being helpful?"

"Helpful? Helpful is putting away the dishes and maybe vacuuming once in a while. Helpful is not lavishing expensive gifts on Grace like she's some whore!"

"The fan was on sale. Doesn't it say that on there? It was only a hundred and fifty dollars. I mean a four hundred dollar fan? Who in their right mind would buy that?" Henry realized he was entering into one of those irrational areas of married life with his not-pregnant-about-to-have-a-baby-of-a-wife. Nothing he could say was going to save his lily-white ass.

"...And the crib, the changing table, the Bose sound system for the nursery? Were those purchase prices wrong too? A carousel? A carousel? What in God's name are we going to do with that?"

Henry cleared his throat, "I thought we could put in the backyard?"

Sometimes Clair thought how in the hell could I possibly love a man as stupid as him? "Are we living in the same house? Have you seen our backyard?"

"I can return the carousel."

"Oh, you will and you'll return the state of the art diaper genie. Who needs a diaper genie that turns everything into mulch? Oh, and you're returning the Bose sound system." Clair was choking back tears. "And while you're at it why don't you return me?"

Henry stared at his wife. The despair in her eyes cut him deeply. "Can't. You're the right color, you're definitely the right fit, and well, you don't shrink when I wash you. Plus you're made with that stain proof fabric I love."

"Yeah, well I'm defective, detestable, and depressed."

He let a small smile escape his lips. "Nice alliteration."

"Do you love me?"

"I haven't tried to return you, have I?"

She sighed. "Are you in love with me? There's a difference you know."

"Since the moment you made that ridiculous request in Starbucks."

"Then how can you not see that the support bra, the maternity panties, the fan, and the fucking swank apartment your parents are buying my sister, the Auntie Mommy of our child, would make me feel like a third class citizen?"

Henry was at a loss. "Huh? You told Grace to let my parents buy it for her."

"Yes, Henry, but I didn't know about the Ugg slippers or the sweater from the Gap. Is there a reason you didn't tell me about any of this?"

"Well, honestly, because I freaked your sister out and I didn't want to upset you. I didn't want you to feel shitty." Henry saw his wife's bottom lip quiver and tried to get everything out in one breath. "I want to be part of the pregnancy too. You and Grace have all these weekend sleepovers planned. What about me? You're not the only one who's feeling the burn here. She's your sister. You've known her your whole life. I've known her for like what, six years? We have no connection, no unspoken bond, and I want our child to know my voice. Seriously, Clair, what are our boundaries?"

Clair, who loved her schmuck of a husband even more at that moment than she ever thought possible, got up, and sat on his lap. "Maybe we should ask Grace?"

"How do we tell her we need more? I've done the research, childbirth isn't pretty. Did you know that the baby's head pushes against the bladder? And all this crap comes out of her?"

Clair kissed him. "We'll figure it out. Just don't stop telling me stuff, okay? And next time ask me before you run out and buy my sister panty-liners."

"You got it." Henry kissed her back.

Chapter 19

Grace couldn't take her job anymore. It was only eight and she was bored out of her mind. She didn't care if she saved a life or not. Well, she'd rather save one than lose one, but as she fielded phone call after phone call of life threatening, not so life threatening, and dumb ass requests for help, she decided that maybe after two years she was done being a 911 Operator. Of course, that concerned Grace. It seemed she couldn't find anything that she felt any excitement for other than sex and food. Maybe she was defective? Maybe she should just keep renting out her womb for cash? The pay was good, the benefits were okay, and if she could live with the morning sickness and the irrational mood swings, she could make a fortune.

"Hey, tubby."

Grace turned to find her coworker, Matt, staring at her. "Yeah?"

"You want to take your dinner break?"

"Nah, I'm good."

"What should I tell the short twitchy guy in the lobby?"

Grace's heart jumped. "Who?"

Matt smiled. "He says he's here to take you to dinner."

Grace sighed. "Little guy, pug Irish nose?"

"That's him. Want me to take care of him for you?"

"Nah, thanks for the offer." Grace walked down one flight of stairs to the lobby and peeked in. There was Ray, leaning against the reception desk holding a bouquet of flowers and wearing a suit. A suit, she thought? He owns a suit? Grace steeled herself and entered the lobby. "Let me guess, you're selling steak knives?" Ray handed her the flowers. "What's the occasion? You rip off another unsuspecting girlfriend?"

He grinned. "I deserved that."

"And so much more, but the sarcasm train stops here. I don't want you visiting me at work, Ray. I don't want you waiting for me outside my apartment. I saw you the other night."

"What's with the boxes? You moving in with that big guy?"

"Not that it's any of your business, but yes." Grace couldn't believe she just lied.

Ray didn't like the sound of that. He didn't like it one bit. "Why?"

She saw the pain in his eyes and felt guilty. "You screwed up your life Ray, not me. I was just the schmuck who kept believing in you, remember?" Grace walked outside, Ray followed her.

"I remember and I know you, Gracie, you believe everyone deserves a second chance. I did my time. I got clean, got a good job." Ray looked like he was on the verge of tears.

Grace felt bad. Her mom used to say she was the only one who could see the good in Ray. She sighed. "I gave you a second chance, Ray. Hell, I gave you a fifth and sixth chance."

He pulled out a packet of Sour Patch Kids and tossed a few into his mouth. "You want me gone? Then I'm gone!" Ray turned on his heel. Grace watched him go. An older woman walked toward her and

Grace handed her the flowers. As she headed into the building, a wave of guilt hit her. Why she felt so guilty after everything he did made no sense. As Grace made her way back up the flight of stairs, she stopped to rest. Wow, she thought, why am I so winded? She touched her stomach. Overwhelmed with emotion she sat on the stairs and wept. Her cell phone rang.

"Hello? Hey, mom. I'm not crying no I'm..." Before she knew it Grace was a sobbing, gulping, sniffling, wet faced, snot nosed mess. "Ray keeps showing up. I told you that. Yes, I did and I now I feel guilty. And, I'm tired, fat— yes I am! I know I'm not showing, but I'm fat." Grace gasped for air and hiccupped, "I think I still love Ray, but what about Jack? And, and, and... my shoes don't fit—uh, huh—and I had to wear my period underwear because I can't fit in anything else. I'm having a baby and it's not even mine!" Grace used the sleeve of her oversized sweatshirt and blew her nose. "Right now? I'm sitting in the stairwell at work."

Less than an hour later, Grace was sitting in her comfy clothes with a cup of soothing herbal tea and a box of Entenmann's cookies on her mom's couch. Her mother had rushed over to Grace's office, scooped her up, and took her home. Diane watched as a now semi calm Grace dunked her cookie into her lukewarm tea and pulled a photo album out of her great grandma Higgins' armoire. Diane made room on the couch next to her daughter. She sighed as she fingered the embossed letters on the cover of the album, then opened to a photo of herself fat and pregnant with Grace and smiled. "This is the awful truth. I'm seven months pregnant."

Grace choked on her tea. "Oh my God! I'm going to look like that in three months!"

Diane laughed. "Well, every pregnancy is different, but there's a strong chance you won't be able to get off the couch without a forklift."

Grace started to laugh. A belly rolling, tears streaming, laugh. "What the fuck am I doing with my life?" Diane pulled her daughter closer. As they spooned on the couch, she brushed some hair out of Grace's eyes and kissed the top of her head. "That night after the emergency room incident, Ray showed. He gave me back the money he took, well I think he did, I still haven't opened the envelope, and he said all the right the stuff, the stuff he should've said two years ago. Then he said he wanted me back and he kissed me. And tonight he was wearing a suit and had flowers and, well, it just seemed that he finally turned into the Ray I knew he could be."

"And if he has?"

"Shouldn't we see if we could make it work? He finally got his shit together."

Diane knew what Ray had done to her daughter. She knew how long it took her little girl to recover from this particular hit and run. Yet, with all of that knowledge, with every fiber of her being screaming at her to tell Grace to run, she knew she couldn't. She had to remain indifferent and not act on the huge wave of fear that was swirling through her body. "Sweetie, just because someone changes or tries to make you believe they changed doesn't necessarily mean that they have changed or that the person they changed into is the right person for you. And what about you? Haven't you changed?"

"Yeah, I guess it's a mixture of—see I told you he was a great guy and he could accomplish all this and wow, he changed for me—and well, it's like wishing for a pony every day and then the pony suddenly shows up."

Diane pulled her arms tightly around her daughter. "Yes, but you have to feed the pony, clean up the pony shit, make sure the pony gets enough exercise, and deal with all sorts of pony like situations."

Grace nuzzled into her mother's body. "You don't think people can change?"

"I don't think you should get back into what was a notoriously bad relationship because of your ego. Sure, it'll feel good to say, 'I told you so' and right now you're all pumped up and giddy at the thought of someone going to all that trouble to fix himself for you, but at the end of the day, are those the right reasons to be in a relationship?" Grace yawned. Her whole emotional roller coaster of a day was finally catching up to her. "What about Jack?"

The mention of Jack always made her smile. "He's great, really great."

Diane caught Grace's yawn and yawned herself. "Then why run to something that has never worked and let go of something that's pretty damn great?"

Grace knew her mom was right. Her mom was always right. She was right about dying her hair cotton candy pink and she was right about becoming a dog walker. "I guess you're right." As Grace nodded off to sleep, Diane scooted closer to the inside of the couch and joined her.

Chapter 20

Grace hated her job. George hated being sober. Diane hated her daughters. Clair hated no one—at least not at this very moment. It was also Thursday. The Thursday. Grace, Clair, George, and a not so happy about it Diane, were finally going to put to rest the great Piceno debate. The three women had various areas of the museum staked out. Diane knew they were there. She also knew that if she didn't ask him out, one of them would do the deed for her. Diane took her normal stroll through the museum. Every afternoon she watched the patrons to see what exhibits they responded to and once in a while she'd engage someone in conversation. In the past month, she had spoken to Sal twice. There was something about this man that fascinated her. He was handsome, but not too handsome, he dressed nicely, but not too nicely, and he strode through the museum with a confidence and bravado that was completely alluring. Diane turned her head in time to catch Clair gesturing for her to look to the right. There was Sal. Diane's stomach lurched. Shit, she was hoping against hope that today would be the one-day he didn't show. Diane told herself to suck it up. She was a grown woman. There was nothing intimidating about asking a man out and yet, the last guy she asked out, she married and then he got run over by a snowplow. Diane stopped in front of the Manet. Maybe she could slip out the back.

"Excuse me?"

Diane turned and found herself face to face with Sal Piceno and George. "Yes?"

George grinned, "Diane, I wanted to introduce you to my friend Sal."

"Your friend?"

"You're surprised I have friends?" He laughed.

George took Diane by the arm and walked her and Sal toward the Roman Greco sculptures. "Sal and I go way back. Don't we Sal?"

"A whole fifteen minutes. George and I got to talking at the snack bar. By the way, have you ever tried the chocolate cheesecake they have? It's terrific." George stopped walking. Sal shyly looked at his feet, then back at Diane. "Anyway, we got to talking and she asked me why I was always here and I confessed that I was trying to get up the nerve to ask out a very beautiful woman. When George asked who, well, here we are."

Diane blushed. "Um, wow, really?" She looked to George for help, but she was already walking away.

"So, what do you say?" Sal nervously asked.

"Uh, sure, I think that would be fun," Diane stammered. Fun, she thought, you sound like an idiotic teenager. Suddenly, Sal kissed her. And, not one of those polite kisses on the cheek, he went in for the kill.

He smiled at a surprised Diane. "That was really nice, don't you think?" Diane blushed again. "And trust me it will make the first date so much easier. We won't have the pressure of wondering what our first kiss will be like." He sighed. "I stole that from a Woody Allen movie." Diane laughed. She liked this man.

"I hope that's the only thing you do before a first date." Sal turned to find Grace, Clair, and George staring at him.

Grace sized him up. "No funny stuff okay? This is a very special lady."

"I believe it. I believe it," said Sal.

"I thank you for your concern, but really girls."

"Really what, mom?" asked Clair.

"Oh, these are your daughters!" he said, with a twinkle in his eye.

George grinned. "Not me. I'm her body guard and lawyer."

Sal laughed. He liked this woman even more because of these three. "When do you get off work?"

"Five," a confused Diane answered.

"That gives me two hours to take these ladies out for coffee and win them over. If I get their approval, how about an early dinner?"

Diane looked at their grinning faces and was overcome by the urge to send them to their rooms without dinner. "Even without their approval—dinner tonight!"

"Terrific," said Sal. "I'll pick you up at five." Diane, unsure of what else to say, nodded her head. As he strode out with them, Diane felt a bit flustered and went to the cafeteria to try the chocolate cheesecake.

"So quit," Sal said. Grace couldn't believe she was getting advice from a complete stranger.

Clair agreed. "He's right. Quit. Now is the best time to do it, you don't need the money. You're already getting paid."

"What am I supposed to do then?" asked Grace.

"I don't know," said Sal, "enjoy being pregnant?" Sal smiled. It had been a while since he felt like what he said mattered. Not that volunteering with the ACLU and The Sisters of Mercy Mission didn't matter. It did matter. It mattered a lot. It just mattered in a different way. These were young people who were seeking him out and it wasn't because their lives were in the shitter and they needed to be rescued. He knew he was being test driven for their mother, but it still made him feel good. "Let me ask you a question..."

Grace grinned, "I don't know who the father is." Everyone cracked up.

"Do you have passion, a real burning passion, for what you do?"

Grace sighed. "No." She answered so quickly she surprised herself.

He turned to George. "Do you?"

"I used too..."

He turned to Clair. "And you?"

She laughed. "Sadly, yes, I enjoy my job."

Sal grinned. "If you're digging holes for a living and you love it, who cares? I don't know a lot of things, but I do know that if you don't have a burning passion for what you're doing in life, stop doing it!" He cut Grace off before she could protest. "I'm not saying to put yourself in financial jeopardy, but it's time to figure out what makes you tick." The girls, we know they're full-blown women, but around Sal they felt like girls, listened with baited breath. "It's not easy finding your passion. You have to cut through the bull-crap, but you know what? If you can't put it on the line with yourself, then why bother? How can you find balance and trust and even love if you can't find it within yourself?"

Grace laughed. "What's the catch? What are you selling?"

Sal's eyes danced. "Do you actually understand that your personal experience in life is to make a positive difference in someone else's? Now you see, Gracie, do you mind if I call you Gracie? She gets it. She's having her sister's baby for Christ's sake, but then after that, what? What are you doing George, how about you Clair? Are you making a difference?" Sal felt a little like a huckster, but at the same time, he knew how everything he just said resonated with his own life. He quit big bucks and the society list when he realized he wasn't making a positive difference in anyone's life.

George sighed. "I'm in recovery."

"So?" queried Sal. "Recovery doesn't define who you are. What's the one thing you'd like to do? Don't think about it, just blurt it out."

And, so, George blurted it out. "Own my own business."

"Now you have the seed of an idea and you can make it happen," Sal replied.

"Not so easy," Clair sighed.

Sal took Clair's hand. "Change what you can. Do good where you see a need."

Clair nodded. "I collect clothes for our church's homeless shelter and I donate money."

"All admirable things," said Sal, "but can you imagine the difference you'd make in someone's life if you actually engaged in a conversation with them? Helped them find a job?"

The girls sat there full of admiration for a man they had just met who inspired them to be better people. "I want to cook," sighed

Grace. "Who the hell are you, Saint Sal?"

"Saint?" he laughed out loud. "You haven't met my first wife. She thinks I'm a shifty bastard with a mommy complex, a gambling habit, and two left feet. And you know what? When I was with her she was dead on, but I changed, I saw the light."

"Whoa Nelly," said Grace.

"Am I laying it on too thick?"

George laughed. "Just a bit."

"You can't blame a guy for trying." Sal bit the inside of his left cheek.

"And you can't blame a gal for wanting a background check before you take her mother out," said Clair.

"So, I didn't pass the test?" sighed a clearly disappointed Sal.

"Oh you did, but if you turn out to be an asshole I will unleash a torrent of financial woes on your ass faster than you can say I.R.S. audit!" Clair slyly smiled.

"Sounds like fun. Listen, I hope I get to see a lot more of you gals, but I have a gorgeous woman waiting for me." He paid the bill and took off to meet Diane.

"You want to own your own business, really?" asked Grace.

"I do," said a surprised George, "and you want to cook?"

"Yeah or maybe bake. Crazy, no?"

"Great. I'm the only one living the dream. I'm a CPA working for the best firm in the city and about to become partner, how boring is that?"

George squeezed Clair's hand. "It's not boring, it's you."

Grace cracked up. "It's not boring, it's you. I love it!"

"I should use that on my next campaign," laughed George.

Chapter 21

Clair and Henry sat in the NG's office waiting for Grace to show up. It was a nice office she thought, but all the pottery, paintings, and even the black and white glamour shot of the Cocker spaniel couldn't distract her from the task at hand. She squeezed Henry's hand. He leaned in and whispered, "maybe we should have spoken to Grace before the session, you know, to give her a heads up?"

Clair whispered back, "I'm a loser. I chickened out four times."

"You're not a loser. You're a wimp. There's a difference."

She jabbed him in the side. "Oh and mister I bought my sister-in-law inappropriate gifts, but couldn't manage to blurt it out while stalking her on the way to work every morning?"

"I'm not stalking her."

"No, it's definitely not stalking anymore; it's more like a drive-by. Now he just knocks, hands me a fortified breakfast or like this morning, a pair of walking shoes, and takes off." Grace models them. "Ain't they sweet? Is it okay if I start with that trainer you got me? I know I said no at first, but now, well, we're five months and things are shifting big time." Grace sat down.

Henry smiled. "See? I knew she'd like Reid."

Clair rolled her eyes. "He's way better looking than the panty liners."

"You can say that again. So what's up? Why the special session?" Grace queried.

Clair felt her stomach contort. "Oh no reason."

Grace wasn't a fool. "What is so hard for you to tell me that you need a medical professional in the room?"

"Yes, Clair, what is so hard for you to tell your sister?" asked Dr. Yael as she came into the room from a secret passageway.

"Wow! You're like Batman," laughed Grace.

She smiled. "More like a renovated hotel with connecting doors. Shall we get started?"

Everyone including Henry looked at Clair. There was no one left for Clair to look at, so she cracked under pressure. "We need more..."

Grace was confused. "Uh, I hope you don't mean time. 'Cause this baby train is pretty much keeping its own schedule."

"No, no." said Henry. "We want more time to experience the pregnancy. We want to be able to touch your stomach without you thinking we're freaks. We want to know what foods you eat that make the baby react and if the baby kicks more at night or during the day. We want to read, or you know, sing so the baby knows our voices."

Grace stared at them. "Wow! So, having the kid for you isn't enough? Well, uh..." She looked at the NG for help.

Dr. Yael smiled. "As the reality of the child sets in and more importantly starts to physically show, it's normal for the parents to feel like they're missing out on a very magical time in their child's life."

"Since when is gaining weight, heartburn, and lower back pain magical?" asked Grace.

"Well, to you it's not, but from a distance... Come on, Grace, a human being is growing inside of you. How is that not magical?" Dr. Yael cracked.

"Okay, okay, but still, more time? That's like impossible."

Dr. Yael looked to Clair and Henry, then back to Grace. "Not if we set some boundaries."

Grace was uneasy. "I get this. You know, your need to be completely immersed in this pregnancy because, well, when I'm not with you it's sorta easy to forget that you're pregnant, but if I were a complete stranger having your kid would you ask me to do this?"

Henry cleared his throat. "I don't know, maybe, but we didn't know what it would be like; what it would feel like to be absentee parents-to-be."

Dr. Yael tried to get the conversation rolling. "Grace, what are your misgivings?"

"Well, I'm not just an incubator. I've got my own life and stuff. I just happen to be having your kid. There are things I need to do for me and I do need some privacy."

"I get it," sighed a disappointed Clair, "but we won't be intrusive. I promise. We'll figure out a schedule that everyone agrees with; we'll put it in writing if you want."

Grace knew this was the right thing to do and that this wasn't her kid; hell it wasn't her pregnancy. "You do know I have a job, so you're just going to have to miss out on some things."

"I thought you were quitting?" said Clair.

"Great idea," said Henry, "you can stay home with the baby."

Grace looked at Henry and sighed. "Uh, the baby is home inside me, remember? You want me to sit around keeping food diaries and in-utero baby activity charts?"

"Why not?" said Clair, "Sal said you could quit."

Grace rolled her eyes. "He's been dating mom for two weeks and now he's Obi-Wan Kenobi?"

"Do you want to quit your job?" asked the doctor.

"To do what, learn to sew?" asked Grace.

"Yeah, sew together the life you want to live," said Dr. Yael.

Grace rolled her eyes. "Okay that was bad— even for you—but, uh, don't you see that as a problem? I'll be barefoot and pregnant with someone else's kid, living in a house I earned by getting knocked up by my brother-in-law. I mean, what kind of loser does that make me?"

"You'd only be a loser if you didn't use the time wisely," NG said while writing in her pad.

Clair smiled. "See? It can work."

Grace sighed. "I guess, but documenting your kid's life in-utero is not the life I want to sew together."

"We can figure out visitation hours and set up a webcam and webpage, so you can post pictures and information and then we won't actually have to be in the room with you every day."

"Whoa, whoa, whoa! Aren't you just jumping on the crazy wagon?" Grace looked at NG. "I want to be fair, but I would prefer not to live in a George Orwell novel."

The doctor smiled. "I'm sure we can figure out a happy medium. Henry, what do you think? You've been very quiet."

Henry looked at his wife and sister-in-law. "The books I've been reading say it's important for the child to hear the parents' voices before it's born."

That melted Grace's heart. "If I do this, there are rules. Never buy me anything again, not for me, not for the pregnancy, deal?" Grace had second thoughts. "Uh, but Reid doesn't count."

Henry smiled. "Deal." And so with the help of the Nubian Goddess, the Higgins sisters were able to negotiate a deal. Grace was to keep a baby journal and in return, Clair and Henry had to stop stalking her. All in all, everyone was happy. Well, everyone, but Jack who was starting to feel like the fifth wheel.

"You gave them every other weekend?" Jack was shocked. As he packed up the rest of Grace's dishes, he tried reasoning with her. "What about me? What happens if the only time I have off is when they're scheduled for a sleepover?"

Grace, who was packing her linens, laughed. "Okay, you're acting like a fifth grader. It's not the end of the world."

Jack was feeling like a petulant child and, so, he continued to act like one. "I'm just saying we barely have enough time together as it is and now this?"

"We see each other twice a week and every weekend. Besides, we'll have more time after I quit my job."

"You're quitting? What is going on here?" an exasperated Jack asked.

For the life of her, Grace couldn't figure out what his problem was. "We talked about this. I'm not happy, so why not quit when I can figure out my life and not have to worry about the bills. Plus, if I'm not working nights, there's more time for us. It's a win-win situation."

Jack looked across the dining room to where she was sitting. "I know, but..."

Grace walked into the kitchen, picked up some of her stemware, and started wrapping it in newspaper. "What's wrong? You're acting weird." Jack hesitated. Grace leveled him with a look. "Quit acting like a girl. And don't lie to me. We said we'd be honest, right?"

Jack leaned back on his haunches and then sat. "Honest? I hate you in orange, honest, or gut wrenching emotional, why didn't you tell me Ray's been calling here and that he came to see you at work, honest?"

As she put the wrapped glass into the box labeled kitchen, her heart began beating really fast. "Oh."

Jack felt his stomach drop as he put the last of Grace's Fiesta Ware dishes into its storage case. "He called when you were in the bathroom and told me everything."

Grace wasn't going to lie; she had no reason to lie. "I didn't think it was important." She smiled at a frowning Jack. "You look so mean right now."

"This is how I look when I'm scared."

That's when she realized he was afraid of losing her. Something about that soothed her jangled nerves. "I'm confused by the whole Ray wants to be back in my life thing, and I didn't want to upset you." Grace noticed that Jack relaxed a tiny bit. "He told you everything? What's everything? That he showed up to my office and brought me flowers, which I gave away—bet he didn't tell you that. Did he tell you I told him to leave me alone for like the fifteenth millionth time?"

Jack didn't like how worked up she got talking about this guy. "He said you said that you loved him and you'd always love him."

The color drained from Grace's face. She sat down on the floor across from Jack. There was no way out of this. "Yeah, well, I do love him, but I'm not *in* love with him. And there's a difference, you know. I love him like you love a twelve year old Retriever who's incontinent, but you're afraid to put him asleep."

"Most people don't put their dogs to sleep because they feel guilty doing it. From what you've told me, you have nothing to feel guilty about." Jack tried to look away from her. It was her eyes that got him; deep pools of green that were filled with so much confusion right now. "You obviously love the guy and if you love him then there's a damn good chance you're still *in* love with him." He really hated this conversation.

"You're right," she whispered, as she leaned against the pile of blue and red-checkered tablecloths from her days as a manager of an Italian restaurant.

"I am?" Now the color drained out of Jack's face. "Fuck!"

"I'm in love with the idea of what he could be, you know? I have this 'what if' haunting me because I wasn't able to save him from himself. It's like with my dad. No matter how many times I replay the morning in my head and change it and I get up and help him shovel, he's still dead."

"So, now what?" asked a very unhappy Jack.

"I don't know." She kissed the inside of his right palm. "But you're going to have to trust me." Jack was scared and confused right now. Grace could see it in his eyes. She had to admit that she was too. "I didn't expect you to show up in my life when you did, or for Ray to come back, or to actually be pregnant, so we just have to take it one day at a time, okay?" Grace kissed him. "Right now though, I need some Cherry Garcia. You up for a Ben and Jerry run?"

"This is where we leave it? You don't know if you want me, the best thing that ever happened to you, or Ray the worst thing that's ever happened to you, but you definitely want ice cream? And I'm supposed to be okay with that?"

Grace knew he was right. "All I know is that I love every minute I spend with you, I have to pee all the time, I need closure with Ray, and if I don't get Cherry Garcia in the next twenty minutes, I'm not responsible for my actions!"

Jack felt a little better. "Cherry Garcia isn't even a flavor."

Grace rolled her eyes. "Why such disdain for the Cherry Garcia? A treat made in honor of the greatest Rock and Roller to ever live—drop the attitude buddy!"

He laughed, "I thought pregnant women craved pickles and chocolate and sex."

"Pickles? That's an old wives tale. Chocolate and sex? Women don't have to be pregnant to crave that. Oooh, chocolate! I want to stop at Ethel M's; they have the best chocolate peanut butter clusters, which would taste so great slathered in Cherry Garcia."

"Good thing you're starting with that trainer."

"Yeah, he's a hottie!" said Grace as she headed out the door.

"What does that mean? Are you gonna need closure with him too?" asked Jack, as he followed her out.

Chapter 22

Grace and Clair had now officially passed from 'now, now what', and the annoying 'you don't say, and the semblance of normalcy' into the fifth month of their pregnancy, which should be called something wittier than the fifth month, but our brains are a bit taxed—sorry if we disappointed you! Okay, so that said, with sisterhood, sobriety, and visitation rights intact, and the stopping of inappropriate gifts, the beginning of new relationships, and some odd food cravings, as well as the reacquainting of old relationships, the Higgins Sisters thought they were ready for almost anything, but they were about to learn that almost anything included a myriad of things that they never would have expected.

Life changes. Grace knew that. She knew that because her life was changing every second, of every minute, of every day. Right now, she was unpacking her kitchen as Jack, George, and the rest of her family brought in boxes and supervised the movers. The apartment had an amazing view of the lake and it was the very first thing Grace had ever owned besides the pink Schwinn Cruiser she bought with her first communion money in second grade. Grace was in a good place. She had stuff to deal with, true, but everybody had stuff to deal with. Something was different though. She felt good. She wasn't sure what it was, but Grace decided to ride the wave.

"I thought I got rid of these?" Grace turned to find Clair holding a box of The Flintstones' jelly glasses. "They're an eye sore."

Grace rolled her eyes. "Yeah, well they're my eye sore and I'm displaying them in my wet bar, so shut up!"

Clair walked the box over to the wet bar, which was snuggled into the corner of her sister's dining room. She liked how that sounded—her sister's dining room. Grace owning something put her at ease. It made her feel that after all this baby stuff was done, Grace was going to be okay.

Grace rushed to Clair, grabbed her hand, and shoved it on her stomach. "The kid officially likes the Flintstones' jelly glasses." Clair felt the kick of her child inside her sister. It was weird. It wasn't the first time the baby kicked and it wouldn't be the last, but would probably always be weird.

"You are an idiot!" George crowed.

"Because I think the Chicago Bulls haven't run a good offensive in two years?"

George carrying an ironing board and a basket of what she hoped was clean laundry laughed. She liked this guy. This guy was good for Grace. "Yes, Jack, you're an idiot."

Jack carried Grace's coffee table and set it down in the middle of the living room. "I cannot believe she's your friend!"

Grace laughed. "She can get you free Nikes for your gi'normous feet."

He turned and bowed. "You're a genius. I'm a size fifteen."

George looked at Grace. "Size fifteen? Really?"

Clair, who was heading down to the van for one last run, grabbed George's arm and took her with her. "Mind. Gutter. Out!"

Jack made his way through the clutter toward Grace who was unloading the last of her silverware. He loved knowing she was in his life. He loved every wonderful, frustrating, sweet, and annoying thing about her, but he couldn't tell her. She had too much going on and with the whole Ray thing hanging over their heads, he didn't want to scare her off. He put his arms around her. The baby kicked. "Nice, he's gonna be a soccer player."

Grace turned her body into his. "Or she's gonna be a Rockette."

"Not my k...," Jack stopped himself, "not on my watch."

"You better be careful," she said as she brushed her lips against his, "I think I'm falling for you. And if I do, boy are you in trouble!"

Jack kissed her back. "Sweetheart, I invented trouble."

"Anybody home?" Sal, looking very dashing in his white oxford and jeans, peeked in the door. Diane, surprised to see him, came up behind him with Clair, Henry, and George. As soon as Diane saw him she lit up. Clair and Grace traded knowing glances. He was carrying a basket. "Just a little something for the little lady. I'm Italian, it's tradition." Sal followed Diane into the dining room. Grace peeked in the basket. "Okay, here it goes—bread, so you'll never go hungry; a broom, so you can sweep away evil; a candle, so you'll always have light; honey, so life will always be sweet; a coin, to bring good fortune for the year; olive oil, for health, life, and believe it or not, to keep your husband, or in this case, your boyfriend, faithful; a plant, so you'll always have life; rice, to ensure your fertility, but that's taken care of, eh? Salt represents life's tears. I recommend you place a pinch of salt on the threshold of every door and window for good luck and according to my grandmother Chetta it also mends old wounds. Oh and... ah, yes, wine, sparkling non-alcoholic wine, so you never go thirsty and always have joy and last, but not least wood, so your home will always have harmony, stability, and peace."

Grace grabbed Sal into a big hug, "Wow! Thanks."

"What is going on here?" Patricia and Henry, Sr. were staring at them. They were both wearing jeans. Grace couldn't get her mind around it. It was like seeing a bear in a tutu—disconcerting, and yet, strangely appealing. "Well?" stressed Patricia.

"Uh, I'm moving in?" said Grace.

"Yes, dear, but where are the movers? The movers were supposed to help you move."

Grace was lost. "Uh, they did. They moved the boxes, put them in the van, moved them up here, and ta-da!"

Patricia gave Grace her patented are you an idiot look, but thankfully Henry, Sr. jumped in before she had a chance to actually call her an idiot. "They're a full service mover. They pack and unpack everything, soups to nuts, so to speak. They'll even cook you a meal if you need it. Don't tell me you packed everything yourself?"

Clair laughed, "I knew we shouldn't have sent them home."

"Home! You sent them home? This place is a mess." Patricia was on her cell phone and dialing so quickly you would have thought she was trying to stop a breach in national security. Within fifteen minutes the movers were back, within thirty minutes they had half the apartment, under Clair's strict supervision, unpacked, with the exception of Grace's bedroom, Clair insisted on setting that up herself, and within two hours the entire house was done. All that was left was a pile of stuff from Grace's storage room— stuff she was determined to sell on e-bay now that she was gainfully unemployed.

Clair cornered Grace in the kitchen. "They seem serious."

Grace watched her Mom with Sal. "She seems happy, but if he hurts her…"

"He won't," Clair matter-of-factly stated. "Do you see the way he looks at her?"

"Well, what if he hurts her, but you know, didn't mean to hurt her? Like his wife comes back from the dead or he gets caught in a robbery and accidentally gets shot? Or maybe, maybe…"

"He gets run over by a snowplow?" said Diane as she watched Clair help Grace unload the dishwasher.

Caught, the girls sighed. "Well, yeah…" said Grace.

"It couldn't happen twice, could it?" asked Clair, albeit nervously.

Diane smiled. "We need to have a little chat."

Grace touched her belly. "It's too late you already told us where babies come from. By the way, you left quite a few things out."

Clair laughed. "Yeah, and we're not talking about in vitro."

"I know. The woman blew through her sex talk like she was running the one-minute mile! Just the old cut and dry when a man loves a woman he puts his penis in her vagina and they make a baby. No mention of how awkward it can be," joked Grace.

"Or, the actual surprise of seeing a penis for the first time." added Clair.

"Yeah and how about the old, not every make and model is the same. Now, that would've helped—a lot!" giggled Grace.

Diane, red with embarrassment shook her head. "Girls!"

They both knew what that tone implied. "What? Too much?" asked Clair.

"What do *you* think?" Diane sternly replied.

"That I'm way too old to be punished and sent to my room," said Grace.

Diane cracked a smile. "Will you please stop talking for one second?" Clair and Grace exchanged looks. Diane jumped in before either of them could react. "The chances that somebody I love will get run over by a snowplow again are pretty slim. Will I get hurt, will I get my heart broken, and will they leave? Maybe. Girls, I'm sixty-five. The chances that my date will have a stroke before dessert is more likely." Diane looked at her daughters and regrouped. "Sal asked me to go away with him on a trip where we share the same room. At least I think we're sharing the same room. I mean that's only logical, right? That I think that we're sharing the same room?"

"Whoa! Where did he ask you to go?" said Clair.

"Canada. Somewhere called Niagara-on-the-Lake. Does location matter?" Diane had been with men since her husband died, but, well, it was always no strings attached. This trip, there were strings attached.

"I just read about that place. The guy's got style, plus he's paying for air fare, so yep, he expects you to put out." Grace smiled at her very nervous mother.

"It's not putting out I'm worried about," snapped Diane.

"Really?" said Clair. "That's a little disturbing."

"Is it too soon?" Diane sighed.

"Well, do you not want to be alone with him in that type of situation like ever or are you ready to pounce?" asked Grace.

"And, as a wise woman used to say, 'we can't make this decision for you.' You just have to figure out if this is the right thing for you or not," Clair deadpanned.

Diane sighed. "I didn't raise you to throw my words back into my face."

Grace grinned. "Are you sure about that?"

"Where did I go wrong with you two?"

"You let me go Goth," said Grace.

"Math camp. Oh, the things we did with numbers!" Clair gave her mom a hug. "Go for it."

"But, use a condom," cracked Grace.

Diane hugged Clair, pulled Grace's hair, and the girls followed their mom into the living room. Patricia was chatting with Sal. She wasn't sure about this one. He seemed nice, but he had a little too much gel in his hair and he was wearing cologne. Men who wore cologne had something to hide. "We thought we'd take everyone to dinner."

"We were gonna get pizza—please stay," said Grace.

Henry, Sr. looked at his wife and picked up on her thoughts like only people who have been married for over forty years could do. "No thanks. Diane, Sal, shall we hit Morton's?"

Diane's entire body clenched. She had never eaten with her daughter's in-laws unless it was some momentous occasion and when she did, she never had a date, but before she could beg off...

Sal grinned. "Sounds terrific."

"Do you think she's okay?"

Henry gave his wife a kiss. "You act like you sent her off to be lynched."

George, in the midst of emptying a box filled with dog paraphernalia, tossed Henry a rubber bone. "Hey, it's your mother we're worried about, not your father. If she finds one reason not to like Sal she'll hound him 'til he's running for the hills!'"

Henry laughed. "If he can survive her he's pretty much set."

George was now picking through leashes and some really nasty tennis balls when she came across an envelope. George being George didn't think twice and opened it. "Jesus, Mary, and Joseph!"

Clair immediately sprang up off the couch. "What?"

George held out the piece of paper in her hand to Clair who took it. "Thirty-five thousand dollars! He paid her back."

Now Henry got up. "Who paid what?"

Clair gave him a look, "I told you, the whole Ray thing. He came by, wants her back, and gave her the money he took."

Henry took the check and studied it. "It's a cashier check." He looked at the date on the check and counted backwards. "In ten days it's useless."

"What's useless?" asked Grace, as she and Jack came in with pizza and beer.

Because he was only married to Clair for six years and he hadn't yet learned how to clearly read her thoughts Henry blurted out, "Thirty-five thousand dollars."

Grace, Clair, and George traded glances. They knew better than to bring this up in front of Jack. Clair immediately put the envelope in her pocket. "My husband is useless. He can't hook up your entertainment center and said he'd pay someone thirty-five thousand dollars to do it for him. Jack, can you help him out?"

Jack knew that whatever they were talking about had to do with Ray. He saw it in their eyes, but he had had a great day with Grace and didn't want to screw it up. "Sure. We've got hours to kill at the station, so I can pretty much build one from scratch. Okay, we've got sausage and pepperoni, feta cheese and spinach, and pineapple and ham for the hormonally challenged pregnant woman who is causing my great grandmother Angela to spin in her grave right now."

"You make banana and fluff sandwiches," Grace said as she brought the pizza into the kitchen, "and that is more acceptable than pineapple and ham?"

"Two entirely different categories of food, but yes," he said as he grabbed some plates and helped Clair get out the silverware and glasses, "okay, who wants a beer?" Jack came out holding a couple of bottles of Coors Light, Henry took one, Clair took one, and Grace grabbed that one off of Clair and handed it back to Jack who opened it for himself.

"What happened to the old—we'll do this together? I'll never know what it's like to be pregnant crap?" intoned Grace.

Clair rolled her eyes. "Fine. George what do you want?"

George was now immersed oddly enough in doggie rain slickers. "A beer."

They all stopped. Grace groaned. "No, seriously, what do you want?"

"A beer. It's not going to kill me. It's been five months, I've earned it," she said defiantly.

"She wants a beer," Jack said.

"Well, she can't have a beer," said Clair.

Grace agreed. "There is no way she's blowing five months of sobriety."

George responded as any mature adult would. "Stop talking like I'm not here. Besides, you're not the boss of me."

Jack sighed. "When you're a fireman there are a lot of guys in recovery. At five, six months sober they think they have it under control; that they can have a beer or a drink and it can be just one and nothing will come of it. That's never the case and they end up on a bender to end all benders, unless...." He looked at George who stared at them. "...You make sure that doesn't happen."

George made a face at them. "I'm not going on a bender." George whined, "will someone *please* bring out the friggin' pizza?"

Grace sat down beside her dear old friend. "Don't judge me," said George.

Grace gave her a squeeze. "I'm no Judy Judgestein; it's not my choice to make. Why the sudden urge for a drink? What went wrong?"

"Nothing," sighed George, "pizza goes with beer. End of the story."

Before Grace or Clair could grill her further, Henry came out with the pizzas and Jack came out with the drinks and passed them around. Clair raised her can of soda. "To the greatest sister ever." Everyone raised his or her bottles and cans. "To her soon to be swollen feet and from what mom tells me, hemorrhoids!"

George had just taken a long sip of her much anticipated cold beer and turned to see everyone staring at her. She wasn't sure if she should swallow or not, but decided too. It was cold and delicious and everything she thought it would be. Then, because everyone was staring, she handed the beer to Jack. "I'm done." Of course George didn't believe what she had just said, but she hoped they did.

After the guys had put together the entertainment center and were run off by chick music, Clair pulled out the check. "You had a check for thirty-five thousand dollars sitting in a box of dog toys?"

Grace watched George catch popcorn in her mouth. "Yep."

George shrugged. "Uh, wouldn't it be smarter to put it in the bank?"

"Yep."

"Did you know it expires in ten days?"

"Yep."

"Tomorrow we're going to your bank and depositing this check," Clair said sternly.

Grace laughed at the look on her sister's face, all stern and motherly.

"You're gonna be a great mom."

Clair's face crumbled into a torrent of tears. George and Grace were so taken by surprise that they sprang into action faster than they actually knew what to do. George put her arms around Clair and brought her over to Grace on the couch. Grace jumped up, almost knocked over the entertainment center, and searched for tissues. "Holy shit! That was a compliment," said George as she kept her arms around Clair and gently sat her down.

Grace came back from the kitchen with a roll of paper towels and a glass of milk. She had no idea why she had a glass of milk. "Do you want me to warm it up?"

Clair took the paper towels and was soon a sobbing, gulping, sniffling, wet faced, snot nosed mess. "I'm no good at diapers and I can't even...when I dropped, uh, huh, uh," Clair struggled to catch her breath, but between the tears and the snot streaming down her face it wasn't easy, "I failed. Babies hate me and now...," she blew her nose, "are you sure you don't want to keep it?"

"Uh, no." Grace and George traded looks. "Clair bear, you're just scared; everyone is scared—especially about having babies."

Clair blew her nose. "George isn't scared. George is never scared."

"Honey, I'm an alcoholic. I drink to abate the fear of just about everything in my life," George said as she tried to lean back into the couch, but Clair was still attached to her body, so she adjusted accordingly. "Just tonight, you know, after you sorta break the habit of drinking like red wine with dinner and tequila shooters with your favorite clients and really figure out why you drink, it comes down to fear."

Grace sat down next to Clair and took her into her arms to give George, who had to be uncomfortable with her body contorted that way, a break. "Fear?"

"Good old fashioned—I lost my first account what the hell am I really doing with my life—fear." Grace knew how much George hated to lose and George knew her friend was about to ask her twenty questions and cut her off. "What set off the waterworks?"

"Last night I babysat our neighbor's kid, you know, the Deckers. They just had their first baby. I couldn't change the diaper, I nearly dropped her off the bed, and then she wouldn't stop crying. She hated me!"

"Don't be ridiculous, she's a baby. She has no idea what hate is; she has to learn that. She was just uncomfortable," said George.

"You know your kid is gonna cry—a lot—right? And it's gonna poop and you're gonna have to cut its fingernails and pull boogers out of its nose?" asked Grace.

Another round of tears came bubbling and by bubbling we mean snot bubbling to the surface. As Clair blew her nose she sobbed. "We're having a baby!"

Grace and George exploded in laughter. Clair knew she was being ridiculous. Grace kissed the top of her head. "Why don't you take a hot shower and relax?" Grace stood up and walked Clair to the master bath.

"Okay," sniffled Clair.

Grace gave her a squeeze. "Just don't rearrange everything."

"Can I do the medicine cabinet? I didn't get a chance to color code the products."

Grace laughed. "Okay, just the medicine cabinet."

As Clair shut the door, Grace turned to George and giggled. "And I'm the one with the raging hormones? Hey, are you hungry?"

"You ate a whole pie and a pint of ice cream. How can you eat anymore?"

"Hmmmm, I'm craving… cinnamon and peanut butter—oh and chocolate."

George knew better than to get in Grace's way when she got like this and followed her into the kitchen. She sat at the table as Grace started pulling a ton of stuff from her freshly unpacked cabinets. "What account?"

"Foster's Beer," replied George as she picked the cheese off of a leftover slice of pizza. "We were under review. Companies do it all the time, but I've never lost an account and I've been under review millions of time." George started cutting the pizza slice into long strips, "It threw me off, I'm not used to losing."

As she lined up green apples, peanut butter, mini marshmallows, cinnamon, butterscotch chips, and walnuts on her counter, Grace asked, "did you get fired?"

"No." George was rolling each individual pizza strip up and popping them into her mouth. "But, well, I lost the account and I didn't care."

"Oh, it's the old—what am I doing with my life if I don't care about my job anymore?" George had finished the pizza slice and was about to start on the next when Grace threw her an apple. "Core it and slice it baby!" Grace took a bunch of apples, grabbed a bowl and some knives and sat with her. "I've done that with every job I've had. I may have no skills, well, other than being a librarian, but you've got a big ass salary plus all those awards and not to mention frequent flier miles, so if you wanted to follow your bliss you wouldn't have a problem living off your last three bonuses." Grace expertly cored the apples. "Besides, you said you wanted to start your own business, right? Well, now that you know you want a change, you can use your time wisely."

"When did you get so smart?" George smirked.

"When my sister paid me to let her husband knock me up and I went into intensive therapy."

"She almost dropped the kid?"

Grace cracked up. "She must have shit her pants."

"Who, Clair or the baby?" asked a laughing George.

"Both!" choked out Grace as she convulsed into peels of laughter. Grace finally calmed herself down, but when a freshly showered and pajama clad Clair came walking into the kitchen, she lost it all over again.

"What's so funny?" asked Clair.

"Drop any babies lately?" asked George as she and Grace howled with laughter.

Clair did her best to put on her angry face…"fuck you"…but she didn't quite pull it off and soon the three of them were in hysterics.

"Oh my God! These are amazing," sighed Clair as she dunked her third cookie into a freshly poured glass of cold milk.

George counted how many cookies were left to make sure that no one ate more than her share and readily agreed. "We need to name them something."

"Hey, speaking of cookies, you'd better not hurt Jack," said Clair.

"Yeah," added George. "He's a keeper."

"Will you stop going on about how great he is!" an exasperated Grace said.

"She's scared," said George.

"Totally! Remember that guy before Ray? David, no Paul, no…" Clair said between bites of cookie.

"Ringo! No, no, it was Jason," said George. "He was sweet."

"I didn't feel the zing-zing."

"Every guy you've rejected is because of the zing-zing. Sometimes attraction grows you know? And, zing-zing, didn't really help with Ray," said George. "You started out all zing-zing, but then he zinged…"

"…Into an asshole." Clair sternly stated. "A tried and true asshole."

"Honey, he was always an asshole. It was the zing-zing that clouded her judgment. So don't fuck this up, okay?" George implored. "A blind man could see you guys have the zing-zing. What's the deal?"

"I've got to finish things with Ray." Grace knew it didn't make sense. It didn't even make sense to her, but it was something she had to do.

"Yeah, well don't finish what you can't start," said George. Grace and Clair stared at her. "What? When you finish with an ex you sleep with them one last time. Don't do that with Ray. That is one whole kettle of crapola you don't want to open. As a matter of fact, I hereby decree that you're not allowed to open it."

"Really?" said Grace. "Well, if we're tossing down decrees, you're not allowed to fall off the wagon. And you missy pop," she looked at Clair, "are not going to throw the baby out with the bathwater."

That made George collapse into giggles—Clair and Grace soon joined her. "Cookies! Like Mrs. Fields, I sell, you bake!" cried George.

In between hysterical gasps for air Grace asked, "are you drunk?" And that started the laughing all over again.

Chapter 23

Hickory Dickory Dock, the mouse ran up the clock, the clock struck twelve and Grace and Clair were lying side-by-side and snoring away on the couch. George, needing to burn the energy that always overwhelmed her once the moon shone brightly in the night sky, started working on her big idea. Used to drinking while she worked, she went into Grace's kitchen, opened the fridge, pulled out the last beer, then stopped. She longingly looked at the bottle in her hand, fumbled for a bottle opener, and opened it. The familiar crack and siss brought a smile to her face. She stood there and thought about all the things that scared her, like her parents' death, being alone, losing her first account, and her own death. Then, there was destruction of the world, trying to land a new account, falling in love, getting fired, the plague, going to the dentist, not being good enough, smart enough, or attractive enough. She was about to take a sip, but quickly poured the beer down the sink. "I am not my fear." She then shakily, but with a small swagger of confidence, walked into the living room.

George took in Grace's amazing view and watched her friends sleep. Clair's hand was resting on Grace's tummy and Grace's head was nuzzled against her sister's shoulder. She picked up the throw blanket off the ottoman and put it on them. They are brave, she thought. They are the bravest people I know. If they can be brave then so can I. With that George turned, accidentally knocked into the entertainment center and the sound of it crashing into a million pieces sent the two bravest people she ever met running for their lives!

We've officially changed the name of the chapter from the Fifth Month to Zing-Zing. You may be wondering why, but as you read on the name change will be apparent. Those that don't get it ask a friend and if you still don't get it, wow! Now, where were we? Oh yes. Grace fell with relative ease into the routine of not working. She rose early every morning to workout with her hottie trainer Reid, she kept a pregnancy journal for her sister and brother-in-law, she sold everything with the exception of a second set of Flintstones glasses on e-bay, which added twelve thousand dollars to the money Ray had given her back. Grace was good, Grace and Jack were good, Grace and the unborn child of her sister were good too, and at five and a half months pregnant, almost all was right in her world.

Clair, who had recently undergone an intense few weeks of interviews with the Board of her firm, the Principals of her firm, and any other person in the free world who had anything to do with choosing the firm's new partner, was still haunted by her babysitting debacle. After practically memorizing the entire series of the <u>What To Expect While You're Expecting </u>books, Clair was more frightened than she had ever been in her life. She spent sleepless nights contemplating whether she had sentenced her sister to an early death or not. Of course, if she didn't die there was all that other stuff that would make life after giving birth excruciatingly painful.

Another thing that consumed her thoughts was the possibility that she would end up with a mutant child whose head was shaped like a goldfish and had the body of a Doberman. All in all, the <u>What To Expect While You're Expecting</u> books were like the original Grimm Faerie Tales where everybody ended up mauled, maimed, or in the morgue. These books boiled down life's greatest joy to a series of hit and run accidents in which there were no survivors because all of the accidents happened at the exact time a fatal Tsunami hit. Their— everything you wanted to know about pregnancy, but were afraid to ask—advice terrorized Clair. She had panic attacks for no reason, well no reason other than the death of sister, her child, and her sanity. And these attacks of which the fair-haired control freak of a sister refused to tell anyone about landed her in the fitting room of The Gap on an emergency phone call with the NG. Dr. Yael, who was in between patients and never took calls at lunch, broke her own rule when her assistant buzzed her that a patient was trapped in the Gap. "Clair, what's wrong?"

"An episiotomy is going to kill Grace and loud noises may make my baby retarded," an out of breath Clair whispered as she sat on floor between a pair of skinny jeans and some basic Gap T-Shirts.

"Is Grace in labor? Where are you? What happened?" Dr. Yael asked.

Clair struggled to keep her composure. "I was shopping for baby clothes..." she paused to catch her breath, "...I saw a pair of pajamas with a cotton tie and I realized that the baby could choke on it. Then I remembered what I read about the baby being choked by the umbilical cord and that made me think about the baby's head and if it was too big it would tear open Grace's, you know, parts, and she could bleed out and die." Clair was sweating. She pulled out a Wet

One, one of many examples as to why her OCD will make her a wonderful mother, and wiped her forehead.

Dr. Yael knew Clair was in real pain, but she was nonetheless highly amused. "Clair, where you are right now?"

"I told your assistant that I'm paralyzed with fear in the fitting room of The Gap." Her heart was beating so quickly it threatened to jump right through her buttoned down white tailored blouse.

"Okay, good. And what time is it?"

"Lunchtime." She took a deep breath and slowly let it out.

"And at this very moment is Grace or the baby in any grave danger?"

"Why, do you know something I don't?" asked a panicked Clair.

"Clair," Dr. Yael sternly added, "is everyone safe?"

"Yes." Clair felt her heart slow down.

"See? Good. Now, whatever you're reading—burn it!"

"But, it's What To Expect While You're Expecting," sighed Clair.

"Burn it—now!" said Dr. Yael. "That is not a pregnancy guide. It's a how to give a pregnant woman a heart attack guide. No one should expect that much. Now, what set this off?"

"From the beginning?" asked Clair.

"I've got time." The doctor said as she rearranged herself on her couch.

"Well, I tried to change a diaper and nearly killed a baby."

Again, Dr. Yael had to stop herself from laughing. "Well, okay, something we can control."

"We can?" sighed Clair as she finally relaxed.

"Of course. You're overwhelmed about motherhood. Why don't we get you some skills to make you comfortable with the whole mommy transformation? There are some really great classes."

Clair smiled. Classes are something she's really good at. "Like diaper changing for dummies?"

"Exactly. I'm going to put you back on with my Assistant, Rae, and she's going to give you the information about St. Stephen's parenting classes, but first can you get up, can you get yourself home?"

As Clair stood up she thought "classes give you control." "I'm good, I think, I mean, I'm standing up. Thanks so much NG, you saved me from insanity."

"NG?" asked Dr. Yael.

Caught, Clair blurted, "uh, we call you Nubian Goddess, Grace and I. She came up with it." Dr. Yael laughed and laughed and laughed and then passed Clair off to her Assistant because she couldn't speak.

Chapter 24

There are things you do in life that you have no idea why you do them. For some, it's the way they put on their sneakers or how they cut their pancakes. There are also things you do that you have no idea why you're doing them while you're actually doing them, such as locking your keys in the car or having dinner with your lying-cheating-embezzling-ex-boyfriend, which is where Grace was right now—having dinner at the Landmark Grill & Lounge with Ray. Grace hadn't told Jack or even Clair or George about this dinner. For the most part Grace had barely told herself it was happening until she met Ray at the restaurant. So far, the dinner had gone well. Ray had a real job selling liquor for a well-known distributor and was making great money. He was out of debt, out of the basement apartment at his parents' house, in recovery, sober for over a year, and seemed to be talking the talk and walking the walk of a bona fide mature adult—everything Grace knew he could accomplish, but two years too late. Grace wasn't bitter or even resentful, but she also wasn't totally sure why she was having dinner with him and she hoped and prayed she didn't do anything stupid.

Grace felt the baby kick and put her hand on her tummy. From the corner of her eye she could feel the older couple at the next table smiling at them as if she and Ray were about to start on this big new adventure, but they weren't. Their adventure was more like the sinking of the Titanic and less like a wonderful day at Disneyland.

Ray noticed her hand on her tummy. "I'm proud of you. Not many people would put someone else's needs over her own, but that's my Gracie, always taking care of somebody else."

Grace bristled, "I'm not your Gracie. I haven't been for a really long time. And for your information, when you love someone you put their needs over your own, but you never really figured that out."

Ray took the hit. He knew he deserved it. "I know. I didn't mean... Listen, it's going to take you a long time to trust me again, hell, to believe what I'm saying."

"Ray, I have no idea what you think this dinner is about or even why I was foolish enough to let you convince me to come, but trusting you again is not an option."

Out of the corner of her eye Grace saw someone that looked like Jack. That's when it hit her. "You know what? Thanks for dinner. Thanks for paying me back, but more importantly thanks for staying out of my life." With that Grace got up and left while Ray sat there bewildered. Grace gathered her thoughts and with the help of the valet, she quickly hailed a cab. Grace got in, told the driver her address and just when she was shutting the door, Ray jumped in beside her.

"You don't mean that," he implored. And so, the cab pulled away with Ray in it. Neither of them was sure what came next. This was always a pattern in their relationship. Grace would get upset and leave. Ray would cajole her back and they would have sex. Patterns once ingrained into your psyche are really hard to break. Soon they were making out like a couple of high-school kids, but try as she might Grace couldn't tune out George's—don't finish what you can't start—that was ringing in her ears. There were a few things that were running through her mind while she was kissing Ray. First, there was, well, Jack and that maybe Ray had changed and then Jack again. As the cab stopped at a light and Ray started fondling her breasts, she was thinking about Jack. She was also wondering if her earring fell off and then she was thinking about Jack. As Ray's hand slipped under her skirt, she was thinking about Jack, that she's pregnant and can't have sex in a cab, more Jack, and then she had one of those out of body experiences she's heard people talk about. As she watched herself with Ray, she realized she didn't like the way she felt in his arms. She didn't like how he smelled like candy or really anything about him anymore and as that last thought clicked, Grace pushed Ray off of her. "No!"

Ray was unhappily derailed. "Are you shitting me?"

The cab suddenly stopped short. "Sorry folks, there seems to be a collision."

Grace practically jumped out of the cab. Ray tried to follow, but Grace pushed him back inside. "No—no! Don't call. No. Don't. I'm sorry. I was wrong. I don't want this; I don't want you or us or any of it!" The cab pulled away. Grace straightened her skirt, so she didn't look like a disheveled slut, got her geographical bearings and cried like a banshee on her walk of shame home. Ray watched her from the window of the cab. For the first time, they both knew she wasn't crying over him or even for him.

Chapter 25

Fifteen minutes after she was talked down from her Gap attack, Clair had made a decision. She was a good study—she always was and she always would be. The knowledge of that gave her the confidence she needed to sign up for The Baby Zone classes at St. Stephen's Hospital. Clair walked into her classroom and was relieved that most of the women didn't look pregnant. Not carrying the child you were expecting took a lot of explaining and with so much on her mind, like how to change a diaper, how to use that bulby thing and get snot out of a baby's nose, how to breast feed, how to cut the baby's nails, how the baby is supposed to sleep in the crib, how to give the baby a bath, and a myriad of other things that were racing through her mind like a run-a-way train, not having the pressure of being visibly pregnant was a plus. Clair took a seat.

"Good morning ladies!" said a short red head. "I'm Marianne and I'm your teacher. Let's get this party started, shall we? Today is all about the diaper. First, we're going to go over your diaper options: cloth versus disposable, which disposable brand works the best and is the best for the environment. Then, we'll touch on to powder or not to powder and then you'll dive into changing diapers and all of that fun stuff!"

Clair took notes about every type of diaper, powder, baby butt cream, wipes, diaper services, and diaper genie modern man had ever created. She felt good. She felt confident. "Are we ready to put to practice what we just learned?" asked Marianne. She felt sick. Before she could muster the courage to vomit, she and the rest of the class were standing in the front of the room armed with their own changing table and large baby dolls. "Okay," said Marianne. "As you all know, babies move…" She held up a remote control. "…and so do these babies." Clair felt faint as a wave of her LSD-diaper-changing-baby-almost-fell-flashback hit her like a ton of bricks. "You have everything you need: diapers, diaper cream, wipes, powder, and, well, the baby." Clair's body was shaking and sweat formed at the base of her neck. "Look at your changing table," continued Marianne, "and make sure you know where everything is, then once you're ready start changing."

Clair nervously found the diaper, the wipes, the cream, and the powder. She pulled out a diaper, like she had been instructed, put one hand on the baby's stomach, took off the old diaper, grabbed a wipe, and wiped the dolls plastic ass while keeping one eye on Marianne as other dolls around her occasionally moved. Feeling confident, Clair lifted the dolls' butt, placed a diaper beneath, and then dropped it— the doll, not the diaper. Clair grabbed the doll before it hit the ground, but her hand slid and as she rushed to secure the doll she punched herself in the face. And that is how Clair earned herself a certificate in diaper changing.

"Wow!" George said, as she stared at Grace and Clair.

Grace had every ingredient ever needed to make the perfect cookie strewn across her kitchen. "Wow, I can't believe she actually has a black eye or wow, I better make Grace a scarlet letter 'cause she's a ho?"

Clair crunched the peanut M&M that was in her mouth. "I'm thinking both."

George laughed. "And I'm the alcoholic?"

"Can we not speak of this ever again?" asked Grace as she mixed together some milk, flour, and eggs. "Let's put it in the middle of a Rubik's Cube, then put that in a vault, then lock the vault, have a complete stranger, or say a monkey, change the combination, then shoot him dead, and surround it with a wall of bees—although, I'd feel bad about shooting a monkey."

George, who was chopping up marshmallows, grinned. "So now what?"

Grace smiled. "Put the peanut butter chips and the craisins in this bowl." George popped a marshmallow into her mouth. "No, you moron, what are you going to do about the Ray vs. Jack thing?"

"There is no Ray vs. Jack thing. It's not a boxing match," she sighed heavily, "it's over. It's done. I know." Grace began separating egg whites. "So I had to make out in a cab with him to figure it out. That's closure. Can we change the subject now? George, how's work, your sobriety, uh, your love life?"

"Oh, sure, use the frustrated-unhappy-in-her-job-alcoholic as a diversion for your messed up life," laughed Clair as she grabbed the marshmallows away from George who was eating more than she was cutting up.

"Love life? I'm easing myself off of drunken one-night stands. I have to figure out what I want in a relationship before I'm making out with a sleaze ball while prince charming is waiting at home for me."

"Bitch!" Grace smacked George in the ass with a dishtowel. "Jack was at the firehouse, not my house." She grinned. "Okay, we need to take those bowls of batter, scoop them onto these cookie trays, then pop them in the oven for ten minutes. Then we need to mix batter for three other cookies, stop picking on Grace, pick on Clair who got a black eye while changing the diaper of a mechanical doll, and help George find her purpose in life—are you game?"

"Does Grace sabotage every relationship she's in?" said George.

"And is she a ho-bag?" said Clair.

Grace sighed. "I take it you're both in?"

Three successful cookies, two disastrous cookies and two maybe, maybe-not cookies later, the air in Grace's apartment was thick with a semi-sweet chocolate peanut butter ambrosia that hung like the smog over California ever since the last batch of cookies, under Clair's not-so-watchful-eye, went up in smoke. The women, battered and smeared, sat on the kitchen floor surrounded by the remnants of their cookie-making crusade and tried to sort out their mess.

"Okay. So, yes for the chocolate peanut butter craisin, no for the coconut lemon, and maybe for the cinnamon semi-sweet swirl?" asked Grace, who was nauseous after she had tasted the last batch of cookies.

"No, yes on those, but no on that Tahitian vanilla mess with the pecans," replied George as she lay down on the kitchen floor.

"Yeah," said an equally over sugared Clair. "No on that cherry vanilla thing with the coconut, maybe on the apple pumpkin spice, and definitely yes on the chocolate peanut butter black and white cookie. That frosting could give you an orgasm!"

George handed the bowl to Grace. "Say no to Ray, say yes to frosting!" The women, who admittedly knew it wasn't that funny, were so hopped up on sugar that they laughed their assess off. "Hey, maybe we can break into the sex food market?"

"Don't make me laugh. No, no, no! My bladder isn't as strong as it used to be," gasped Grace, as she patted her pregnant tummy.

"So, what's the next step?" asked Clair.

"Well, a business plan would help. The one I did is really bare bones. A package for potential investors and maybe a tasting?" suggested George.

"I can look over your plan and see if I can help beef it up. What about packaging and a place to make the cookies? Where are you getting your ingredients? Clair asked as she pulled her tired ass off the floor.

George and Grace exchanged looks. "Why don't you run the business? I can do the marketing and Grace, well, she does the baking and shit."

Clair smiled. "I'm about to become a mom and about to be named partner. I don't have time for it."

"You could consult. I've got a few months until I'm ready to blow."

Clair knew she was right, but going into business with them was something that needed careful consideration. "I'll think about it, okay?"

"Great! Now help me up off this frickin' floor," laughed Grace.

George stood up, grabbed Grace's arm, and pulled her sorry ass off the floor. "So who's cleaning up this mess?"

Chapter 26

In every mother-daughter relationship there is a rite of passage. Getting the first manicure/pedicure together, buying her first bra, her first crush, her first kiss, getting her driver's license, etc. In the arena of mother-daughter rites of passage, the mother sided issues aren't as fun. Grace and Clair figured that what they had to look forward to was taking away her driver's license, buying her large print books, reminding her to take her medication, praying that she never broke her hip, and the like. What they never expected in a million years was a mother-daughter shopping spree that involved buying lingerie for a romantic weekend away with a man who most definitely wanted to have sex with their mother. Ew, gross!

"OH MY GOD, NO!" said Diane as she stared at herself in the fitting room mirror. "This is not underwear. This is not even a bikini bottom. This is a string. Why in the hell would anyone in her right mind want to wear a string? You know—HERE!"

"Mom," said Clair, "you can't wear your white Granny undies."

"Fine, but I'm not wearing dental floss either. It's indecent."

"Isn't that the idea?" cracked Grace.

"No, it's not the idea." Diane, to prove her point, opened her fitting room door. Grace and Clair instinctively recoiled in horror and closed their eyes. "I want to be sexy and tasteful. Think Grace Kelly, even Sophia Loren—not Pamela Anderson!"

Clair opened her eyes first. She nudged Grace to do the same. After getting over the shock of their mother standing in front of them in a lace baby pink scallop bra and matching thong they studied her as one does works of art. They took in her shapely legs, studied her arms, which weren't flabby due to her weight lifting and aerobic regime, and her surprisingly flat stomach. All in all, they were confident that the apple didn't fall far from the tree and that their bodies would age as gracefully as their mom's.

Grace put her hand on her expanding pregnant stomach. "Amazing, but, well, you definitely need a trim." A confused Diane looked to Clair.

Clair had to agree. "You so need a trim, but clothes off and all – in-all you look great."

"What do you mean by a trim?" asked Diane. Clair looked at her then down at her, you know. "Oh, oh, uh, there. I don't look like a whore do I?"

"A whore? Oh, God, no! Very tasteful, very sexy." Grace turned to her Clair. "But maybe a different bra?"

"Yeah, the DKNY Belle Du Jour, you know, with the little bow."

"And maybe with the Cheeky Boy short in the Chinatown Red. Now that is hot."

Before Diane could respond, her daughters disappeared and returned with armloads of lingerie. After being poked, "I don't think that's supposed to hug like that," Said Grace.

Prodded, "Mom, can you just move that? What is that?" asked Clair.

"My nipple," sighed Diane.

Cupped, "Wow, well you know what they say, more than a mouthful is a waste," grinned Grace.

Lifted, "Why does your ass do that? Is mine gonna do that?" asked Clair as she put her hand on the bottom of Diane's ass and pushed it up.

"What is it doing?" asked Diane, "I can't see behind me."

Turned, "You're not dizzy. We have to see it from every angle," sighed Grace.

Studied, "Nope, it makes her legs look like cantaloupes," laughed Clair.

And on one occasion, spanked, "Look at that. He's gonna love that!" Grace smacked Diane's butt.

With all of that, Diane emerged from the experience with six hundred dollars' worth of fancy underwear. As they waltzed into Nordstrom's Restaurant, she had, believe it or not, more confidence in her body. "Now, clothes; your wardrobe consists of sweatpants, high waisted jeans, and dress slacks circa 1998." Clair walked to the counter and ordered them all the lunch special.

Grace suddenly exhausted, put her feet up on the extra chair and closed her eyes for a moment. "You okay?" asked a concerned Diane.

"I don't think I'm going to make the clothing expedition. Do you mind?" said Grace.

"How about we send you home in a taxi, you take a nap, and then we'll treat you to dinner and a fashion show?" said Diane as the waitress dropped off three glasses of lemonade.

Grace nodded her approval. "I'm in. So, are you prepared for sex?"

"I'm past menopause, I don't need the pill."

"We know that," said Clair. "Do you need condoms? Plus we have to get you a wax. Do you want to buy some sex toys, get some KY Jelly?"

Diane choked on her lemonade. "I don't wax my legs. At my age, I barely have enough hair to shave."

"We don't mean your legs, Mom," smiled Grace.

Diane felt her cheeks grow red. "I thought you said I had to trim it?"

"Yes, by waxing it. Makes wearing a thong so much more comfortable," said Clair, "you should do it too, Gracie, before the big day. Makes the whole birthing thing less icky."

Grace took a sip of her lemonade and then grabbed her tuna melt almost before the waitress set down their food. She was suddenly starving. Pregnancy is way weird, she thought. "Oh, right, I've heard that too. Less icky, but does it make it less painful? It better be less painful if I'm going to get on my hands and knees and let some tiny Vietnamese woman rip the hair out of the one barrier between my bladder and my underwear." Grace noticed their Mom wasn't eating. "Mom, are you okay?"

Diane sighed. "Maybe this is a bad idea?"

"In the realm of bad ideas, there are so many to choose from," sighed Grace. "Having Clair's baby, dating Jack while having Clair's baby, letting Patricia buy me an apartment, wearing bangs through most of the eighties, dying my hair orange for the most of the nineties, my belly ring, the stork tattoo on my ass, and The Spice Girls reunion."

Clair rolled her eyes. "What's a bad idea, mom?"

"Sal-me-us." Diane finally took a bite of her sandwich. "I think I'm in love."

"As in 'til death do you part you don't want to wake up next to anyone but him for the rest of your life, love?" asked Clair.

Diane nodded as she took a sip of her lemonade. "Freaky."

"Oh my GOD did you tell him?" asked Clair.

"Nope. And I'm not going too."

"I get it," sighed Grace.

"You would." Clair shook her head. "I don't know how you idiots function in life. Don't you think it's sad that you're more comfortable with one night stands?"

Grace cracked, "hey, that's not me, that's her."

"She's got a point," sighed Diane. "After your Dad, I just didn't want to get attached in that all seeing, all knowing, all loving forever way."

Grace saw her mother's eyes well up with tears. "Yeah, what she said. Now, back off bucko or this kid is staying in here way past its due date. We're romantically challenged—we get it, then move on."

Clair picked up what was left of her tuna melt. "Fine," she said between bites, "but it's time for the two of you to fucking grow up!"

Diane sighed. "What's with the potty mouth? I raised you better than that."

Grace grinned. "You coined the phrase stupid-fucking-sack-of-shit when I was five!"

Clair sighed. "You're really not gonna tell Sal how you feel?"

"No. I want to be positive," stammered Diane.

"And she won't know if she's positive until she knows if they're sexually compatible. Nothing is worse than loving a man who can't deliver," laughed Grace. "I saw this couple on Jerry Springer and they had to get a sex surrogate. Hey, maybe that will be my next job—from surrogate mother to surrogate sex starter-upperer."

Diane drolled, "are you going to run your business out of a cab?" Grace almost toppled out of her chair, Clair howled, and as Diane rolled with laughter, and as the entire restaurant looked on, she felt proud that she and her daughters were making a spectacle out of themselves. She was even prouder of the relationship she was able to have with them. She wondered if it would've been possible if her husband were still alive. Well, she thought, thanks to an errant snowplow she'll never know the answer to that one.

Chapter 27

As the moon rose higher in the sky, an ominous wind blew—a telltale sign that something wicked this way comes or more accurately something wicked this way sat in the swank apartment across from the lake on the floor of her shoe closest. Grace was amongst her once cherished shoe collection with her wide, sweaty, and swollen feet. Besides a pair of Keds and some flip-flops, she had absolutely no shoes to wear. She also had nothing to put over her ever-expanding ass. No one had warned her about that. She had no idea why her ass was growing in proportion to her stomach because the baby was not growing in that part of her body. And, so it may be safe to assume that the rain and hail that were now beating down on the city of Chicago was due in fact to the wailing, sobbing, Grace. To top off the shoes that don't fit horror was the fact that at this moment she weighed the most that she had ever weighed in her life, was the horniest that she had ever been in her life, and she was about to meet Jack's parents for the first time—all while five and a half months pregnant with her sister's child. It was not going to be a good night. Rain made her hair frizz, Keds were inappropriate footwear for dinner, her last pair of pantyhose had just ripped, and the Liz

Lange striped polo dress she had planned on wearing to this casual little get together made her look like a pregnant zebra. The baby kicked and Grace immediately put her hand on her belly. "Listen kid, I love you like you're my own, but seriously enough with the growing. Aren't you getting cramped in there? If I get any bigger, I'm going to need a forklift to carry me around." Grace, exhausted, lay down and as the thunder and lightning slowly joined the cadence of the hailstorm that was going on just outside her window, she drifted to sleep.

"I think I found her," said the slightly Italian accented voice that was coming from the sweet faced, green-eyed blonde who was staring down at Grace. Grace, whose eyes weren't completely opened yet, was confused. "Are you okay dear?" asked the voice.

Grace opened her eyes. She knew where she was, but didn't know who was staring at her. "I think so."

"Gracie, Gracie, are you okay?" asked a panicked Jack, as he came rushing into her bedroom.

Grace was still confused. "I think so. What's wrong?"

"It's nine o'clock. You were supposed to meet us at the restaurant at seven, remember?"

That's when the clothing, shoe, panty-hose ripping nightmare flashed before her eyes. "Oh my GOD! No! I was getting dressed. I just laid down for a second." She looked at the blonde and the strapping barrel-chested white haired man who came up behind her and cringed. "You're Jack's parents?"

"Yes dear," said the blonde.

Grace was mortified. She was about to get up when she suddenly felt wet. "Uh, why don't you go fix your parents a drink and I'll, uh, finish getting ready."

Jack had no idea what to do. There on the floor, smelling the tiniest bit like urine, was the love of his life and standing over her, hopefully not picking up the tiniest smell of urine, were his parents. "Sure." Jack guided his parents out the door as Grace struggled to her feet. Once he had his parents safely ensconced in the living room, Jack came back in time to save Grace from losing her balance and landing on her ass.

"I'm so sorry. I don't know what happened. My shoes didn't fit, my pantyhose ripped, and I looked like a pregnant zebra and then, I think I peed myself. I felt everything get all warm, but it was probably a dream."

Jack had no idea if he should laugh. "It wasn't a dream," was all he could say.

"Oh my GOD! I wet the bed. I mean the floor, I wet the floor?" She looked down at her dark cherry hardwood floors, saw the damp sheen of pee and was mortified. "Your parents must be starving." Then it hit her. "I smell like pee. I just met your parents for the first time and I was passed out on the floor smelling like pee. Oh my God, if I had a cup next to me they would've given me a quarter! Get them out! Out, out of here—like now! We're so broken up!"

Jack smiled. "Uh, no, but I'll order some dinner while you fix yourself up and we'll just start over." He kissed Grace, went into the master bath, came out with a towel and some spray ammonia, cleaned up the pee, tossed the towel into the laundry basket and headed out the door. "Why don't you take a shower and relax?"

"Relax? How am I supposed to relax?" implored Grace.

"By taking a shower," he said as he closed the door behind him.

Jack was right. A shower had calmed her down. She was still mortified, but at least she no longer smelled like a kid learning how to be potty trained. Grace brushed her wet hair and pulled it back off her neck into a soft bun. She used to wear her hair like this when she was on the local swim team. Her dad used to call her the swimming ballerina. Grace smiled at the memory of her Popsicle, then sighed. She was ready to meet Jack's parents for the second time. The moment she walked into the living room, the welcoming aroma of lamb chops and roasted potatoes wafted over her. She watched Jack help his mom in the kitchen as his father busted his chops about the Cubs. While the threesome laughed and joked, Grace realized she wasn't wearing any shoes and was about to go back into her bedroom when Jack's mom caught her eye. She smiled at Grace and her face lit up. Grace, who had always wondered where Jack had gotten his own crinkly smile and laughing eyes, finally got her answer.

"Here she is. I hope you don't mind. I commandeered your kitchen. Seemed like a waste to order out when you had all the fixings for a great meal right here." She wiped her hands on Grace's apron and walked over to her. "I'm Millie," she said as she took Grace by the arm and led her over to her husband. "And this cranky old man is Joe."

Grace wasn't nervous anymore. "Nice to finally meet you. Sorry about earlier. I didn't mean to worry you."

Millie shooed Jack from the kitchen. "Grace and I will finish; set the table with your father."

As Jack scooted out he pulled Grace into a kiss..."Hey, you"...Then did as his mother instructed.

Grace blushed as she watched Jack walk away. "So, what do you need me to do?"

Millie handed her a knife, a loaf of bread, and a cutting board. "Not break my son's heart and slice the Italian bread." Like Jack before her, Grace did as his mother instructed.

"I think that went well," Jack said as he loaded the dishwasher.

"Well, let's just say that considering the way it started, it ended better than anyone anticipated." Grace placed a new garbage bag into the kitchen trashcan and caught Jack smiling. That's when it hit her. She loved him. Oh shit, she thought. She totally loved him. She was in head-over-heels-don't-want-to-be-without-him-in-love, love with him. Grace felt sick to her stomach, excited beyond belief, and scared to death. She felt her heart beat faster. Her breath caught in her throat as she tried to speak she sounded like a wheezing bulldog. "What's with the smile? You got a secret?"

Jack grinned. "I'm just relieved that my parents liked you."

"What? You thought there was a chance they wouldn't? Let me rephrase that. You thought that before you found me lying in a pool of my own urine that they wouldn't?"

"I knew they'd like you, but my mom cooked for you. She didn't cook for my ex-wife 'til we were married and by then we were getting divorced."

"Oh, I thought she just wanted to show me how proficient she was with knives because she threatened my life a few times."

Jack laughed. "She's all bark, no bite."

"Really? 'Cause I'm thinking she's more Bonnie and Clyde and less Mama Celeste." Grace looked down at her feet. "I can't believe I was barefoot and pregnant all night. I'm a freak!"

Jack took her hand and led her to the couch. "Well, you're my freak," he said as he kissed her gently and sat her down. "So," he nervously said as he looked around her apartment, then took her feet and started massaging them. "Maybe we should go away together, you know, before the baby is born."

Grace, who was lulled into a relaxed state as he worked out the knot between her heel and arch, was intrigued. "Why?"

"Why? What do you mean why?" asked Jack.

"Well, going away is a big milestone. It's the capper to the all-exciting, sometimes dreaded, not sure if we should do the deed, deed doing event sealer. And, because you're never putting out, why bother?"

An insulted Jack stopped massaging her feet. "You're kidding me, right?"

Grace, realizing she had hurt his feelings, tried to back track. "Of course I am." She leaned over and kissed him. "Actually, I'm not. I think you should just put out already." Jack was pissed and pulled away from her. She had no idea why she was pursuing this line of thinking considering that she had just figured out she was in love with the guy and, of course, she wanted to go away with him. "You have to look at it from my point of view. After I have this kid, we're not going to be able to have sex for at least two months, and from all the books I read, I may not be in the mood for sex for at least six months, or, hell, maybe a year. What happens if I end up experiencing post- partum depression or if I have a C-section? I won't be able to move my abdomen for like eight weeks and there's all the other gross stuff that goes down in that area that puts you off sex for quite a while. We would be together for at least one, maybe two years and no sex, which is fine if we were Amish, but I'm not Amish. And besides, they have more sex than that. I mean really, what else are you gonna do if you don't have TV? How many barns can you raise? So, why go away for a long weekend and be tortured by the fact that you don't want me?" Grace immediately felt like an idiot.

"Don't want you? Are you serious? Is that what you think?" Jack sighed. "I take so many cold showers at the fire house the guys have started calling me Frosty!"

"Oh really?" giggled Grace as she climbed onto his lap and began kissing his neck.

He kissed her long and hard. "Really. Not going away for a weekend doesn't make any sense. Although, being tortured by my fabulous body certainly does." He pulled away from her. "This is about Ray, isn't it? You think you'll feel more secure in our relationship if we seal the deal."

Grace knew he was right, but she wasn't about to give in. "Oh and you didn't want me to meet your parents for the exact same reason? Isn't that why your mom kept threatening my life?"

Jack knew that she was right, but he wasn't about to give in. "Come on, this asshole has been hanging over our heads since our first date. If you need to have sex with me, so you can feel like you're over him then obviously you're not over him. And trust me, Grace, I'm sick and tired of having this conversation."

"Oh believe me, I'm over Ray— I'm so over Ray. Do you want to know how I know I'm over Ray?" Grace stopped. She was still feeling guilty about her cab ride with Ray and knew telling Jack about it right now would be huge mistake. Grace half whispered, "maybe we should stop having this conversation."

"What does that mean?" Jack felt the color drain from his face.

Grace started to tremble. She had no idea what she was doing. Picking a fight with a guy you just realized you were in love with was one of those things you weren't supposed to do. All the advice columns she had ever read told her that. "I don't know."

"What is it about this guy that gets you so worked up?"

Grace steadied herself against the overstuffed Greenwich chair. "I thought he was the love of my life. On paper he's a complete loser, but he knew how to make me laugh. He was the first guy I had sex with sober, he was the only one who believed I could be a rock star, and just when I thought he was a complete asshole he would say or do something so unbelievably sweet. He broke my heart." Grace shook off the Ray nostalgia and regrouped. "Or maybe I'm so worked up because I'm a hormonal mess and there's the whole who-are-you-to-me- who-am-I-to-you-issue and, oh my GOD, I don't know what the fuck I'm saying—I plead the fifth!"

Jack had no idea what she wanted. She had no idea what she wanted and, so he thought that meant she didn't want him. "Maybe we should just call it quits before anyone gets hurt."

Grace didn't like the sound of that at all. "Yeah, well make sure your mother knows you broke my heart and not the other way around."

"Really?" he asked a bit too hopefully. "If I walked out that door right now and we called it quits, I'd break your heart?"

"Yes," Grace answered so quickly she almost gave herself whiplash. "And I don't think I'd recover." She tried to stop talking, but couldn't. "At least with Ray I'd know it was going to happen again and I'd have my exit strategy prepared."

Jack had no idea what to do next. "Oh."

"That's it, 'oh?'" Grace sighed. "Oh like in, so you thought you felt the same way, but you don't." Jack still said nothing. Grace nervously began to chatter, "and of course you weren't aware of the

fact until I made a fool of myself. Well, that's the last time I fall
asleep in my own pee. Self magazine said it was a turn on, not a turn
off, but once again, as with the bad advice on ruby coral lipstick,
they were wrong." What Grace didn't know was that Jack was in
shock. His heart was beating a hundred miles an hour. He was
definitely sweating. His palms were itchy. He wanted to stand, but he
was afraid his legs wouldn't support him. Once he gained his
facilities, he pushed all his weight onto his feet and stood up. So far,
so good, he thought. He walked over to Grace, pulled her to him and
kissed her passionately and led her to the bedroom. "Ooh," said
Grace, as shirts and skirts were taken off and shoes and belts hit the
floor. "Ooh," Grace whispered while Jack caressed her pregnant
belly and teased her lips with his.

"Nice tattoos," murmured Jack as he managed to erase every
memory Grace ever had about sex with anyone else, but especially
Ray. As we stated before this isn't one of *those* books and it is a
story of two sisters—not the legendary tale of Paul Bunyan, so while
we can truthfully state they did the deed, we can't tell you a whole
hell of a lot more. As for the morning after, we're not going there.
Why? Well, honestly, we weren't invited and really, shouldn't some
things be left to your over active imagination?

And, so The Higgins Sisters had now officially passed from
now, now what through the annoying you don't say, and the sun was
setting on zing-zing, which you must agree was an aptly named fifth
month of their pregnancy. What other surprises, disasters, natural or
otherwise, were waiting for them over the next few months? No one
knew. Well, you would if you'd just turn the page. Now, you should
turn the page, now!

Chapter 28

The Higgins Sisters entered the next phase of their lives that we like to call now or never. So far, all was going swimmingly. That's what people usually say when life motored along without a hitch, but there are many definitions of the word swim. Some use it to describe the actual act of going for a swim and if you know your fifth-grade English then you know the drill. So, life going swimmingly was for the most part in the eye of the beholder. Right now, the beholder was Grace and the swimmingly was George, who was not so much swimming along with life as much as swimming in it, and the moment Grace heard George's, "sooo don't be maaad," she assumed it was alcohol.

"Where are you?" asked Grace as a whiff of musk covered her when she grabbed one of Jack's shirts out of the laundry basket and hurriedly put it on. She enjoyed the fact that the shirt of the man she loved was sitting in the laundry basket of her bedroom. "George, George… are you there?" Grace could hear some background noise and a bit of commotion going on somewhere in the land of the drunk.

"Where am I? Hey, you, cowboy, where am I? Bad Diva? Sad Beaver? Oh, sad beaver, mine is so, so sad. No really it is, it's a sad beaver. Huh, oh Red Kiva, I'm at Red Kiva Graceieieie."

"Why the fuck are you all the way on Randolph Street?" implored Grace as she put on her flip-flops, the only thing that fit her feet now, and grabbed her jean jacket. It tended to get chilly in Chicago toward the middle of September, especially after two a.m. Grace checked to make sure she had her keys, cash, and headed out the door.

"Tampons..." slurred George.

"I am not stopping for tampons on my way. I have one in my purse. I think. George what the fuck is going on?" Grace buttoned her coat in the elevator and rushed out as soon as the door opened.

The doorman, alarmed at seeing a pregnant woman racing somewhere in the middle of the night, came running over. "You okay, Ms. Higgins? Is the baby coming?"

"No, I'm fine. Just six months. Need a cab though." Ben nodded and within minutes he got Grace into a cab.

"What is going on? What happened?" Grace told the driver where she needed to go then settled back into the seat. Man, she thought, I hope I have enough cash on me.

"Don't be mad, please. Guess what? Turns out you can only like advertising if you're drunk. Turns out there was a reason you couldn't...hey, hey, I told you I don't need you to make my beaver happy. Back off!"

Grace heard what sounded like glass breaking. "George! Find a seat in the back where no one is, can you do that for me sweetie?"

"Sure. I can do that. I'm doing that right now. I'm gonna go sit at the bar with my buddy. What's your name? Sven. My buddy Sven is going to make me a drink. Right Sven? Coffee? But I don't want coffee. Can I have coffee with a touch of Irish? But, I don't want tea, I want hot chocolate with whipped cream."

"George, George focus. Okay, sweetie, tell me what happened?"

"I quit, by quit I mean I got fired. Now let me tell you, last night, no tonight, no, the night before the night that was the night of...oh fuck! Anyway before my big maxi pad presentation, I couldn't think of any more ways to describe ab-sorb-en-dent, so I came up with—now this is good—it's better than a diaper. They didn't think it was funny. They asked me if I was drunk and I said no I was completely sober and I was. I asked the man if he had ever worn a maxi pad 'cause it feels like a fucking diaper and that's when I excused myself and packed up my office and get, I mean, got or is it getting loaded?" George took a deep breath. "It looks like a pee pad for a dog—if I had a dog...I should get a dog, I have time now."

"No, Georgie, don't get a dog."

"Really? I always wanted one. A dog would be nice. A dog would keep me company and lick my face and pee on my rug. I want someone to pee on my rug. Although, there's a really good chance that I might do it tonight!"

"I know dear. Someone to pee on their rug; it's what everyone woman craves," Grace said.

"Gracieeee do you know what my worst nightmare is? Wearing a maxi pad and corduroys. It gives me shivers. It's worse than brown slacks and black shoes. The corduroy is so thick and it crunches and the maxi pad it crinkles and swishes like tape caught on your ass. It's a scary thing, a scary cornu, cornucop, cornocopulation of sounds like a horror movie. I think I'm gonna be sick!"

Now that sent shivers down Grace's spine. "Oh! Do you feel pukey-pukey or just you know pukey?" This was their code for becoming a drunken vomiting mess. Pukey-pukey meant you were gonna heave now and pukey meant if you ate you might be able to stave it off.

"Pukey, except now I'm not vomit free in 93!" The cab pulled over, Grace asked him to stay, then rushed into Red Kiva. Vomit Free in 93! She hadn't heard that in a while. Grace opened the smokey glass doors and saw George sitting in her black straight leg trousers and her DKNY striped long sleeve cardigan, and smiled. If you didn't know better you would think she was one together chick until you saw that she was missing a shoe, her shirt was stained and her pants were really dirty at the knees. Grace sighed; she was probably crawling around the bathroom floor again. The toilets are always too low for a woman of George's stature and crouching that far down is hazardous to your wardrobe. "Hey let's get you home, okay?"

George, who was by no means an ugly drunk, smiled at her friend and pulled her into a hug. "Okay dokey. Hi, ho, Hi-ho it's off to…we go," Grace smiled at the bartender, who upon noticing she was pregnant, got George who fell twice, tripped off her one shoed leg, then spun and hit her head on the cab door, into the cab for her.

"Thanks," said Grace as she gave him a twenty-dollar tip, then told the driver to take her back to where he picked her up and slid into the backseat with her drunken friend. She pushed George's hair out of her eyes and patted her hand. "How you doing?"

George tried to focus on Grace, but she just kept moving in slow motion like a bad sci-fi movie. "I thought I'd feel better by having a little drinkie, you know? I just want to puke. If I had had just one more drink I'd be a delight, you know? I'd be a Noel Coward play all witty and sparkling, but I went too far. Now I'm

David Mamet all dark and edgy." The cab turned and George slid further away from Grace. "Oooh, I'm not making sense. I'm like Ella Fitzgerald. I'm all scooduddle-dee and rattatatata!" Suddenly, the fact that she was missing her shoe fascinated her and she kept leaning over and sweeping the floor with her hands. "I thought I could do it, I thought I could be a team player even though everyone knows when you go from the head of the Nike account to partner on maxi pads they're shoving you the door—shoving the door in your place," George gulped some air and continued, "please don't send me to rehab Gracie, please. It doesn't help anyway"

Grace's cell phone suddenly rang. "Hello? Sal? Is everything okay?"

"Let me sum it up for you doll. Jack came home to find you gone. Your cell phone has been busy for about an hour and he's freaking out. Your mother's a nervous wreck and Henry is trying to convince Clair that you didn't run off to Mexico to sell their baby on the black market!"

George grabbed the phone. "Sal? Sally boy, how's it hanging? You make me think of a song." George paused to find her singsong voice. "Ride Sally Ride... how you doing?"

"Have you been drinking?"

George laughed. "Me, drinking, ha! It's what I do."

"Why kiddo, you were doing so well?"

George turned to Grace, "he wanna to know why, why? I am extremely dehy-dehy-dehydrated by life. Oh, and I asked a man if he ever wore a maxi pad. I asked my boss if he ever wore a diaper. Turns out, they didn't. Lost my edge, Sally boy, lost my edge and it's not in the lost in found, I checked. So, here I am. No more jobie, all-all-all alone, and the batteries on my vibrator died. Just like that!"

George attempted a snap, but it was more of a swish and suddenly handed the phone back to Grace, as she desperately tried to open the backseat window before she got all pukey-pukey in the cab.

Jack raced to the cab as soon as it pulled up.

"I'm sorry, I'm sorry. I didn't think. I just wanted to get to her as fast as I could," Grace said in her defense.

"Uh, lady, get this mess out of my cab." Grace turned her attention back to George as Jack scurried to help. They were both trying to pull a drunken-vomit-drenched George out of the cab when Sal and Diane showed up.

"She fell off the wagon?" Diane asked, as Sal took over for Grace.

Grace and Diane followed them into the building. "She jumped off and at one point, the wheel actually fell off the wagon and she just dragged it around until her knees were bloody and she became one of those people without any nerve endings who can't feel pain," Grace said as she attempted to adjust George's puked stained cardigan to cover her breasts.

Diane took her daughter's hand. "Are you okay?"

"I'm worried about her. I've never seen her like this before and I've seen her in just about every position known to man."

"There's no business like show business, like no business I know..." George belted it out like she had just downloaded the Tourette's show tunes catalog. They exchanged looks and silently agreed to ignore the singing.

"So, what do we do?" asked Diane.

"Rehab. I know a good one. Some fellas down at the station have gone; it's an A plus place." Jack suggested.

"She won't go," sighed Grace.

"We have to do something. I can't stand to see her like this." Diane noticed George was missing her shoe. "What happened?"

"Don't ask me. She's gonna be pissed that she lost a Jimmy Choo in the gutter somewhere."

"It's a hard knock life for us. It's a hard knock life for us…" George belted this one out. Jack and Sal were so startled they almost dropped her.

Sal hit the sixth floor button again. "We can't force her to go to rehab, but she can't live alone, not right now. If we want to get her sober and keep her sober we're gonna have too…" he stopped, perplexed. "Where is her family?"

"I love you." Diane gave Sal a kiss. "We're her family. Her father died when she was a kid and her mom passed a few years ago."

Sal, stunned, took a moment. "You love me? She loves me?" he laughed, as he caught Diane's eye. "Oh, now you're trapped baby. There's no way off the Sal love parade." Diane grinned.

Jack looked at Grace. It hurt him to see her so worried. "What do we do?"

Sal was about to say something when the elevator stopped on the third floor and little Mr. Watermeyer shuffled on in his pajamas. He looked at George and then at the group. "Just getting the morning paper."

"You do know the elevator is going up Mr. Watermeyer?" asked Grace.

He smiled, "I didn't say I was going to buy the paper. Mr. Harris keeps his television blaring all night, so in the morning I steal his paper. It's my own little good morning ritual."

George suddenly perked up. "Good mornin'! Good mornin'! We talked the whole night through! Good morning'! Good mornin'! To you..." George sang to no one in particular.

Mr. Watermeyer waited to see if anyone did anything. "It's great to stay up late. Good mornin', good mornin' to you..." he added in a surprisingly sweet voice. Suddenly George and Mr. Watermeyer were keeping harmony, "when the band began to play. The sun was shinin' bright, now the milkman's on his way. It's too late to say goodnight..."

The elevator stopped. As they lugged George out, her eyes locked in on Mr. Watermeyer. "So, good mornin', good mornin'! Sunbeams will soon smile through..."

And as the doors closed Mr. Watermeyer bowed, "good mornin', good mornin', to you..."

Sal and Jack leaned against the wall for support. Lugging a six-foot red head was no easy task, especially if she was one hundred and fifty pounds of drunken dead weight. Sal nodded to Grace, "you know kid I'm in recovery—have been for over twenty years. We can do this if we keep her away from alcohol, but if we do then she should stay here."

Diane chimed in, "he's right. She loves you too much to drink in front of you."

Grace sighed, "yeah, but not enough to call someone else to clean up the mess."

Jack added, "They're right."

Grace opened the door. "I know, I know, but I can't do this alone."

The next day George woke up confused, clean, and in a lot of pain. While she tried to put the pieces together from the night before, she discovered that Diane had gone to her apartment and packed her clothes, Jack had tossed every product that had an ounce of alcohol in it, and that Sal was taking her to an AA meeting—his AA meeting. George was a little nauseous and a lot grateful that she hadn't woken up with another tattoo on her ass and so she thanked them the only way she could by bursting into tears.

"Well, at least it's not 'Old Man River,'" cracked Sal.

George stammered between tears. "Mommy, daddy. Show tunes." Was all anyone understood once George took the crying, heaving sobs, to a whole new level.

Clair recovered from the—has my sister absconded to Mexico with my unborn child fiasco—and was readying herself for that next big stage in her life. No, not motherhood—partnership. As she sat outside the conference room, she realized that this dream of hers had made it from the practice list where it sat between marry Ralph Macchio and invent a new calculator, to the laminated list that had become her calling card of life's goals. A secretary came out and smiled. "They're ready for you now," she said motioning for Clair to follow her in. Clair stepped into the glass conference room. There they were Cleary, Kelly, Trees, Brady, and Verbouwen sitting in their crisp designer suits and freshly ironed shirts.

"Morning," Kelly smiled. "Clair, as you know you're one of our most valuable employees."

Trees interjected, "we're all big fans of yours."

"But," Brady smirked, he was never a Clair fan, "things have changed. You're about to become a mother and you won't want to be at the office as much."

"So, partnership isn't really a viable option anymore," added Verbouwen.

"You're right," Clair heard herself say. The partners weren't sure how to react and neither was Clair. "I don't want to work eighty hours a week," she heard herself continue, "I don't want to work an hour a week." Whose voice is that, she thought, as she motored toward a road she never imagined she'd take. "I don't want to be here—*at all!*" Clair realized she was quitting.

Kelly asked, "You're resigning?"

"I think I am, but it won't official until we've negotiated a fair severance package. Now, we all know that not making me Partner because I'm about to become a mother isn't technically against the law, but if you don't play nice, I'll let every client know what you did and then I'll sue for back over-time pay, which I never pursued in the past because I had been promised the partnership and didn't want to rock the boat, but now I'm rocking the boat, hell, the cradle!" Wow, Clair thought, that felt good.

The partners exchanged looks. Kelly sighed. "I'm assuming you'll wrap up the quarter for your clients while we negotiate that fair severance package of yours?"

"Of course." Clair walked to the door and shut it behind her. Once she safely made it past the secretary, she raced to her office, pulled out her cell phone, and then stopped. What did I just do? Who should I call? Henry? She wasn't ready to deal with his questions. Grace? She was dealing with George and the cookies right now. Her mom was away with Sal most likely having tons of sex, which she didn't want to think about and that's when it hit her.

Henry, Sr. handed Clair a drink. "What are you going to do?"

"Stay home with the baby?" Clair queried, as she shot back her entire drink.

He laughed. "Are you asking me or telling me?"

"I don't know." Clair shook her head. "Can I do this? I mean everything changes when you're the one who stays home, don't you think?" Clair motioned to her father-in-law to see if he wanted his drink freshened, he shook his head no.

"Change is good." Henry, Sr. said. "If you're okay with not going back to the whole career thing, you'll be fine. After four months of Patricia being home we nearly killed each other, but we were home together and sometimes that gets a little dicey."

"I thought she went back to work?"

"After Henry she did, but not after Charlie." Henry, Sr. immediately regretted what he said.

Clair sat up. "Charlie? Who the hell is Charlie?"

Henry, Sr. took in the Manet over the fireplace. "Charlie? I meant Henry."

"Who is Charlie?" Clair implored.

Henry, Sr. sighed. He couldn't back out of it now and he knew he could trust Clair. "Our first child," he said. "Patricia decided to be a stay at home mom. It was odd to see her so content changing diapers and making baby-food. She literally invented Baby's First Foods for Charlie," Henry got wistful. "Charlie," he whispered. "An easy baby, easy to laugh, easy to love." He refreshed his drink. "He died, SIDS; I went in to check on him," a shaken Henry, Sr. stopped speaking as it all came rushing back, "we weren't sure if we'd have another child. After Henry was born, Patricia didn't go near him. She'd feed him, but the rest was up to me. She couldn't shake the feeling that she was a jinx. The first year, she barely touched him.

She wouldn't, not until she was sure he wasn't going anywhere, by then, well, I was the official stay-at-home-parental-unit and the rest is history." Before Clair could even formulate a concise thought he interrupted her, "well that was melodramatic. For the record, Henry has never been told." He cleared his throat and got a hold of himself. "Listen, if you want to stay home, stay home, it's your decision. If you get bored, go back to work."

Clair felt so helpless right now and just wanted to give him a hug, but figured he wanted to move on, so she did. "You're right. Plus, I can always take on some clients and work from home. Actually, I was curious about your thoughts. Grace and George are starting a cookie company."

"You quit your job to start a cookie company?" Patricia walked in the door.

Clair and Henry, Sr. both jumped. "What? No? How did you...?"

Patricia went straight to the bar and made herself a Martini. "Oh one of those idiots Brady or Cleary, frankly I can't tell them apart, called to make sure we didn't part ways with the company because you were parting ways. What the hell is going on?"

"They weren't going to make me partner because of my impending motherhood and I quit." Clair sucked down what was left of her drink.

Patricia grinned. "They give you the old—you won't be spending that much time at the office song and dance?" Patricia, drink in hand, gave Henry, Sr. a peck on the cheek and then slid in next to him on the club chair. "I've used that a lot." Patricia studied her daughter-in-law. "Why don't you come work for me?"

"Whaaat?" Clair said that louder than she expected.

"Let me guess, you'd rather take a chance on a cookie company?" Patricia drolly stated.

Clair smiled. "Who knows, maybe I won't go back to work."

"Some women are built to stay at home, some are not. Trust me, you're not."

Clair knew Patricia was probably right. "Maybe I'm not, but I'd like to try."

Patricia got a far-away look in her eyes and sighed. "You should try. Every mom should, but if you're unhappy, your kid will hate you and you'll hate yourself." She shook off her melancholy. "So, have you told my son yet?"

"No, I was waiting for the right time," sighed Clair.

"Well, don't tell him before or after sex. He's an Erickson, so his mind will be on other things and Lord knows you can't tell them anything during sex."

Clair cringed. What is it with grandparents-to-be being so talky-talky about their sex lives?

Chapter 29

Grace stared up at the scrabble ceiling as she waited for her OBY-GYN, the lovely and talented Frigidaire, and Clair to show up.

"Henry couldn't make it," Clair declared as she walked through the door.

"Just as well. He always gets weird when they hoist me up here. We finding out?"

"Nope. This is the only surprise you can count on these days." Clair moved her over and sat on the edge of the table. "Man, you're huge!"

"Yeah? Well whose fault is that?" Grace tersely stated.

"Hey, you know that thing we talked about?" Clair looked up at the ceiling.

Grace cocked her head. "The mom telling Sal she loved him thing, the me and Jack having sex thing, the Patricia talking about sex thing, the you staying at home thing, the George pigging out on sweets thing, or the you becoming CEO of our cookie company thing?"

"Those are a lot of things. No one can say our lives are dull. I'm thinking specifically of the CEO cookie company thing. Let's do it!" grinned Clair.

"Really?"

"Really. If we can do this baby thing we can totally do the cookie thing."

Before an excited Grace could speak, Frigidaire finally walked into the room. "And, how are mom and auntie mommy doing?" Clair yanked Grace's hair and immediately jumped off the table.

"Owww," Grace grinned, "that is the best ten bucks I've ever earned."

Frigidaire laughed. "I'll take it off your bill."

"Oh no you won't. She foots the bill. I want cold hard cash."

Frigidaire shook her head. "You got it. How have you been feeling?"

"Pretty good. Can't hold my pee as well as I'd like and sometimes pooping is uncomfortable. Other than that, I'm good. How's Junior?"

Frigidaire pulled up the gown and covered her belly in gel. "Let's find out." She turned on the monitor, picked up a wand and when she touched it against Grace's belly they saw their little miracle.

"Junior got bigger," said Grace as a crying Clair held her hand. "You have to stop crying every time we do this. When the big day actually shows up you'll under perform in the—my sister's a saint and wow here's my baby crying department."

Frigidaire put the wand down and motioned to Grace to open up her legs. "Well, let's check under the hood." Her head disappeared for a few moments. "Good to go," she said when her head popped up. "I'm going to give you a prescription for a stool softener. If the pooping gets difficult start taking it. Okay, I'll see you ladies in a month." She pulled off her gloves and started to leave, but Grace stopped her. "Sue Ann will give you your ten bucks when you make your next appointment."

"Thanks," laughed Grace as Clair rolled her eyes. "What are we going to call it?"

"The baby? We can't decide."

"No," said Grace, as Clair helped her off the table to get dressed. "The company. Let's see, a recovering alcoholic with a sweet tooth, a woman pregnant with her sister's child, and an OCD, recently unemployed accountant, who paid her to be her baby's mama all adds up to what?"

Clair laughed. "Let's pick out the good words: sweet baby, sweet rum, sweet accountant, sweet..."

"Jesus," giggled Grace. "Sweet vagina, sweet ass, sweet cheeks, sweet life, just plain sweet, or sweet auntie mommy."

Clair smacked her. "Sweet stack, sweet stork, sweet money, sweet stuff."

"Sweet mamas," said Grace as she buttoned her shirt.

"Sweet mamas," echoed Clair and helped her put on her flip-flops. "Now that's a keeper."

And, so a star may not have been born, but it was a name they could all live with.

Chapter 30

Clair initially woke up at five a.m. Thrilled that she didn't have to get out of bed, she went back to sleep, but then much like the Chinese food she ate the night before, an hour later she woke up feeling oddly unsatisfied. She listened to Henry shuffling around the kitchen, no doubt eating his cereal over the sink and had no idea what she was supposed to do on her first non-vacation, non-sick, non-personal, non-workday since she was seventeen. Clair, being Clair, decided to make lists—to do lists. There was the baby list, the house list, and the Sweet Mamas list. Then, when all the lists were done, she rolled up her sleeves and got to work. In less than eight hours, Clair had reorganized the kitchen, living room, and family room. Now keep in mind Clair has OCD, so that meant that what she deemed unlivable or in need of organization, the rest of the free world aspired too.

After eating lunch, she realized that the only real mess was her photos. As much as she loved organizing, there was something unwieldy about getting a few hundred photos under control. Clair was glancing at some snapshots when she stopped mid shuffle. Her father, with his shaggy brown hair and big blue eyes, was staring back at her. The sight of him caught her breath. It was summer; they were at the lake. He was tan and healthy and laughing, he was always laughing. Clair closed her eyes and tried to remember the sound of his voice, but like him it was lost forever. It was time, she thought, to put more pictures of her father around, so her kid would know who he was. The pain of losing him had dulled. It was no longer sharp and prickly, but had somehow turned into a nice memory. Not the losing him part, but the knowing him part. That part was now like a hymn or a sweet hum or a song you remember from childhood that makes you smile. Clair took in the photos that were strewn upon the rug and thought "this is going to take some time."

"Are you kidding me?"

Clair pulled herself away her organized boxes of photos as Grace and George walked in the door. "Wow!" said George as she took off her shoes and joined Clair on the rug. "What are you doing?"

"What time is it?" Clair asked as she snapped shut the final box.

Grace followed George into the living room. "Six. Did you do this all day?"

"Yep." The boxes were color-coded, so Clair easily pulled a green box marked childhood and handed it to Grace. "We wore some ugly shit."

Grace handed her the email she had sent them. "You expect us to get all of this done in a week?" She sat and opened the box of photos.

"She's been freaking out all day." George grabbed her caramel suede messenger bag and pulled out a folder. "Halloween!"

"It's not even October yet, why the hell would Halloween freak her out?"

"Think about it, Clair Bear, how do we usually spend Halloween?" George asked, as she handed over a thick Sweet Mama's folder to Clair.

"Like drunken sluts," Clair cracked. "Oh, shit! Well, George can be a sober sex kitten and you can go as Garfield."

Grace was staring at a photo of her father and gave her the finger. She forgot the way his smiled crinkled at the edges of his mouth. "It's your fault I'm reduced to dressing up as a fat lazy cat that gorges herself on lasagna," sighed Grace, as she pulled open a blue box labeled high school. "What is with those pants?"

"All you notice is the pants? I'm color coded right down to my socks. I'm thirteen and in a leisure suit I probably fought Grandma for and you never said a word!"

"Oh, we said a word," George laughed, as she took a look at the photo. "We just said it behind your back!" Clair grabbed a photo of Grace from her Death Parade years and dangled it in front of her.

"Man, I was hot," sighed Grace, as she took in her too tight vinyl pants.

"You had to be," laughed George. "You have the voice of a dead trucker on crack."

Grace watched Clair and George as they laughed. "You never appreciated us!"

"Honey," guffawed George, "you sang off key, your keyboardist was constantly reinventing Three Blind Mice, you never performed sober, and your drummer used a wooden spoon. What was there to appreciate?"

Grace laughed. "We got paid in beer. How could anyone not appreciate that?"

"How the hell did we get from there to here?" asked Clair.

"I know. It's so weird—there's, like, missing years," sighed Grace.

"That's because we weren't sober," offered George. "Well, except for Clair. You only got drunk once."

"Yeah and somehow it got me knocked up!" Deadpanned, Grace.

Clair bit her lip. "Popsicle's been gone eighteen years. It's so weird. He would be so excited to see this baby."

"Especially since both his girls are involved. He would've been a great grandpa. The kind that would always have Cracker Jacks," smiled Grace.

"How can we still miss him so much?" asked Clair.

"I still miss my parents," sighed George. The sun started to slip from the sky and as they helped Clair put away the photo books, the late September breeze floated in from the open windows. "Life goes too fast."

"These nine months seem to be going pretty slow if you ask me," cracked Grace.

"Are we really doing this? Or, is Sweet Mamas going the way of Grace's forty-nine other occupations?"

"This can work—unless you want off the train?" said Clair.

"This," Grace put her hand on her belly, "and Sweet Mama's are the only things that have made sense in a long time."

"Okay, so then no turning back, but we need ground rules." Clair spied Grace as she tried to stand while doing the pee-pee dance.

"Help me the fuck up—unless you want urine all over your floor!" Grace yelped. George and Clair jumped into action. "Who the hell are our investors? We keep talking about having a tasting, finding investors, who are these people?" Grace raced off to the bathroom.

"Well," said Clair. "My old clients and Henry's parents' friends, Henry's rich college buddies, I have a list of potential companies looking to invest, and hedge funds."

"I can hit up some of the vendors I've used in the past plus the clients I left on good terms with, but..." George added..."Clair's right, we need ground rules. First, we make all decisions together. If we don't all agree, we don't do it."

"And no one gets a salary for at least a year," added Clair. "Can you do that? I know Grace can, I'm paying her a fortune to kick out that kid of mine, but are you good?"

It was moments like these that George envied Grace her little sister. "I'm good. They had to pay me out because they violated my contract when they took away a client I brought in. Oh, and you would not believe how much money I'm saving by not buying booze." George answered Clair's confused look, "honey, come on. When you're wearing five hundred dollar shoes you don't drink the house wine!"

The toilet flushed, Grace washed her hands, and then opened the door. "First order of business, dinner."

"I refuse to eat anymore pizza. That's all we've eaten for the past week." George took in Grace's ever expanding seventh month stretch. It was moments like these that her jealousy over not having her own little sister went bye-bye.

Clair laughed. "No pizza, majority rules!"

"But, I get two votes," chuckled Grace.

"No. You. Don't," said George. "And no playing the baby card."

Grace put on her shoes and smiled. "Baby card? Like I'd play the baby card?"

Clair grabbed her keys, started out the door, then paused. "I want a tattoo." Clair felt nervous, but emboldened. Grace and George exchanged looks. "Now!" And with that, Clair headed out the door.

"Shotgun," said George as she followed her out.

Grace shut the door and tried to catch up. "Sitting in the back seat makes the baby nauseous, so…"

When you're sober, getting a tattoo hurts like a motherfucker, or so we've been told, especially if the tattoo was of a stork to match the tattoos of the two reformed drunken idiots you were going into business with. For the next few weeks, these stork assed babes hit the ground running. Well, not literally running, so much as in Grace's case, but they got their shit together. They researched factories, found paper stock, finalized their business plan, created a brand look, and a strategic marketing plan, and as late nights turned into early mornings and vice-a-versa, the passion of building something from nothing kept them going.

Chapter 31

"Are you sure you don't want me to leave?" asked George, as Henry and Clair settled in for the night. It was the last Saturday of the month and it was baby-bonding time for the parents-to-be. George felt like a fourth wheel, but with Sal and Diane gone again and drinking no longer on her life's agenda she didn't have any place to go alone that she trusted herself to be. There were too many bars in Grace's neighborhood and too many reasons to get drunk still floating around in her head.

Clair came out with a tray of snacks. "Hey, did you look over the revised business plan? I added in the marketing costs and the production fees for the packaging."

"Yeah, I just have a few questions like the insurance issue. Henry, do you know if we have to insure the factory that makes the cookies or can we just ride on the insurance they already have?"

Before he could answer, Grace, fresh faced and bushy tailed in her new pregnancy jeans and a fresh white cotton Gap maternity top, came out from her bedroom. "Hey! You promised me a night out. That means out!" Grace took the tray from her. "I haven't been out in public in over three weeks."

George sniffed. "It's not our fault your boyfriend keeps covering everyone's weekend shifts."

Grace put the tray in the kitchen and scooted Henry to the door. "He's on his make extra money kick. I finally get the guy to put out and then he disappears."

"I wanted to stay in and chill," said Clair as she hesitated putting on her shoes.

"Screw that! We haven't left this place unless it was to go to your house or to sample paper products." Grace grabbed George's arm and practically pulled her out the door. "I have about three weeks before I balloon up like the Hindenburg, so put on some lipstick and show your baby's mama a good time! There's a cheesy romantic comedy playing at the Three Penny at seven." Clair and George exchanged looks. They knew they had no choice but to follow Grace out the damn door. "I bought tickets and then we can have dinner at Rocks or Lincoln Station; I made reservations at both."

Before long, they found themselves in the theater waiting for the cheesy romantic comedy to start. George and Grace were on line at the concession stand while Henry and Clair found seats. "Okay, what's your poison?" asked Grace. "And, really, no more red vines; you've gone through three jumbo containers. How do you not have lock-jaw?"

George looked around. Everyone seemed happy and alcohol free—even the damn teenagers. Weren't they supposed to be pissed off at the world? "Maybe I'm gay."

Grace searched through her bag for her buy one get one free movie watchers coupon. "The queen of the one night stands is gay?"

"Ever think that was a warning sign?" said George.

"A warning sign? You're an idiot. Trust me you're not one of those late in life lesbians." Grace finally found her coupon. "Shouldn't you be sober for a while before trying a new sexual orientation? You experimented in college, right? That held you for thirteen years—another six months won't kill you."

"Maybe." The tall, good-looking guy standing in front of the poster of a huge robot distracted George.

Grace followed her gaze. "See, you're attracted to guys. Oh man, that's Rich."

"Who?" asked an interested George.

"Jack's friend. The bait and switch guy." Rich noticed Grace and smiled. "Shit, I'd better say hello. You wait here." George tried to follow her. "You're not ready for Mr. Never Dates Anyone Twice to push your buttons."

"He could push anything he wanted," purred George.

"Go buy candy," said Grace as she made her way through the lobby. "Hey!"

"Who's your friend?" asked Rich, as he eyeballed George one more time.

"She's a living breathing human being who deserves a guy who will treat her with love and respect and not toss her out like yesterday's trash because she's looking for a committed relationship."

"Feeling a bit hormonal, eh?" Rich laughed. "Okay, I deserve that, but really, Gracie, I'm just a guy looking for love."

No matter how hard she tried, she couldn't hate him. "You're looking for a one night stand. So, are you on a recon mission for a buddy?" Grace looked around the lobby trying to pick out the poor, unsuspecting woman.

"Actually, I'm waiting for a very nice woman who figured out from the moment he sat down that Jack wasn't me."

As Grace tried to process this she forced a smiled. "Maybe I'll meet her if she lasts longer than a week." They laughed. "Well, I'd better go." Grace strode quickly back to George who was buying more junk food than four people could actually eat. "He's still dating."

George said, "he's single, isn't he? What's the big deal?"

"Not him, Jack's dating," said Grace as she handed over her twenty.

"What does that mean Jack's dating? Is that code for something?" A confused George handed money to the girl behind the counter and grabbed her stuff.

"It's code for he's still doing the bait and switch for that schmuck. And, I felt guilty about the cab ride," Grace fumed.

"Yes, but sweetie, you should feel guilty. I think you should chalk this up to being even."

Grace followed George into the theater. "How are we even if he doesn't know?"

George whispered, "but, you don't want him to know."

"I know something he doesn't want me to know and now that I know what am I supposed to do?" Grace hotly whispered, as she found Henry and headed for their seats.

"The opposite of whatever it is you think you want to do. You know Jack. He's not doing anything but having coffee."

"Hey, I did something that I don't want him to know. How do I know he didn't do something he doesn't want me to know?" said Grace as she angrily took her seat.

"That is the point of the don't ask, don't tell rule." George cut Grace off as the lights went down. "At some point, you transition from dating to seriously dating; that time in between doesn't count. You don't need to know if he dated other people while trying to figure out if you were the one. You don't ask, he doesn't tell." George cut Grace off again. "I fucked up—not you. I broke our deal and fell off the wagon, but that's no excuse for you to derail your relationship with Jack."

"I'm just saying, I think I should…"

"Shut up!" yelled some guy who was sitting about two rows behind them. Grace promptly did just that, but she couldn't keep her mind from racing.

The movie sucked. Cheesy romantic comedies with high concepts like clumsy girl meets rebound boy usually do. But, it sucked enough to occupy Grace's mind from the Jack thing for at least part of the evening. George managed to distract her during dinner and as soon as they got home, Clair grabbed the big book of baby names hoping it would divert her sister for the rest of the night. George passed the Grace sitting duties on to Clair and beat a hasty retreat to her room. A still miffed Grace got into her pajamas and climbed into bed. Clair and Henry entered for their usual good night routine.

"So, we're all in agreement on the nays— no Tilda, Frida, Elaine, Geraldine, David, Sexton, Adrian, Angelo, Robert, or Fredo," said Henry.

"Fredo's a strong name. No one messes with a kid named Fredo," said Grace.

"No one plays with a kid named Fredo either." Clair came to the door, toothbrush in mouth and said between brushes, "he or she needs a non-threatening, non-alienating, can't rhyme with any body part name."

"What she said," deadpanned Henry.

Clair stressed, "the right name sets the tone for the kid's entire life."

"Yeah, well, they called me Grace," she paused to look up the name, "as a reformed slut, I am in no way good will or a vision of the Grace of God." She punched a pillow and put it behind her head. "And they called you Clair. No offense, but you're an OCD freak not clear, bright, famous, illustrious, or French."

Henry grabbed the book from his sister-in-law. "See? Henry means the ruler of the home." He was about to make a crack when Clair leveled him with a look. "Let's face it, none of us have the right name. What would your name be if you chose it?"

Clair climbed onto the bed. "I was always envious of George. I thought it would be cool to be named Scout like in *To Kill a Mockingbird*. No one expects Scout to be a girl, so I'd be Sam or Cameron or Ryan."

"I'd go with something tough and ethnic like Anthony or Joe. Henry is so WASPY!"

"You got beat up a lot, eh?" asked Grace. "Me, I'd go for Natasha or Lana. Something earthy and sexy," Grace yawned.

"How about Michael or Gabriel for a boy?" asked Henry who was now submerged in the book.

"Maybe." Sighed Clair. "But I'd rather do Gabriel and Michael for a girl."

"If we use all the boy's names for girls we're shortening our list of choices."

"But, if we like it for a boy and we also like it for a girl, then we double our choices."

Henry smiled admiringly at his wife. "I like how you think."

"Yeah, she's devious." Grace leaned back. "Lights out people!"

Clair turned out the lights then snuggled next to her sister. Henry put his hand on Grace's tummy, leaned in, and whispered goodnight to the baby. Clair did the same. Grace stared out at the full moon while her sister and her brother-in-law held hands on her belly. There was something comforting in a big moon she thought. There was also something comforting about lying in the middle of so much love. Grace knew George was right. Being upset about something as ridiculous as bait and switch Rich was idiotic, especially if you consider what she did, which was far worse and telling Jack about it to make them even or if she was being honest, to make herself feel better was a dumb move. What she really needed to do was to finally tell Jack that she loved him. All this hinting around wasn't getting them anywhere. Saying it out loud, that made it real. It made them real. Grace sighed satisfied with her decision.

"Man!" whined Henry as he hopped off the bed and ran out of the room.

"Come on!" a pained Clair added as she rolled off the bed.

"Your kid craved the chili cheese fries, you live with the consequences."

Clair playfully pulled her hair. "You're lucky you're carrying my kid."

"You can say that again." Grace watched her beat a hasty retreat out of what was no doubt going to be one gas filled room.

Chapter 32

"George! What the fuck?" yelled Grace, as she stepped over the huge basket of clothes that had taken on a life of its own. She woke up cranky today because Jack had to work last night and no matter how hard she tried, she couldn't convince herself that that's all he was doing and so cranky was how she was going to stay.

George, who was somewhere under the pile, was also annoyed. "What?"

"What are you doing?" asked a peeved Grace.

"Laundry," sighed George. "I'm separating the whites from the colors and the colors from the black 'cause as you know, black isn't officially a color. It's gonna take me all day to get this crap cleaned."

"Who's going to help me make all these friggin' cookies? We've got two weeks to perfect these recipes," Grace trilled. "This is about team work, remember?"

"Well, if I don't do laundry, I'm either raiding your closest," snarked George. "Including your underwear drawer or going shopping and Sal says I'm not allowed to replace one addiction with the other."

"Fine, but if I go into premature labor it's on your head." Grace wasn't about to bake alone, so she called Clair, who called Diane, who brought Patricia because they were in the middle of trying to plan Clair's baby shower when Clair called.

Grace pulled a cookie tray out of the oven when George came in. "Operation laundry completed?" She asked.

"Completed, Captain." George said as she grabbed a cookie off the tray and popped it into her mouth. "Shit! Hot, hot, hot!" she yelped, as she stuck her mouth under the faucet to cool it off.

"All of those years of drinking didn't dull your reflexes, but sadly quitting didn't improve your manners." Patricia handed George a paper towel.

Diane sighed. "Okay, how many more of these do we have to make?"

"Two." Clair grabbed the next recipe from Grace's hand. "What does that say? Oatmeal?"

Grace stared at it perplexed, "cornmeal?"

George grabbed it from her, "caramel."

"Really?" Grace and Clair cocked their heads.

"Girls, you're not exactly inspiring confidence right now," sighed Patricia.

Diane quickly changed the subject before George went on the attack. "So," she said to Grace, "what about a shower?"

"I took one this morning. Do I smell? Since the whole pee thing with Jack's parents, I'm a little paranoid."

Patricia was confused. "No dear; it's tradition for the sister or mother to throw the baby shower."

"I'm making her a kid and now I have to make cupcakes and punch and entertain everyone with clothespin games?"

"No sweetie, I'm officially throwing the shower," said Diane.

"Good," sighed Grace, "I don't have any more time. I'm rehabbing George, starting a cookie business, and last time I checked I had ten toenails to make."

Clair laughed. "We get it. You're creating life, Mom's throwing the baby shower."

"Hey, at this shower no one is wrapping string around my belly to figure out how big I am."

"This is Clair's shower, not yours," George said as she gave Grace a nudge.

"Okay, sis, it's your call. Baby shower games—yeah or nay?" whined Grace.

"Oh God, nay, nay, nay," implored Clair. Grace smiled triumphantly.

"So, your mom and I are going to buy the baby furniture and Grace should probably purchase the layette," Patricia said.

"I have to get her a present?" Grace suddenly felt put upon and left out at the same time. "I'm having the kid and now I have to buy her a layette? I don't even know what that is." Overcome with emotion Grace took off. "I have to pee—again!"

"She's hit operation emotional meltdown," Diane sighed.

George swallowed a laugh. "Let's get these last two cookies baking before auntie mommy finds something else to cry about!"

Two hours later with the last of the cookies done, Clair cleaned the kitchen while Patricia looked over their business plan with George. Grace and Diane packed cookies into some red and white boxes. Grace tied one of the boxes with red ribbon and put a Sweet Mama's sticker on the top of the box. "Voila!"

"I'm impressed," Diane said, as she squeezed Grace's hand. "I really am."

George, feeling restless, got up. "Anybody up for a walk?"

"Totally," said Grace. "We can finish these later."

"You girls want to start small, right? asked Patricia as she peered out from over the business plan.

"We want to stay small," said Clair. "The goal is to be in specialty grocers, so that we can create snob appeal. You know, the old—you can't find us everywhere, so we must be good—cache." Clair nudged Grace, who nudged George, who turned to see Patricia working up some type of equation with her pen and her calculator. "Did I miscalculate something?" asked Clair.

"Can you make any of these cookies with mayonnaise?" Patricia queried.

"Why the hell would we do that?" asked Grace. She of course answered her own question when her brain caught up with her mouth, "Oh."

Clair and George traded looks. "What are you thinking?" asked Clair.

"Well," said Patricia, "we do cookies, but we've been looking to acquire something with a bit more, as you said, snob appeal. Mrs. Fields isn't snobby enough. Besides, the bitch won't sell and Rachel Ray went with Nabisco."

"Like the baby food. You went from Baby's First Foods to an all natural signature line, Baby's Finest Foods; it's selling really well," George said.

Impressed, Patricia smiled as Grace offered up, "why don't we experiment with some mayonnaise recipes and if nothing pans out, no harm, no foul because we still have the investors tasting."

Patricia liked them, Grace and George, more than she'd admit and Clair was like the daughter she never had, but going into business with them, that was a whole other story. "I like how you think."

As life progressed for the Higgins Sisters, in terms of the everydayness of said lives, not much changed. The baby continued to grow in Grace's belly and the cookie business continued to be perfected under their watchful eyes. The invitations for the investors tasting would be ready to be mailed in precisely one week. By using her powers of deductive reasoning and her <u>Miss Manner's Perfect Etiquette Guide</u>, Clair determined that the invitations must be mailed out by next Friday in order to give everyone the proper four weeks to respond. All in all, life was good. Henry and Clair had finally decided it was time to paint the baby's room and get all the stuff they had bought out of the garage and into the house.

Grace, on the other hand, had more pressing matters to attend to. More important than the three mayonnaise cookie recipes or even the child that was constantly pressing against her bladder, was Jack and looming in the Jack category was the old—do I really love him and should I tell Jack that I love him—dilemma.

"You're thinking too much," said Dr. Yael.

"Or," countered Grace, "maybe, I'm not thinking enough?"

"You're not trying to figure out string theory," Dr. Yael continued. "But, this web of intrigue you've spun is ridiculous. The deal is you're terrified of not being loved in return." Grace hated when the NB was right. "Was it this complicated for you when you told Ray you loved him?"

"No," whined Grace. "But, look how that turned out!"

"But, Jack isn't Ray."

"Jack is nothing like Ray, but well, Ray needed me."

"So, you have to be needed in order to be loved?" Dr. Yale studied her. "Jack clearly wants you. Isn't it better to be wanted than needed when it comes to the romantic relationships in your life?"

"Of course." Grace put her feet up on the couch. "I mean it is, right?"

Dr. Yael caught the look of fear in Grace's eye. "Okay, let's do some free association. You know what love is, right? Your definition of love?"

"Well, according to Charlie Brown it's three kinds of ice cream, finding your skate key…," Grace cautiously offered.

Dr. Yael rolled her eyes, "and according to you?"

"It's calm, peaceful, challenging, fun," Grace said.

"Who do you love?"

"Jack, Clair, Henry, this baby, my mom, George, ice cream."

"Who are you in love with?"

"Jack," Grace smiled "And ice cream."

"Grace," Dr. Yael smiled, "stop thinking. Just be."

"Just be? I'm not sure that's me," Grace huffed.

"Try saying this whenever you panic about it: just be calm, just be quiet, just be."

"Will this work for anything? 'Cause we have our investor tasting coming up and I'm scared shitless. Plus, Patricia is toying with the idea of actually investing in us or buying us and that totally screws with my mind."

"Why?"

"Let's see. She bought me a place to live and then this? I don't mind being a kept woman, but that's too much even for me."

"So, what's the downside?" asked Dr. Yael.

"Well, we'd never know if we could have made without the mother-in-law who decided to humor her daughter-in-law."

Dr. Yael stretched. "From what you told me she's a pretty smart lady who wouldn't view humoring her daughter-in-law as a sound investment. Am I right?" Grace nodded yes. "Okay, so it's time for you to move on from being the doubting, nothing ever turns out right Grace to being the confident, believing in yourself Grace."

"What does that have to do with Jack or the cookie thing?" an exasperated Grace sighed.

"If you don't know that then I can't help you and I'm not just saying that because our time is up," Dr. Yael cracked.

"Are you ready?" asked Clair.

"For what?" asked Grace, as she pulled her ass off her sister's couch to go to the bathroom, again.

"To mail our invitations and, well, Lamaze?" Clair hurriedly said as she licked the last envelope shut.

"You want to send out Lamaze invitations?" Grace huffed.

"Henry and I signed us up for Lamaze." Clair leaned against her yellow kitchen wall waiting for Grace to get her fat ass out of the bathroom.

"Well, you guys should have fun, might even be the talk of the class with no actual baby bump to speak of," Grace said as she opened the door. "Seriously, you want me to go through huffing, puffing, deep breathing natural childbirth?"

Clair deadpanned. "You can still have an epidural."

Clair rolled her eyes and handed her a pile of envelopes. "Okay smart ass, let's get these going." Clair picked up a box of envelopes, opened the door, and waited for Grace who grabbed the other box on her way out.

"This is a lot of invitations," a nervous Grace sighed.

"One hundred and twenty-five to be exact." Clair shut her door and put a huge bucket of candy on a table at her front door with a sign for kids to help themselves.

Grace pulled out a couple of pieces. "Now where the hell is this mail box?"

"About three blocks away."

"We're walking three blocks?" Grace bellyached.

"You need to walk," Clair said. "Frigidaire gave explicit instructions to keep you mobile."

Grace sighed, "I love to walk." She stopped when the baby kicked. "Your kid keeps pressing against my bladder or jumping around when I'm trying to sleep and now the new thing is whenever I put on a seatbelt I get jabbed. What is that?"

"Payback," deadpanned Clair, as she watched a group of five year olds trek from house to house. She couldn't believe she was about to have one of those. "What do you think we're having?"

"A ten pound watermelon, but what do I know?" Grace sarcastically offered.

"No seriously, they say a mother knows."

"I'm not the mother. I have no idea. I'm detached—in a good way, but detached nonetheless. It's healthy. It's big. It's a baby. That's what I know."

"Oh, well that's good I guess. Mom and Patricia think it's a boy."

"Well, they've had kids, they should know. I guess. I mean does it really matter?"

Clair nudged Grace to cross the street. "I know, you're right. A healthy kid is a healthy kid, but, well, a boy? How can I be a mom, a good mom, to a boy?" Clair asked.

"You're kidding me, right? That's ridiculous."

"This from the woman who just came back from a session with the NB because she's afraid to tell the man she loves, she loves him?" snarked Clair.

They stopped as a parade of loud young girls went past. "That, I understand," sighed Clair. "Princesses and Barbies." She pointed out a few boys dressed as super heroes. "That, I don't get. And puberty? If boys don't get periods, what happens to them?"

"Hormones, hair, hard-ons, plus their voices change and they start having wet dreams, but that's why you have Henry."

They crossed to where the mailbox stood. Clair started mailing. Grace, with a degree of difficulty, sat on the curb. When she was done, Clair sat down next to her.

"Do you think I'm a—doubting, nothing ever turns out right Grace?"

"Yes," Clair answered a little too quickly.

"Wow, you sure you don't want to think about that?" a hurt Grace asked.

"Nope." Clair looped her arm through Grace's. "You're completely amazing, but don't believe it."

"Okay, Dr. Phil." Grace put her head on Clair's shoulder and thought about Sweet Mamas, the baby, and Jack—not necessarily in that order. She finally understood what the NB meant. "Our lives are never going to be the same again."

"In a good way, right?" a nervous Clair asked.

"Absolutely," Grace said. "Hey, did you see that? Hey kid, come here." A five year old dressed as Batman walked over with his mom not too far behind. "Did that lady give you a Zagnut bar?" The kid looked at her like she was nuts.

His mom held up the prized possession. "You have good eyes."

"When it comes to candy, I'm a heat seeking missile." Grace was very excited. "Zagnut! I thought they went out of business."

As the woman walked off she tossed out, "it looks like she's running out.'

Grace nudged Clair and tried to stand up. "Can we please, please, please go trick or treating there?"

"Aren't we a little old to trick or treat?"

"Come on, I'll be the Stay Puff Marshmallow guy, you can be a Ghostbuster!"

And, so while the Higgins Sisters moved from now or never into the all-important take the plunge of their eighth month, life as they knew it was perpetually in motion, but what they were about to discover is that life can sometimes give you motion sickness.

Chapter 33

The phrase "take the plunge," much like the word swimmingly can mean so many things. There's the obvious—to literally get wet and then there's the whole jump in, take a chance, try something new connotation the phrase has. Grace was teetering between literally getting wet via her water breaking and jumping in, taking a chance, and saying those three little words—I love you. Grace who was mumbling, "just be calm, just be quiet, just be," found herself counting down the minutes as they drove to meet his family.

"Do we have to do this?" Grace asked Jack as he pulled her out of the car.

"Come on, they're my sisters." Jack took her hand.

"Yeah, but no husbands, boyfriends, or kids? That's like dinner with the members of the board. It's not really fair, is it?" Grace hoped her bladder held out. "Your mom told them the pee story, didn't she?"

Jack bit his tongue, then gave the keys to the valet. "They wanted to meet you. It was either this or Sunday dinner with the entire family."

"Okay, but for the record I'm hormonal. I'm crying over everything and I'm not being held responsible if I have a meltdown and if things take a turn for the worse, you'd better fake a seizure for me."

Jack kissed her firmly on her lips. "I promise, I won't let them hurt you. Okay?"

Grace held her breath as they entered Harry Caray's Italian Steakhouse and rounded the corner into the bar. Jack nudged her. There they were, the Faccinelli sisters. The oldest, Toni, was knocking back cocktails like they never let her out of the house; next to her was Donna, dark haired, about five-five if she was lucky; next to her was Tina, who did not look like the sweet schoolteacher Jack swore she was; and rounding out this group was Debra. She had Toni's legs, but wasn't as tall, and Donna's thick hair, but wasn't as dark, and she totally had Tina's hot body.

"Hey, you!" Debra said in her thick Italian Mid-Western accent. "How's my brother?" She pulled Jack into a hug and turned to Grace. "You are just as beautiful as Jack said you were."

Grace blushed. "Thanks. Nice to meet you."

"Did you fucking walk?" asked Tina, as she ordered another drink. "I was ready to gnaw off my arm for Christ's sake!"

"Ignore her," Donna added as she gave her brother a hug.

Toni grabbed her fresh drink, swept past her sisters, stopped long enough to give Jack a peck on the cheek, and continued moving. "Move it or lose it; our table's ready! Nice to meet you doll."

Jack gave Tina a look. "What's with the drinking? Is she on shore leave?"

Tina grabbed his arm as they followed Toni to their table. "Michael came home with his latest girlfriend. She's got tits out to here, a skirt up to here, a nose ring, a belly ring and—drum roll please—she's bald!"

"Geezus! I think I need a drink!" Grace sighed.

Donna grinned. "She's artistic."

"She's nihilistic—there's a difference!" Debra put her arm around her sister. "She's here to piss off mommy and she is living up to her end of the bargain."

"Well, for his sake I hope she's good in bed," laughed Jack.

"Amen to that," Tina growled as they found their seats.

"He's eighteen," Debra sighed.

"He's twenty one." Donna shook her head. "Can't you keep track?"

"Be grateful I remember which ones came shooting out of my own body," laughed Debra.

"They shoot out?" asked Grace hopefully. "Like faster than a speeding bullet?"

"You wish!" Donna said, as she grabbed the basket of rolls.

Toni took a menu from the waiter. "Let's not freak her out. It's her first kid and thank God she doesn't have to keep the ungrateful no-good-rotten-son-of-a-bitch."

Debra smiled. "No one says, 'I love you,' like a drunken, disgruntled mother!"

"So, Grace," Tina drawled, "why are you having your sister's baby?"

Donna grinned, "I thought I heard something about a drunken pact?"

Grace kicked Jack under the table. "I blame Nancy McKeon, Melissa Gilbert, and your brother who on our first date told me about his amazing sisters and how they'd step in front of a bullet for each other."

"A bullet doesn't necessarily mean I'll lend them my fucking body for a year," laughed Tina.

"You do know," Toni stressed, "that the word fuck and every variation of it is not and will never be an adjective, right? You're a teacher!"

Grace leaned over to Jack and kissed him. 'What was that for?" He asked.

Grace almost said those three little words, but panicked. "For being you."

Debra caught the exchange out of the corner of her eye and smiled. "It's time to order some fucking dinner."

Dinner with the four Faccinelli women wasn't as bad as Grace had thought it would be. For reasons she couldn't explain, surviving dinner made her feel more secure in the whole Grace-Jack relationship thingy. So much so, that the entire ride home Grace tried to say those three little words. When they got into the car she was planning to say, "dinner was great; I love you," but she only managed the dinner part. Then, while they were at a red light she tried a witty variation of "Stop! In the Name of Love!" but it came out more as "STOP! There's a dove above." Obviously, she was channeling her days as a member of Death Parade. Finally, as they pulled up to her apartment and Jack got out to open the door, Grace was ready to take the plunge until she realized she had to take the plunge of another sort and it wasn't her water breaking.

Jack made his way around the car, opened the door, and helped Grace out. "Want me to walk you up? I have a half hour before I'm on."

Her lower intestines were seizing and she felt the need to be in the bathroom, NOW! "No, no, go, I'm fine." Grace kissed his cheek.

"Thanks, for tonight," Jack said. "It meant a lot to me."

"Me too." She felt a huge wave of gas getting ready to blow and scurried away. "Call me later, you know, if there are no fires or other disasters."

"Will do." Jack grinned as he got back into the car.

Grace raced into her building, smiled at her doorman, Ben, did the pee-pee dance while waiting for the elevator, while in the elevator, and then all the way to her apartment where she burst through the door, blew by a confused George, ran to her bathroom and tried not to topple over as she put on the light, pulled down her pants and navigated her ass to the toilet seat where she let it rip. Grace was disappointed. The pain she felt couldn't just be gas. That twenty-one-gun salute came out of her at such a force she could've sworn it left bruises. "Yowza," Grace whispered as her teeth clenched and her stomach muscles hardened. She tried to relax. "Just be calm. Just be quiet. Just be," she told herself. Grace hoped and prayed that whatever was moving through the pipeline was getting ready to land. Her breathing got labored, so to distract herself she mentally listed everything she'd eaten that day. Granola and yogurt for breakfast, a peanut butter and jelly sandwich for lunch, an apple, some strawberries, a banana, some Wheat Thins, and a baked potato, spinach, and filet mignon for dinner. As her body began to tremble and sweat poured down her back, she deduced that the granola with its sadistic honey nut clusters, was causing her the pain. Grace wondered how the hell she could give birth to something that was gonna weigh at least eight pounds if she couldn't handle taking a dump.

"Are you okay?" a concerned George called through the door.

An exhausted Grace answered, "I think I have to go to the emergency room."

George immediately opened the door. There was Grace with her hair matted down, covered in sweat and sporting a splotchy red face. "Oh my God!"

Grace, on the verge of tears, sighed. "It won't come out."

George quickly deduced what the problem was. "Oh. Wow. Uh, how bad is it? Is it like stuck?"

"I don't know. I think so," Grace moaned.

"Okay, okay," George said, as she tried not to panic. "How about we walk you around to loosen it up? I'll make you a cup of hot water, too, that may help push things along."

Grace leveled her with a look. "You'll make me a cup of hot water?"

"Can you stand? Do you need help?"

Grace sniffled. "Can I keep my underpants down? Just in case?"

"Maybe we should just take them off?" George pulled Grace's panties off and tossed them into the laundry basket. "Let me get you up." George almost had her standing.

"It's coming, it's coming!" Grace plopped down on the toilet, but it was just gas.

"Whoa!" George said, and then helped her up again. Grace leaned against the sink as George ran a washcloth under cold water and dabbed at her face and neck. "Maybe we should try walking?"

George put her arms under Grace's torso and they edged their way out of the bathroom and into the living room. As they took one walk around, Grace stopped. "I can't do this, I can't do this."

"Maybe you need to wiggle it a bit," George did a little twist to demonstrate what she meant. "Do you want me to call an ambulance?"

Grace could see the headline: "Constipation Forces Pregnant Woman to Call Ambulance." The article would then state that the pregnant woman was in pain for over seventy-two hours before taking a dump that landed in the Guinness Book of World Records. "For constipation? I can do this. I've been doing this all my life. Maybe you're right and I should wiggle it out?"

As Grace did her version of a shit wiggle, George put on the teakettle and called Clair who picked up on the first ring. "Grace is like in a lot of pain."

Clair slipped into her Keds and grabbed her coat. "What's wrong? Did you call an ambulance?" The teakettle whistled in the background. "You're boiling water! Is she having my baby?"

George poured the hot water into a mug and grabbed some concentrated lemon out of the fridge and squirted it in. "She's been trying to take a shit for over an hour and can't."

Clair stopped in the middle of putting on her jacket. "Oh, whoa!"

"She's all red faced and sweating and she doesn't look good."

"Call an ambulance, now."

"She doesn't want one." George peeked in on Grace who was shit wiggling away in the living room. "She's doing a shit wiggle—that might help."

"I'm calling the doctor and heading over. If Fridge thinks she should go to the hospital, we'll drag her if we have too. I'll be there as fast as I can."

George walked over to Grace carrying the hot mug of water. "Did it help?" she asked, as she handed Grace the hot water. "Drink it as fast as you can."

Grace drank the water. She felt her temperature rise, could feel the warm liquid as it permeated her body, and burned her tongue. She slowly rocked back and forth as she crouched down on her haunches and, then cradled herself as best she could on the living room floor. George raced to the bathroom, ran cold water on the washcloth again, and then ran back to the living room. She sat on the floor with her friend who was now lying on her side, grabbed a pillow for her, and put the damp cloth on the back of Grace's neck.

Forty-five minutes later, nothing much had happened. Well, nothing other than George trying to calm Grace and creating a new mantra that would help her feel at one with the problem at hand. Grace was writhing in pain on the living room floor as she kept repeating over and over, "be the shit, love the shit, free the shit."

A freaked out George was repeating the same mantra as she paced around the living room while waiting for Clair. "Be the shit, love the shit, free the shit—just push."

"If I push any harder, I'm going to give myself a stroke. Shut. The. Fuck. Up!"

Clair finally opened the door, white paper bag in hand and was on the phone with Frigidaire. "Yes, okay. I have it right here, but... Okay, I'll tell her," she hung up.

"What the fuck took you so long?"

"I had to pick up a prescription for a stool softener. Grace never filled hers. Hence, the problem," Clair said as she raced to Grace's side. "Are you okay?"

"Hence? What are we in <u>Pride and Prejudice</u>?" Grace looked up at Clair with flushed cheeks and pillow marks on her face and groaned, "I need an epidural. And for the love of God—if you ever loved me or even thought one fucking nice thing about me you will never speak of this, ever!"

Clair felt so bad. "Frigidaire says you're going to be fine. This happens a lot."

George walked over to them as Grace groaned. "What is happening to me?"

"Well," sighed Clair, "it seems eating for two has some setbacks. With your prenatal vitamins and your body saving every bit of nutrients from your food to give to the baby, if you don't take your stool softener it can create a situation with the pooping."

"A situation? Losing your dry cleaning is a situation. This is a God damn emergency!" Grace whimpered.

"She says you have to keep pushing to get it out."

Grace could no longer hold back her tears. "Are they trying to prepare for me for the baby? If having a baby is worse than this, just kill me!"

Before George or Clair could answer her, Jack, holding a bouquet of flowers, opened the door. All he saw was Grace on the floor in the fetal position. Well, the fetal position for a woman who was eight months pregnant and Clair and George crouched down beside her. He panicked and ran over to her.

"What are her vitals? What happened?" He started taking her vitals.

Grace did not want him to see her like this. "Oh my God, no! You have to leave! Why are you here? Get him out of here. NOW!" A sobbing Grace begged him. "Leave, leave, leave. I don't want you to see me like this." Utter humiliation gave Grace the strength she needed to crawl to the bathroom.

Jack freaked out. "What the fuck is going on?"

Clair followed Grace while George grabbed Jack's arm and stopped him from doing the same. Grace's knees welcomed the cool black and white tile of the bathroom floor. Once she was as close to the toilet as she could get, Clair helped her up and sat her down. "Make him go home—NOW! And you leave, leave me alone!"

Clair quickly left and closed the door behind her. For twenty minutes she, George, and Jack paced in the living room as they heard the most unimaginable sounds coming from behind that door. Grace pushed like she had never pushed in her life. At this point she felt so hot and sweaty she pulled her arms out of the sleeves of her dress and worked it as best she could over her head where it got stuck on her hair clip. Grace struggled to pull it loose, but it wouldn't budge. Tired and cranky, she left it where it was and closed her eyes for a few moments. She whispered to her pregnant belly. "Sweetie, Auntie Mommy is very sorry for whatever discomfort this may be causing you." And then, with all the energy she could muster, she made her final sweat inducing-eye-bugling-body-trembling-I-really-think-I'm-going-to-die-push and slowly, but surely, the eagle landed.

Covered in sweat, arms trembling she grabbed the toilet paper, wiped her ass and caught her breath. Well, she thought if I can do that, I should be able to have a kid. That's when she started to laugh. The realization of the impending labor hit her. The fact that it was going to be so much more painful than what she just went through wouldn't hit her for a few weeks. For now, Grace was grateful for the stool softener she would soon be popping like M&M's and the promise of the epidural when in the throes of labor. She grabbed a washcloth from the tub, ran it under the sink and then patted down her face. When her body finally stopped its tremors and the feeling returned to her legs, Grace pulled herself off the toilet and flushed. That's when she heard that water rising-toilet-hissing-shit-so-not-going down sound. A horrified Grace turned to see what the problem was. "Holy shit! It's a God damn cannon ball!" she whispered as she stared at the biggest, roundest, hardest looking piece of human feces she ever had the misfortune to call her own. It didn't move. It was too big and too dense that the water had no choice but to fill up around it. "Go down, go down! Please go down," she anxiously pleaded, willing it to flush away, but it wouldn't listen. Grace, who hadn't stood for the past three hours, had a bit of head rush, her legs began trembling and then her knees gave out. She grabbed the towel rack to steady herself, but it popped out of the wall and clattered to the ground. Grace landed on her ass with a thud. That was all Jack needed to storm into the bathroom. He found a disheveled, naked, dress sitting on top of her head, crumpled on the floor Grace. She sighed. "It wouldn't flush."

As Clair and George raced in behind him, Jack knelt down and gently pulled the dress off of her head. "Are you hurt?" he tenderly asked.

"No." Grace struggled to get up. Jack got into position, helped Grace onto her feet and lifted her into his arms. As he carried her out the door, he spied the plunger in the corner and kicked it over to Clair and George. "Good luck ladies!"

Grace, exhausted, sweaty, and reeking of God knows what, felt so loved and safe in Jack's arms. "I love you," she whispered. Jack smiled down at her. "No, no I don't mean it as a thank you," she implored. "I love you. In that all seeing, all knowing, all loving forever way." Then she called herself an idiot and nestled her head into his chest.

Jack carried Grace into George's bathroom. "I love you, too. In that all seeing, all knowing, all loving forever way." Then he sat her down, put her feet inside the tub, took off his shoes, climbed in, grabbed a washcloth, turned on the water, and started to give her a sponge bath. They were quiet. Grace, exhausted and happy about her declaration and his reciprocation of love and Jack, relieved and happy about her declaration and his reciprocation of love—no words were needed.

"HOLY SHIT!" broke their reverie as Clair and George screamed in unison.

"It's a God damn cannon ball!" yelped Clair.

"Well, the diamond you get her better weigh as much as that!" gasped a hysterically laughing George.

And as Jack gently ran the washcloth across Grace's back, her sister and best friend were about to experience an entirely different meaning of take a plunge or in this case take a plunger, but really, why quibble?

Chapter 34

Once Frigidaire confirmed that mother and child were okay and that Grace had miraculously avoided getting hemorrhoids from her bathroom catastrophe, it got Clair to thinking. About what you ask? Well, as a mother-to-be who wasn't about to experience the joys of labor, she had plenty to think about. What color to paint the room, where to put the crib, is it tempting fate to set up the baby's room before the baby was born? However, one thing she kept coming back to was something Sal had said the first day they met. Imagine what you could do to help someone if you actually got involved. "I'm one lucky girl," she thought,"and I should be doing more for other people." Clair's interest, or as Henry called it, obsession with world peace, the environment, organic food, organic baby products, and saving the children reached the breaking point one drizzly Saturday when they had gotten up before the crack of dawn to make it to the recycling center, a peace rally, and a compost class. After Henry had gone to Home Depot to replace all their light bulbs with eco-friendly light bulbs, he came home to find Clair cleaning puree off the ceiling when an attempt to make her own baby food went awry. "No more!"

Was all Henry could manage as he watched his wife, mop in hand, standing on the kitchen counter and cleaning their ceiling.

"No more what?" Clair craned her neck to see if she could find any splatters.

Henry walked over, lifted her off the counter, carried her to the kitchen table, sat her down and looked her in the eye. "I appreciate that you want to save the world, the polar bear, the eco system, and children born into war and poverty. Not all in one day, okay? There are limits of what we can do and how we can do it. So, instead of doing everything at once, how about we pick one or two causes and do the very best we can with those?"

"I just don't want to be one of those people who give money," Clair said.

"If we give money to the right places we can do a lot of good. We have a lot of money and, so we can do a lot of good." He stopped her from arguing. "We will make this house as environmentally sound as we can." Henry kissed his wife. "We will vote in every election, we will volunteer. I'm even open to composting, but we will do it all within reason, okay?

Clair grinned. "I guess I have been going a bit overboard." Henry laughed as his wife leaned in and kissed him. "But, I think we should start funding micro-financing to people living in third world countries."

Henry stopped laughing. "Excuse me?" And thus was the battle cry of the Clair Higgins save the world revolution.

George hung up the phone. "That was another yes!" Clair and Grace high-fived. "So far, we've got seventy-five potential investors attending. You know, when most women find themselves unemployed or knocked up they're not as lucky as we are."

Clair squealed. She was so excited because George had said exactly what she wanted to say. "I've been thinking and doing research and…"

"Driving everyone crazy with your new found zeal to save human existence!" cracked Grace.

Clair ignored her. "I found this organization called Kiva that provides micro-financing to people living in third world countries. I think we should give a percentage of every sale to them. We can help women get on their feet with a small amount of money. Well, what's small to us is large to them."

"She's got a point." George grabbed a trial tin of cookies and broke it open.

Grace poured George a glass of milk and sat down. "You're preaching to the choir. It would be nice to give that shot to another woman, but what happens if Sweet Mama's is a bust?"

"We can still take a chance without losing our shirts and most women in third world countries barely have a shirt!" Clair implored.

"Enough, Joan of Arc, next thing you'll be telling us you have visions of Angels," laughed Grace.

"I'm in!" said George and Grace as they clinked their milk glasses.

Clair beamed. "Now, how do I tell Patricia I don't want a baby shower? It's a waste of money and all those gifts, I don't need them."

"Ease your way into it. Mom doesn't care, but with Patricia it's a whole other level of social obligation."

"Why don't you donate it?" George asked.

"Donate it?" asked Clair as her eyes lit up.

George explained, "since you're going all Oprah on us, why not have the baby shower, but donate the gifts to charity?"

"Oh, that's a great idea!" Clair reached for the milk and cookies then peered at George. "Hey, this investor tasting is in less than two weeks, are you sure you have everything under control?"

"Man, you can turn on a dime, eh? It's marketing, it's my thing. If I need your help I'll ask," George sighed.

"If she doesn't see to-do lists everywhere, she doesn't trust the system," Grace cracked.

"It's a disease. I'm working on it," laughed Clair.

"Maybe we can find you an OCD support group," George said, "or you can come to my AA meetings." Clair and Grace laughed. George grinned. "You know, I like this. Our business has a better chance karmically if we're attached to a charity. God loves that." And with that, Grace set out to perfect her cookies, George set out to perfect the tasting, and, well, Clair set out to perfect the world.

"White?" Patricia sniffed, as she looked into the baby's room. "White?"

"Henry hates the color yellow and I can't stand the color green and nothing else seemed appropriate for a baby's room."

"Once you hang the pictures and get the crib and changing table put together it will look great!" Diane scooted out of the way for the two Henry's and Sal as they carried boxes of furniture into the baby's room.

Henry, Sr. put down the box he was carrying. "Who's putting this stuff together? Is the store sending someone?"

Henry smiled. "Nope, I'm doing it." He then put down his side of Sal's box.

"Alone?" An alarmed Henry, Sr. asked. "Need I remind you of the camping debacle of ninety-one, the Christmas tree massacre of ninety-five, and the entertainment center crash of just six months ago?"

Henry sighed as he looked at Sal, then at his wife. "He's being dramatic."

"No," Patricia said as kindly as she could. "He's being accurate. How hard is it to put together a tent and a pop up tent at that? And if I recall, that Christmas your grandmother was nearly impaled by the star. Are you really sure you want to put together your child's crib? The place where your baby sleeps?"

Sal spoke up. "He can do this. We can do this. I'll help him. I've put together a ton of cribs. It's time for Henry to man up. If he's having a boy, we better show him the error of his clumsiness, so the kid doesn't take on his ways and if it's a girl, well, daddies are supposed to be able to take care of everything."

Henry laughed. "Thanks for the vote of confidence, but if by we you mean my father, he's worse than I am."

"I am not!" Henry, Sr. argued. "I built a perfectly respectable tree house."

Patricia pulled Diane and Clair out of the room. "You boys go ahead and prove your manliness, but remember our grandchild will be sleeping in that crib." Clair trailed behind them as they headed toward the kitchen. "How did you decide on bed times and disciplining and stuff like that?"

Diane looked over her shoulder at her daughter. "We did what felt right."

"Why?" Patricia asked as she made her way downstairs.

"All the baby books say that you should make sure you're on the same page and don't have such different parenting styles that you confuse the kid."

"Just understand that as Grandparents, if we disagree, we'll do everything in our power to undermine you," cracked Patricia. "Rule number one, spanking is a last resort."

"Potty train them by the time they're two and a half." Diane followed Patricia into the kitchen.

Patricia sat at the table. "Don't let your kid intimidate you; you're the boss."

"But, not an asshole—there's a difference," said Diane.

Clair sat down overwhelmed. "What if I do it wrong? I could create a serial killer or worse a conservative republican."

"We haven't even had the baby shower yet. One day at a time," Diane said.

"About this baby shower," Clair hesitantly ventured, "I was thinking—no gifts." Clair took a cheesecake out of the fridge and hit the button on the coffee maker.

Patricia was mildly offended. "Over the past thirty years I've been forced to attend the wedding, baby, and divorce showers of every person I've ever known and since you insisted on a small wedding I didn't get my payback, but now?"

"She doesn't have to have gifts. It's not as if they need them," defended Diane.

"There are two great organizations Newborns In Need, which provide newborn kits to impoverished families in the U.S. and The Mennonite Central Committee that sends the kits to hospitals and refugee camps overseas. If we include the organizations wish list in the invitations we could donate everything." Diane gave Clair a squeeze as she cut herself a slice of cheesecake.

"Do you really think a diaper genie is going to save the world?"

"No, but we have more than we need and I'd rather share it with someone who needs it then let it go to waste."

"Fine, but if there are no gifts and no games, Grace is getting her ass on a scale and we're guessing her weight." Clair hugged Patricia. "And to show you that I'm serious I'll match every gift you get," Patricia peered at her. "Any other big ideas you'd like to share?"

"Do you think the Country Club will let America's Second Harvest pick up the leftover food?" Clair asked.

"I'll see what I can do." There was a loud thump from the baby's room, followed by a long expletive rant. Patricia sighed. "Promise me you'll have a professional check that crib."

"I promise," laughed Clair. And Clair, never one to break a promise or hurt her husband's' feelings, hired a professional handyman who came over a week later and put the furniture together correctly.

Chapter 35

The Art Institute of Chicago had a small event room that Diane was letting them use for their investor tasting. George had somehow managed to transform said room from a sterile white box into a cornucopia of colors. The Sweet Mama's logo cleverly hung around the room, there was a cold milk fountain and a hot chocolate fountain, an ice cream station, and to top it off the Kappa Gamma sorority girls were dressed as milkmaids. "So?" asked George. "What do you think?"

"Who did you blow?" Grace deadpanned.

"Well, to be honest the posters were done as a favor from an old boyfriend who I did blow in a past life. And as an alumnus of the Kappa Gamma's, I got them to do this as a part of their community service hours." Grace started to say something, but George stopped her. "Look at this!" she picked up an old fashion lunch pail that was adorned with the Sweet Mamas logo. "We're going to put sample cookies, our business plan, and containers of cold milk into these as take home gifts. And by we, I mean the milkmaids."

"Oh my God, you blew the budget! By blew, I mean spent all our money. Please tell me you negotiated a great deal while you were on your back," a panicked Clair sighed.

George chided, "don't worry. I stole them. The agency had a couple of hundred left over from Christmas a few years back and I smuggled them out a few weeks ago."

Jack strolled in wearing a power suit. The girls whistled. "You clean up nice."

Grace noticed the Kappa Milkmaids eyeing Jack and pulled him close. She looked around the place and was suddenly a little spooked—like Sweet Mama's could actually be the thing she did with her life, not just the thing she was trying to do. "Don't you think we should check on the cookies?" she asked. "Some of them might have broken. No one likes a broken cookie. I know I don't."

"Let's check the cookies," Clair said, as she transferred Grace's looped arm from Jack to herself. George followed behind them as Henry walked up with his parents and Sal and Diane in tow.

"The place looks great," Sal said, as he looked around.

Diane gave him a kiss. "It certainly does."

"They just might pull this off," said Henry, Sr.

Patricia noticed a Kappa Milkmaid eyeing her Husband and immediately looped her arm through his. "They just might."

"What gives?" asked George, as Clair counted the rows of cookies.

"Why are you so calm? This is a big night for us. A BIG night don't you get it?" An exasperated Grace sighed as she checked the baskets for broken cookies.

George watched them. "Yes, I get it. Enjoy the moment."

"Hey, I was fine until Grace did her whole check on the cookies thing," Clair said.

"Okay, this is a big night. So, let's start it the way a momentous occasion should be started." George went to the fridge and pulled out a bottle of sparkling cider and poured them each a glass. "We've been through a lot—death, a lot of death, and drunkenness, a lot of drunkenness, bad hair, bad clothes, bad men, new relationships with alcohol and the right men, and now we're about to welcome a baby into the tribe." Grace and Clair cheered. "We survived all of that with our friendship intact. And bitches, to be honest, I can't think of any two people I'd rather be in business with! Whatever happens tonight, we did good, and so—to us!" Grace and Clair cheered some more.

"Tonight, we don't take no for an answer!" Grace looked at George, "unless it has to do with sex, drugs, or alcohol."

"Amen!" Added Clair and George. They all clanked paper cups and drank.

As the night progressed, it became clear that eating free cookies was one thing, but getting people to invest in them was an entirely different glass of milk. "People are impressed," Sal remarked, as he put his arms around Grace and Clair.

"Yeah, but not enough to pull out their checkbooks," sighed Grace.

"No one is pulling out their checkbooks until they've studied the numbers. By the end of the week, you'll have some bites."

"How's our girl doing?" Grace smiled at George who was across the room.

"Is she keeping her nose clean?" asked Clair as she smiled at her mom.

A nervous Sal put his hands in his pocket. "I want her to move in with me."

"George?" Grace said a bit too loudly.

"Mom?" Clair said a bit too loudly.

"Mom?" a confused Grace said, as she pulled them into the kitchen. Clair started to speak, but Grace stopped her. "Let him talk!"

Sal squirmed. "I want to ask your mother to move in with me."

"Hey, she's a grown woman. If she wants to shack up, well then more power to her." Grace gave him a peck on the cheek. "So, you'll move in with her?"

"Well, I was thinking of buying a new place in the city and having your mom sell the house. She could put that money directly into her retirement fund or…"

"You'd sell our house?" Clair disappointedly sighed.

"Our house?" Grace echoed.

"Nothing is set in stone. Hell, she might say no."

Clair managed a smiled. "Well, you have our blessing. You make her happy." Sal kissed them and got out of the kitchen before they could change their minds.

"Sell our house? That's surreal." Grace checked the remaining cookie baskets.

Clair began counting rows again. "Our rooms won't be our rooms anymore."

"Our rooms haven't been our rooms for over a decade." Suddenly, Grace felt a little wet where she hadn't felt wet before.

"Are you okay?" Clair stepped closer. "You have a funny look on your face."

Grace looked down. "I think my water just broke!"

Clair freaked. "What? Oh my God! Oh my God! OHMYGOD!"

The next thing she knew Grace was on the way to the hospital with Henry, Patricia, and Diane in tow.

Grace stood with Diane as Henry filled out paperwork, Clair called Frigidaire, and Patricia dealt with her hospital phobias, which meant that every ten or fifteen minutes she had to step outside to free herself from the germs that the inconsiderate sick people had brought into the hospital.

"Frigidaire's here. She's waiting for another woman to dilate. The poor thing has been in labor since noon!" Clair grimaced.

Grace panicked. "Noon? Noon? She's been in labor since noon? That's inhumane—that's ten hours of inhumane!"

Henry came over with the clipboard. "I know I should know this, but what's your middle name?"

"Anne," snapped Clair.

"Uh, honey, I meant Grace."

"I don't have one. Someone was so overwhelmed, she couldn't figure out what went with the name Grace and, therefore, I've been middle nameless my entire life, which, by the way, made the nuns label me a troublemaker and a trollop. I had to take a saint's name for my confirmation to get them off my back!"

"Really? Heloise is a saint's name? And all of that bad behavior had to do with the fact that you had no middle name?" Diane mocked.

Grace cracked a smile at the exact second Frigidaire showed up and Patricia entered the emergency room lobby for the twentieth time. "How are you ladies doing?"

"Do these people have to be in here?" Patricia stared down everyone waiting for emergency help. "Especially him, I mean really." They followed Patricia's gaze to an unfortunate fellow with a steel rod protruding out of his left foot.

"Grace, Clair, why don't you come with me?" The Higgins sisters followed Frigidaire into the emergency room. "Hop up, let's check you out." Grace dropped trough, as Frigidaire got ready to check under her hood. Clair took Grace's hand as she hopped up on the table. The doctor took one look and sighed. "Well, it seems you wet yourself." They were confused, so she tried to speak more clearly, "as in, peed your pants."

"I what?"

"You peed your pants." Frigidaire took off her gloves. "It happens a lot when you're this far along, it's hard to tell."

"You peed your pants?" Clair bit her tongue and tried not to laugh.

Grace's face turned beet red and Clair lost it. As her laughter rang through the emergency room, rod-in-my-left-foot fainted from the pain of, well, having a steel rod imbedded in his left foot and Patricia, fearing she'd catch something from him, ran outside.

As Grace got ready to embark on the walk of shame—different, of course, from the walk of shame of her youth that most often happened after too many margaritas and a one-night stand—interesting things were happening at the cookie tasting. The maids they were a milking and the cookies were being chowed down. So much so, that the Kappa Gamma's were serving them hand over fist.

"Put that coffee down," Sal said to a startled Henry, Sr., as he held his cup under the hot chocolate fountain. "Sorry, I always wanted to say that—best Mamet play ever."

Henry, Sr. added, "coffee is for closers."

Sal looked at the crowd. "How many people you know here?"

Henry, Sr. followed his gaze. "Let's just say the leads aren't weak."

"I'm a charming guy, you're a charming guy and like the master said, only one thing counts in this world, get them to sign on the line that is dotted. You game?"

"Give me the Erickson leads. We need a talker or someone who's married to or dating a talker," Sal said.

Henry, Sr. locked onto the biggest talker he had ever met. "Videtti, he owns the biggest trucking company in the city, he's standing about three feet away in the grey suit."

Sal followed his gaze. "Well, let's get him to part with a little money. Give me a two minute lead."

Henry, Sr. watched Sal as he strode over and then casually walked in the other direction until he rounded his way back toward Sal. Henry loved the hunt. As a golf pro, it was all about the hunt—casually suggesting a game of golf because you can't find someone of your own caliber to play with, never letting them win, but never letting them think they can't. Off-handed suggestions like the way they stand that can have an immediate effect on their stroke and then, by the end of nine rounds, they're begging you to take them on as a client. Henry, Sr. smiled and slapped Tom on the back. "Videtti, how's the king of the four wheelers doing?"

"Videtti, as in Videtti trucking? You're that Videtti? You're a big thinker!" said Sal.

Tom smiled. "Trust me, I'm no genius. I bought a truck and started hauling people's crap around because I wanted to avoid college." Tom shook Henry's hand.

"So, why are you here? I can't even get you on the golf course, but you'll spend the night eating cookies?" Henry, Sr. grinned.

Tom sheepishly smiled. "Long story, short version. I'm dating Nancy Clay. She was a client of your daughter-in-law's. Anyway, she heard about the whole baby gate partnership debacle, got a bug up her ass, and feels she needs to support up and coming business women and, so here I am."

Henry, Sr. had his in. "You know the girls plan on giving ten percent of every sale to Kiva to finance micro-loans for women in third world countries?"

Sal jumped in, "you invest in a company like this and you get a partial charitable write off. It's the wave of the future. Help others, while you help yourself. It's a win-win!"

Tom was intrigued. Henry patted Sal on the back. The man was a genius. "Sal knows what he's talking about. He's a lawyer, works for the ACLU." Henry noticed some women from the club and now that he and Sal had their patter down he was going in for the kill. "Will you excuse me? Call me this week, we'll set up a game." Henry, Sr. left Tom in capable hands and took off after his new prey.

Henry, Sr. and Sal worked the crowd and before long, women were in line waiting to talk to George. She quickly came up with her pitch, every woman deserves a chance, and shrewdly used the she's having her sister's baby saga to her advantage. It was gold, pure gold. As the cookies ran out and the crowd thinned, George had over seventy business cards, ten promises of meeting for lunch, and two women actually pulled out checkbooks in hopes of putting a down payment on Sweet Mama's. George was happy. George was beyond happy and, as she bounced with the first sense of joy and excitement she felt in over three years, she found herself standing outside waiting for Sal, Henry, and Jack, and craving of all things pizza. Sal came out and she pulled him into a hug. "You are brilliant!" Henry, Sr. came out on that last line.

"Hey, don't I get one of those?" he said, as Sal laughed.

George hugged him. "I cannot believe that we didn't even consider talking about that. We're actually going to get an investor out of this—an investor!"

Henry's phone rang. "Boy or girl?" was the first thing he said. "Oh, oh, but, everyone's okay? Sure, I'll have Sal drop me off on his way to Diane's, meet you at home." He hung up then did his best to keep a straight face. "False alarm."

"Her water didn't break?" George was confused.

"No." Henry, Sr. struggled not to laugh.

"But how could she think her water broke if it hadn't?" Because she had visions of cookies and decimal points floating in her head, George was behind the curve on this one.

Sal burst out laughing. "Oh, the poor thing!"

Jack walked up. "No one at the tasting was what I would consider poor."

"Grace. False alarm."

Jack grinned. "I know, she called me. She's been having a tough couple of weeks."

"Jack? Jack Faccinelli?" A leggy brunette walking past with a group of friends stopped to chat. "Jennifer Weston."

Jack immediately tensed when he saw her. Henry, Sr. and Sal were intrigued and George still stuck in her confused state didn't notice her. "Jennifer, how are you?" He walked a little bit away from the group.

"Well, to be perfectly honest I'm disappointed you didn't call me." She leaned in and put her hand on his arm as her friends walked discreetly away.

"I told you," he stressed as he pulled his arm away, "that I wasn't going to call you. I was doing a favor for a friend. That's it."

"But we hit it off." She stepped closer to him.

Jack had no idea how to handle this. He stepped back. "I'm sorry if I led you on, but I'm not interested."

"You kissed me. What guy kisses a girl if he's not interested?" Jennifer stepped closer.

Jack could feel the sweat beading on the back of his neck. He had kissed her— once. Rich had begged him to do this bait and switch and then got stuck on an attempted robbery. He called Jack and asked him to take her to dinner. The next thing, he knew he was on a date. The whole night all he could think about was Grace and how she admitted she might still be in love with Ray. Rich showed up just as Jack was getting her a cab and Jennifer had chosen that moment to pull him into a kiss—a pretty great kiss that most men would have taken advantage of, but not Jack. He had visions of Grace dancing in his head. That's when he knew he was in it for the long haul and that if it came down to it, he had no choice but to let Grace break his heart. "I was trying to figure out a relationship."

Jennifer had nothing to lose but her pride. "That's not what that kiss said."

"That kiss was a mistake," a defensive Jack replied. God, he thought Henry and Sal must think he's an idiot, an idiot whose ass they're so gonna kick.

Jennifer couldn't tell if he was bluffing or not. A lot of men lay claim to the phantom girlfriend just to be nice. "Really? Well, who's the lucky girl?"

Jack sighed, "If you must know, her name is Grace"

"She peed herself?" George yelped. "Grace actually peed herself?"

Jennifer was taken aback. "You're dating a woman who pees herself?"

George had finally stepped out of her fog, noticed Jennifer, and immediately went into fight mode. "She's eight months pregnant. She thought her water broke. Hit the road! There's still time for you to drink yourself silly and go home with a total stranger." Jennifer, smart, like most brunettes, took the hint, turned on her heels and left. George turned to Jack. "Grace said you were still doing the bait and switch and I didn't believe her."

"No, no, no, that woman was from ages ago." Jack found himself panicking. "How does she know?"

Henry and Sal, not wanting to miss a word, stepped closer. George sighed, "Rich told her. Well, he didn't tell her, per se, as he alluded to it."

"I stopped as soon as Grace and I had our first date, but then…"

Henry, Sr. sighed. "Jennifer makes quite a stop sign." Sal laughed and elbowed him.

"No, it's not like that. Rich begged me as a favor. It was a long time ago." Jack felt himself sweating. "I swear, one time—never did it again."

"How long ago?" George sniffed. She wasn't about to let him off the hook.

"I don't know two, three months…"

A relieved George sighed. "Oh, well then you're even. That's around the time Grace made out with Ray." And as soon as she said it she knew she had done a very bad thing.

"WHAT?" Jack immediately balled his right hand into a fist.

Sal and Henry exchanged looks. "This is getting good," said Sal.

George had to think fast. "Don't get your panties in a twist. You kissed little miss slutty pants didn't you?"

Jack knew she was right, but he was still pissed off. "But Ray? Ray? I thought that was over and done?"

George looked to Henry and Sal, but they were no help. "Hey, you guys didn't know where your relationship was heading or even how you felt about each other. She needed to figure out the Ray thing, they went to dinner to talk, they kissed, end of story."

"You said they made out." Jack stared her down.

"Okay, they made out. Grace left the restaurant when she realized how much she cared about you. Ray followed her, they fought, ended up kissing, which got a little heated, but Grace stopped. She wasn't about to jeopardize what you had." Jack calmed down a bit. "What was the deal with miss slutty pants?"

Jack felt like a fool. "I don't know. I was falling for Grace too fast and I couldn't control it. Then the whole—I might still love Ray thing happened. I was confused and…it was one kiss, I regretted it immediately." Jack turned to Henry and Sal. "I swear, I love her!"

Henry, Sr. patted him on the back. "No use crying over spilt milk."

"I have to talk about it with her, right? So we can move past it?"

Sal snapped, "bad idea. George is right—call it even."

"Don't be an asshole!" Henry, Sr. said. "Admitting to an innocent indiscretion three months later won't do anyone any good."

"But…" Jack wanted to tell her, and well, he so didn't want to tell her.

"You know, she knows, there's no reason for you both to know, you know," Sal growled.

George leveled Jack with a look. "Don't ask, don't tell. We never had this conversation." She looked at Sal and Henry, Sr., "and that means you too—loose lips, sink ships!" They agreed. "Great! Now, if you hurt her in any way, I think I can speak for all of us—we will bring down such a world of hurt you'll never recover from it, okay? Okay. Now, let's get pizza. I'm sure miss peed her pants could use some cheering up."

Jack wasn't sure about the whole don't ask, don't tell thing, but he had to admit he was relieved that the whole Ray thing had happened long before Grace had told him she loved him because that meant that now they were on solid ground.

And, so, as the Higgins Sisters moved from take the plunge of their eighth month, they were about to discover that solid ground tended to get a bit squishy. And that peeing your pants aside, somehow you'd inexplicably end up back to the now what phase in your ninth month. Who knew?

Chapter 36

Clair sat on the bed with her sister while Diane went through her closet. "I can't believe you wore that."

Diane shook her head. "It was the seventies. There are a lot of things no one believes about the seventies."

Clair pulled up Grace's shirt and kissed her tummy. Grace didn't flinch. She was used to the patting, the reading, the singing, and all the other stuff one does to a pregnant belly with the hopes of leaving a lasting impression on her child. They had no real boundaries any more. It was getting harder to tell where Grace started and Clair ended. "We need more pictures," Clair said, as she ran to get her camera.

Grace rolled her eyes. "Seriously, more pictures? This is a big step—shacking up with Sal. You ready?"

Diane finished boxing up the clothes she was donating to Goodwill. "I think so. The house goes on the market this weekend. You're okay with it, right?"

"Of course, why wouldn't I be? Sal's a great guy." Grace stared off into space as Clair came back with her camera. "We're lucky Popsicle didn't bite it in the house."

"Grace!" Clair admonished.

"I'm just saying if dad had died in the house it would make it harder to sell."

Clair's eyes wandered to the window. She gasped, "Snow!" They turned to look. A slight sadness permeated the room.

"It's really coming down." Diane turned to Grace who was fiddling with her husband's old Burberry hat. She felt a bit melancholy when she saw it. There were things of her husband's she could never bring herself to get rid of and now she had to revisit them again. "You should spend the night."

Clair ran out of the room. "I'm ordering the pizza, now!"

Diane sat next to her daughter. "Speaking of ready, are you ready?"

"I can't wait to get this kid out of me!" Grace joshed. "We've done the Lamaze thing, watched all the scary birthing DVDs, and now, I've just gotta pop it out!" Grace leaned against her mother. "I kind of wish we were doing a C-section like in the good old days. Knock me out, wake up in full hair and make-up with a kid and a martini. That way, there are no memories of the actual birth. I knew it was going to be hard, but, it's just, I'm not going to keep the kid and I'm…"

"Scared?" Diane and Grace turned to Clair who had the phone in one hand and the take out menu in the other. "Me, too." Clair climbed on the bed and snuggled next to her mom. "I can change a mean diaper, but there's all that other shit."

Diane kissed Clair on the cheek and squeezed Grace's hand. "It's not going to be easy, but you're going to be fine. I promise. We'll be okay, we've always been okay." Diane watched the snow as it started to come down harder. "We better order that pizza"

Grace grabbed the menu. "No mushrooms or green peppers, gives me gas."

"What doesn't give you gas?" Clair grinned.

The full moon illuminated the night sky and the fresh fallen snow shimmered in its glow. Grace then padded down the hall to the kitchen; she was hungry again. As she peered in the fridge, she caught a glimpse of the calendar that hung on the counter. It was Sunday, December second. Grace stopped. December second. The day their father died. Grace leaned back against the counter. From where she was standing, she could see her dad's hat, his old navy pea coat, and the red striped scarf Clair made him sitting on top of the box of stuff for Goodwill. Before long Grace bundled up, shovel in hand, and stood in the front of her parents' house. She let the cold air invigorate her, then stretched her arms, and began shoveling. The measured scrape-scrape-scrape of the metal shovel against the cold cement woke Clair who sleepily looked out the window. Her movement allowed the cool morning air to sneak under the blankets and wake her mother who followed her to the window. They were both staring at Grace as she pushed the shovel down the front path. "What the hell?" Clair whispered, as Diane got dressed.

Soon, all three were shoveling snow. Grace glanced at the front bench where the box of her father's clothes sat. Clair followed her gaze then crouched on her haunches, made a snowball, and slowly rolled it across the front lawn. Diane did the same. With only the sound of the wind and crunch of the snow beneath their feet, the Higgins family built themselves a Popsicle. By the time the neighbors awoke, it was clad in their dad's old navy pea coat, his red striped scarf was whipping in the wind, the Burberry hat was weighted down with pebbles from the walkway, and instead of a corncob pipe and two eyes made out of coal, he had an old wooden spoon and two eyes made out of pepperoni. Days later, when the snowman melted, they couldn't bear to part with his clothes. Instead of sending them to Goodwill, they packed them away and stored them in Clair's garage. From then on, the night of every first snow, they ordered a pepperoni pizza and built themselves a Popsicle.

Chapter 37

As the days passed, the whole—when is she having the baby thing—was starting to get on everyone's nerves. Clair had washed, dried, and even ironed everything her newborn would need at least three times. She couldn't sleep because she was always waiting for the phone to ring. She couldn't organize because she was always waiting for the phone to ring. She couldn't do anything because she was always waiting for the phone to ring. Henry, who had recently discovered the boundaries of what Clair couldn't do, used his time to finish the crossword puzzle. "What's a seven letter word for broiled?" he asked his wife as she sorted her underwear drawer, again.

"Sautéed," she sighed. "You're never going to do the crossword again."

"Never?" Henry wryly asked as he lowered the paper to watch his wife.

"One phone call and it's over!" Clair finished her drawer and started on Henry's. "This is it. The last quiet time we'll ever have. After this, no more nothing!"

"No more nothing?" Henry stifled a laugh. "I wonder if it will be a boy or a girl."

"Who cares? We've got our unisex name and we're ready to go." Clair took a moment to really study Henry's face. "I hope the baby has your eyes."

"I hope the baby has your smile and your laugh, I love your laugh."

"Oh God no! No child should cackle like the Wicked Witch of The West." Clair climbed on the bed with her Husband, snuggled next to him, and they sat there silently trying to piece together their best features and picture their child.

Henry suddenly filled with fear that something might happen to her, to them, or to their child, quivered with emotion. "I can't imagine doing this with anyone, but you. You know that, right?"

"That has to be the sweetest thing I've ever heard." They kissed as Henry lowered himself next to his wife. "Honey, the phone might ring," she whispered into the nape of his neck, "Oh what the hell, if we're not gonna have time to get a crossword puzzle done then when the hell will we have time to do this? Make it quick, but not too quick!"

As they waited for the big moment to arrive, Jack was rubbing Grace's shoulders. "Do you really need to go for eight weeks?"

"Oh, please, after this pregnancy I need to go for six months, but we can afford eight weeks." Grace bent her head as Jack kneaded the back of her neck.

Jack kissed her. He loved that she smelled like fresh lemons and caramel. He blurted. "I know—about the cab and, you know—Ray in the cab, with you."

Grace leaned against his chest and smiled. "And I know about your last bait and switch." A relieved Jack laughed. "No more skeletons," she said. "We're adults having an adult relationship. Our past is our past—over and done!"

He kissed her again. "Okay, so let's talk about our futures. Do you want kids—I mean of your own?" Jack massaged her neck and shoulders.

Grace let out a small sigh as Jack worked out a knot in her neck. "Do you want to know if I want to have your kids or do you want to know if I want kids in general?"

"Oh. I don't know." Jack obviously hadn't really thought the question through.

"You ask the big questions then you run from them?" Grace peered into his somewhat frightened face. "I'm in it for the long haul. Baby or no baby, middle age, old age, diapers or no diapers, I don't care as long as I'm with you."

Jack smiled. "Whose diapers, ours or the kids?"

"I'm hoping the kids. Hey, who said anything about kids? I said baby. Singular."

"Aw come on, you don't want an only child do you? The kid needs someone to play with, fight with—trust me."

"I'm not having a Faccinelli basketball team. Two is my limit." Grace pulled the blanket around them. "When we're old and gray and you're wearing Depends, I'll still love you."

"Hey, I'm not the one who thought their water broke." Life, Jack thought, doesn't get any better than this. "Grace, will you marry me?" He asked.

"Not until I've gotten rid of the baby weight," she murmured. "Will you marry me?" Then pulled his head toward hers and kissed him.

"Not until I've gotten you a ring." Jack grinned as she snuggled against him and drifted off to sleep. Yep, life was good.

Grace yawned and drew the blankets tightly around her. She was going to miss taking naps in the middle of the day and having people hold doors and give up seats for her. For all her bitching and moaning, pregnancy wasn't that bad. Grace yawned again then sat up and smiled. It was hard to believe that in the course of a year she fell in love, started her own cookie company, and was about to give birth to her own niece or nephew. "Hey, Sal's waiting downstairs. We've got a meeting in fifteen minutes. You okay by yourself?" George asked as she emerged from her bedroom.

"Yep," Grace was tired of waiting for this kid to pop out. "Besides, Jack's coming over for dinner, so I'll only be alone for two hours."

George was putting on her coat. "Are you sure? Two hours is a long time."

"Clair or Henry or his mother or my mother calls every hour on the hour. I'm good. We're only a week past our due date. Everyone needs to relax."

George sang and did a little dance. "Relax. Don't do it. When you want to go to it."

Grace winced at that sound of George's voice, but managed a smile. "Thanks."

"For what?" George asked.

"For never stealing any of my boyfriends, taking me to the most exciting places I've ever traveled to—drunk or sober, our fabulous tattoos, your friendship, and, well, everything in between."

"Yeah, well, your boyfriends were all morons; I didn't want you to date them, why the hell would I date them? As for a the rest, you're easy to travel with, you don't expect me to put out when I'm drunk, once our asses start to sag our tattoos won't seem like such good ideas, and let's face it, if it wasn't for your family I'd still be a drunk." George grinned. "See ya later!"

Grace waved to George as she left. The phone rang. Grace dug around for it and finally located it under the cushions. "Hey, Clair. No labor pains. No water breaking. She just left. No, Jack will be here soon. I'm fine. If you and Henry happen to be in the neighborhood, stop by, but," she cautioned, "not without any Don Pablos. Hey, spicy might kick our labor into gear. Bye." Grace got herself off the couch and stretched. Don Pablos sounds good she thought. If I leave now I can be back before Jack or even Clair got here. Liking this idea, Grace slipped into her furry Crocs and threw on her coat.

A few blocks away into her walk Grace pulled out her cell phone and left explicit where am I now messages for her mom and Clair. Then she let the tantalizing smells pull her into Don Pablos. In between ordering the chicken tostada, the fajita platter, and making sure they gave her two large orders of chips, Grace suddenly felt wet again. Chalking it up to well, peeing herself once more, she moved over to the pick-up line.

"Grace?"

"Yep," she answered before turning and seeing Ray.

"You're huge."

"Ray!" The woman next him chided as she jabbed him in the side, "I'm Nicole."

"Nice to meet you." Grace abruptly cringed from pain. "Don't mind me. Must've been the peanut butter and jelly I had for lunch."

Ray was spooked. "Man, you're ready to pop, eh?

"I'm a week late." Grace silently counted to sixty like they taught her in Lamaze. "So, you come here a lot? Did you get the chicken tostada? It's my favorite." Hit with another tightening in her abdomen she doubled over in pain.

Nicole grabbed her arm and moved her out of the way. "I think you're in labor."

"I probably just peed myself. It happens all the time. Not all the time, just in the last two months...oh, oooh, okay, yeah, I should go. Nice meeting you." Grace shuffled for the door as her number was called and debated whether or not to pick up her food.

Nicole grabbed her ticket and handed it to Ray. "Get her food and meet us outside." A confused Ray did as he was told as Nicole helped a protesting Grace. "I have three kids, I know labor pains. We're getting you to the hospital."

"Really, you did this... Aaaaah... three times?" As soon as they were out the door, Grace searched for her cell phone. She took a deep breath and dialed. Hit with a rocking pain, Grace dropped the phone; Nicole picked it up for her. Grace's hands were trembling, so Nicole held the phone against her ear. "Clair, my water broke, for real. I'm in labor," she looked at Nicole, "right? I'm in labor?"

Nicole took the phone. "She's in labor; we're putting her in a cab and taking her to the hospital. Who am I? Ray's girlfriend. Yes, that Ray. What hospital?"

Grace yelped, "St. Stephens," then doubled over in pain as Ray came out with her food. "Did they give you extra chips?"

Nicole handed Ray Grace's phone as she hailed a cab. Grace's phone rang, Ray went to hand it to Grace, but she was occupied with another labor pain. "Hello?" He tentatively asked. "Yes, this is Grace's phone. Who am I? Uh, Ray. Where's Grace? She's uh, otherwise occupied right now." The caller hung up as Ray scrambled to help Nicole get Grace into the cab.

"We should go with you," Nicole said, as she opened the door.

"Noooo," said Grace, as she slid into the back seat.

"Then Ray should go with you."

Both Ray and Grace yelped, "NO!" then Grace sighed, "I'm fine. Really, you're an angel. Ray's lucky to have you. Thanks for everything and look, dinners on me. Extra chips, so the meal never ends," Grace shut the door.

Nicole told the driver what hospital to go to then popped her head into the back of the cab one last time. "You sure you're okay alone?" A shaky Grace nodded yes as the cab took off with a lurch.

Ray watched the cab drive away when Grace's phone rang again. "Hello? Yes, this is still Ray." The caller hung up again. "He's pissed."

Nicole pointed to Grace's cab as it pulled further away. "Don't fuck this up the way you fucked that up, got it?" Ray definitely got it. Nicole took Grace's phone from him and redialed the last number. "Hello? No, this is Nicole. Calm down. No, seriously calm down. Here's what happened…"

Chapter 38

The ride to St. Stephen's was relatively smooth—if you consider holding on for dear life, panicking over the amount of time between labor pains, and the fact that the driver reeked of cigar smoke, smooth. "Just be calm, just be quiet, just be." Grace repeated and repeated and repeated to herself.

"Good, lady, good. Keep saying that. It helps," the driver said.

"Just be calm. Just be quiet. Just be." The cab abruptly stopped.

He pounded on the horn and leaned out the window. "Get the FUCK out of the way; I've got a woman in labor here!"

"Just be calm, just be quiet, just be," Grace groaned in pain.

"We'll get you to the hospital before the kid shows up."

"Just be calm, just be quiet, just be." The driver picked up on the cadence of Grace's mantra and as the cab bobbed in and out of traffic they were soon both chanting, "just be calm, just be quiet, just be," until the cab pulled up to St. Stephens' emergency entrance. Then full-blown panic set in and Grace threw her mantra out the window.

"Grace!" George yelled as she came running up with Sal who paid the driver.

A nervous Grace babbled, "how did you know I was here?"

"Clair called," Sal said, as they walked her inside.

"You were with Ray?" George asked. "Jack called me in a panic. I didn't know what to say."

"No, no, nooo. I bumped into him at Don Pablos."

An excited Clair and Henry came racing up with a nurse who immediately put Grace into a wheel chair. "We're having a baby!" The nurse started wheeling her away.

Grace yelled, "George. I was at Don Pablos. I bumped into Ray and his girlfriend and went into labor. You have to tell Jack that. It was a coincidence. I didn't sneak out in the throes of labor to meet with my ex! You have to tell him that!"

Clair turned to George. "His firehouse is four blocks away, a block away from the diner where they had their first date."

George turned to Sal. "Operation Jack, here we come." Sal laughed as they headed out the door, stopping only to kiss Diane, and direct her toward the expectant parents-to-be.

Labor wasn't exactly the way Grace had imagined it. There was a lot of waiting in between the pain and there was a lot of pain. Diane shoved some ice chips into Grace's mouth. "What is with the ice chips?" Grace mumbled. "Unless you're about to pour vodka down my throat, no more ice chips! How long does this take? Aaaaaaah!"

Diane tried to comfort her. "Well, it depends on how far you're dilated."

"And we're about to find that out," Frigidaire said, as she breezed into the room with Henry and Clair on her heels. A nurse came in, Frigidaire put on her gloves, and Henry looked away.

"Three centimeters," Frigidaire said, as she took off her gloves. "We've got a while."

"Can you measure that again? I'm feeling at least five," Grace whimpered.

"Grace," Frigidaire calmly said, "you're fine. The baby's fine. Labor is not a race. I'll be back in an hour."

"An hour? An hour? Where is Jack? Could somebody please get me Jack?"

As Frigidaire left, the nurse innocently asked, "is Jack the Father?"

"NO!" Clair, Henry, and Grace exclaimed at the same time. "I'm not even the fucking mother." Grace groaned.

The nurse had no idea how to react to that. "Okay, well, only two people can be in here at the same time. Somebody's gotta go."

"I will," sighed Grace. Diane laughed, then kissed her daughters and headed out.

"I don't think I can do this," Grace said. "No, really. I'll give you back all the money and the apartment— just don't make me do this!"

Clair took her hand. "You'll get the epidural soon."

"But, not yet you're only three centimeters," added Henry.

"I'd like to see you three centimeters dilated!" Grace groaned as another wave of pain hit. "What? Didn't your research tell you what to do when your baby's aunt turned into a fucking bitch while trying to pop out your kid?" Henry pulled an iPod out of his jacket, put the headphones on Grace and turned it on. "Ohhhh—what the fuck you think Journey's gonna make me not hurt? Maybe if you got fucking Steven Perry to fucking tour again starting here in this room it might fucking help!" Grace groaned, as Clair gave Henry a kiss before he went scrounging on the floor looking for the iPod Grace had just thrown.

While George and Sal stood in front of Jack's firehouse, George grabbed his arm. "I may need you more tonight than ever." Sal looked at her confused. "If you thought vodka was my weakness—wrong. Firemen, firemen, firemen! No woman can resist, no woman. They willingly pledge to run into burning buildings, plus they cook and clean. Seriously, perfect men!"

"I'll try to hold you back, tiger!" Sal opened the door and looked around.

George sniffed the air. "It smells like hamburger helper—don't you think?" Seeing no one she started to poke around. "It's so clean in here. Where do you think they keep the Dalmatian?" They finally came upon a couple of firemen lifting weights. She turned to Sal as the first fireman noticed them. "He's not too hot," she gratefully sighed. "I'm going to be okay. I'm wearing clothes more flammable than he is!" The rest of the firemen turned to get a look at her. George whispered to Sal, "if you really loved me, you'd set yourself on fire."

Sal mocked her. "Alcohol and men make you stupid." He addressed one of the firemen. "We're looking for Jack, any idea where he is?"

A tall, heavy-set fireman put down his weights. "He's upstairs."

George smiled. "Well, make him slide down the pole we need to talk to him."

He smiled. "Ma'am, we don't slide down the pole unless it's an emergency."

"Any pole or specifically that pole?" Sal pinched George on the arm. "Ow, trust me it's an emergency."

The Fireman stared at her. "Are you drunk?"

"Nope, sober. Here's my chip." George pulled out her chip and then called upstairs, "Jack! Gracie won't have the baby without you." The firemen stopped what they were doing. George headed for the stairs, Sal and the firemen followed. "Come on, don't be an ass." George climbed the metal staircase. "She loves you enough to hold back the birth of child that isn't even hers because she wants you there." Finally, there was movement behind door number three. "Grace just happened to go into labor when she bumped into Ray is that so hard to believe? Yes, but is it more unbelievable than the fact that she's giving birth to her own niece or nephew?" The door opened. "You're not Jack."

"Yes, I am. I'm just not your Jack." He watched George as she walked down the stairs. "But I could be your Jack!"

Another of the fireman shrugged. "You didn't say which Jack you wanted."

Sal laughed. "Faccinelli."

George stormed down the steps. "Why didn't you stop me?"

"Can anyone really stop you?"

George turned to find bait and switch Rich standing at the door. She smiled big. "It depends on what they're trying to stop." Sal took her arm and led her out. "Bait and switch Rich, right? What are you doing here?"

Rich grinned. "Jack heard you were on some sort of a mission and wanted me to stop you before you did something…"

"Stupid," George laughed. "Thanks boys. Sally boy, let's get some Starbucks on the way, hospital coffee sucks!"

Rich watched them leave, thought about it, and followed them out. "I can help carry the coffee."

"How is she doing?" Jack asked Diane as soon as he saw her. Henry, Sr. and Patricia immediately walked over.

"Great. She's great." Diane said. "Nervous, but good."

"Where have you been?" Henry, Sr. asked with the tiniest bit of attitude.

"At work, I came as soon as I heard." Jack was confused.

Patricia stared him down. "If that was the case, you would've been here before any of us."

Diane, grateful that they felt close enough to her daughter to defend her honor, sighed. "Do you want to see her?"

"Thanks." Jack followed Diane down the hall. "I came as fast as I could. I had to find someone to cover my shift, and then I had too..."

"Shut it, don't bore the messenger. You're here. You obviously love her—that's good enough for me, but break her heart I break your ass. Capiche?"

Diane poked her head into Grace's room and waved Henry out. Grace screamed in pain and Jack, suddenly frightened, hesitated. Henry nudged him into the room as he walked out. Jack smiled at Clair. "How's everyone doing?" Grace moaned as Clair kissed her on the forehead and left. Jack nervously rolled on the balls of his feet. "Your mother just said capiche." Grace looked so small to him and pale. When did she get so pale? Seeing her so vulnerable scared him.

"She went all Momma Celeste on you, eh?" Grace struggled to smile.

"You sure you're okay?" Jack looked around for something useful. She was tired, covered in sweat, and, yet, she still took his breath away.

"No, but the doctors swear I'm fine. Five centimeters dilated—close, but no epidural!"

Jack awkwardly bobbed and weaved until he went in for a tender little kiss that became a more passionate lip lock. Jack grinned and then took her phone out of his pocket. "I met Ray."

"I knew you were feeling a bit too cocky the moment you walked in that door."

Jack pulled up a chair. "He seemed nice, but he's no Jack Faccinelli."

"No," Grace softly said, "he's not."

"She's nice, Nicole, real sweet." Jack took Grace's hand. "So this is really painful, eh?"

"It was, but now it's not so bad." Grace loved him so much she wished this pain was for their own kid.

"I have to admit, I'm a little jealous."

"I'm sure they'll let you have an epidural if you ask real nice."

He laughed. "No. Although, maybe... I just mean, I wish this was my kid."

Another wave of pain hit Grace, so hard it took her breath away. She managed to choke out. "Me, too." Grace suddenly screamed so loud that Jack jumped.

"I'll get a doctor."

Chapter 39

And, so the Higgins Sisters went from now what to now-now-now! In order to spare you the gory details and to preserve some of their privacy, we're not going to rehash everything that happened in the delivery room. In a nutshell, there was the epidural, and then there was pushing, crying, pain, being told to stop pushing, crying, pain, more pushing, epidural kicking in, so less pain, more crying, crowning, which is so not what we thought it was, more pushing, more pushing, more pushing, baby born, baby has ten fingers and ten toes, more crying, more crying, more crying, icky after birth, jubilant Clair and Henry, jubilant and exhausted Grace, new baby girl, and finally, a passed out Grace. So, basically the birthing experience can be summed up as passing a shit ball to the tenth power. The nurses cleaned up the baby as best they could. Clair and Henry hovered over their little one as Grace was wheeled first into recovery and then into her room.

"She doesn't look like I expected my baby to look," Clair whispered.

"What did you expect?" asked Henry.

"I don't know. Isn't she sweet? She looks like her daddy." Clair nuzzled her.

"Hello, Charlie girl—it's me, daddy. I'm so happy to meet you." Henry started to cry, which made Clair start to cry, which made Charlie girl start to cry.

Chapter 40

George, Sal, Diane, Henry, Sr., Patricia, and Rich paced, slept, and tried to remain calm as they waited for news. Throughout the night, George did her best to avoid Rich. The guy just refused to leave and that was too dangerous for her blood. When Henry, Sr. dragged Rich with him to get food, Sal sat down next to George. "What gives? I thought you liked this guy."

"I've never dated sober. What do you people do?" George queried.

"Being in recovery doesn't mean you're dead, but because you're in recovery you're in the power seat. You have to take things slow, get to know him, become friends, and no nooky until you're ready. By the way, we play Scrabble."

"I knew it," George said, as Sal got up to give his seat to Rich, who came offering donuts.

George shyly took one. "You've seriously got nothing better to do?"

Rich smiled. "I like the view."

George tried to dissuade him. "I don't drink anymore."

"Any liquids or just the alcoholic kind?"

"Some other guy is gonna show up in about ten minutes and claim he's the one I'm supposed to be talking too, right?" She took a bite of her jelly doughnut.

"I get a bad rap," he said, as he wiped some powdered sugar off her cheek.

"So do I, sometimes." George smiled.

"See, we have that in common." He grinned.

"Maybe we do, maybe we don't." She coyly smiled.

When Henry, Sr., Patricia, and Diane met their granddaughter for the first time they all wept. "So," Henry said, "this is Charles, but we call her Charlie."

Patricia began to tremble and grabbed Henry, Sr.'s hand. She hadn't heard that name in such a long time. "Charles? Charlie? Why would you…?"

Clair smiled warmly, "I told you we were going to pick a boy's name for a girl and we like Charles. It's a great name."

Henry, Sr. caught Clair's eye and smiled gratefully. Diane kissed her granddaughter's head. "May I hold her?" As Diane took her in her arms, her husband's face flooded her memory. "She looks like your father," she cried. "She's got his nose!"

"I know." Clair said as she stood behind Diane and hugged her.

When Grace finally woke up, it was darker than dark out. Jack was sleeping in the chair next to her bed and Diane was asleep in the chair next to his. She tried to move a little bit, but when she did she was in pain. It wasn't earth-shattering pain; she had, after all, just experienced earth-shattering pain. Grace looked over at the nightstand and was surprised to see a picture of Clair, Henry, and the baby. She studied it closely. She sure was sweet and she had her Popsicle's nose. Grace bit her lip hoping she could stop herself, but she was helpless against the wave of emotion that served up everything she had experienced in the last year. Jack heard her crying, climbed into her bed, and held her in his arms. Grace cried for a long time. She cried for herself, for her dad, for Henry and Clair, for her mom, for Jack, for Charlie, and for every child in the world she couldn't protect because that's how she felt right now, that she had to protect every child in the world. Somewhere, beyond the point of exhaustion, Grace stopped crying and fell asleep. When she awoke the second time, Jack had left. Her room was filled with flowers and with the grateful eyes of Henry, Sr. and Patricia as they smiled down at her.

Grace laughed. "So in the history of awkward moments this is one for the record books, eh? How's my niece?"

On cue Clair and Henry entered. "Meet your Auntie Grace, Auntie Grace meet our Charlie."

"Ooohhh, hello, Charlie girl." Grace took her in her arms and stared down at her in wonder. "Aren't you precious? You're so precious." Grace started to well up.

An emotional Patricia tucked an envelope under Grace's pillow and then pecked her on the cheek. "Thank you doesn't seem to cut it." Before Grace could answer, Henry, Sr. did the same exact thing envelope and all. "It really doesn't." A teary Patricia quickly darted out of the room and Henry, Sr. followed his wife.

Grace looked at Henry. "Your family has to stop giving me things." He took a picture of Grace and Clair with Charlie, a picture of Grace and Charlie, and then he gracefully left the room. "So? I baked her at three hundred and fifty degrees like you said."

"She's perfect." Clair sat on the edge of the bed. "Charlie, this is your Auntie. She's the reason you're here. Thanks, for this," Clair said, as tears poured down her face.

Grace burst into tears. "You're welcome!"

"So, you know, after all the pushing and the crying and the dramatics in the delivery room, you're going to have to be the Godmother."

Grace hugged Charlie closer to her chest. "See, I *am* your Auntie Mommy."

Clair playfully slapped her as Diane came in. "No hitting the birthmother. It's against the rules. Now give the baby to Grandma, it's my turn to hold her!"

She reluctantly gave her the baby. "Hey, mom." Grace started laughing. "This turned out so much better than her ninth grade science project."

"A booger from a dead dog turned out better than her ninth grade science project!" They looked up to see George smiling at them. "Can Auntie George sneak a peek?" George crossed over to the left side of the bed, squeezed in next to Diane, and stared down at this little miracle. "You've done good, both of you. Hello Charlie, I'm your Auntie George. Your Auntie Grace and I are going to teach you all the things your mommy doesn't want you to know—like how to wear make-up!"

"And, how to cut curfew," added Grace. She looked up, saw Jack standing at the door and waved. Clair followed her gaze, saw Henry standing next to Jack, smiled at him and waved.

And that was it. The pregnancy was over—the precious Charlie girl had safely made it into the world unscathed. That's it you ask? When we were first told this wondrous tale, we asked the same thing.

More of the joys, sorrows, and hilarious complications that followed in the wake of the first year after the pregnancy have been told to us, but for you? Well, you'll have to wait. Why? Because like life, the story isn't really over and quite frankly, this book would be longer than *Gone With The Wind*, but because you have been such good sports we'll leave you with this...

What you just read was the almost totally true story of two sisters, but this modern day tale of love lost, love won, impatience, sacrifice, friendship, sex, loyalty, honesty, and at times indecision, drunkenness, flatulence, and cookie dough is far from over. Clair and Grace, with the help of their good friend George, as well as both Grandma Erickson and Nonie Higgins, will be back to continue the saga of the hilarious bedwetting, wedding stopping, cookie making, mistaken identity ridden, drunken, impatient, diet hating, unruly, loyal, heartbreaking, law breaking, joyous, and at times crazy, Higgins Sisters... and friends.

ACKNOWLEDGEMENTS

I must thank the wonderful Melissa Peterman, a remarkable and brilliantly funny woman, who gamely went on this journey with me and made it a joyful, fun-filled adventure. I must also thank John and Riley Brady who good-naturedly put up with our writing schedule, John for his array of colorful outfits and Riley who played with me and shared his toys.

The Figueiredo's Linda, Paul and Jacklyn who always have my back and always make me laugh. The Morewitz's Brian, Kira, Georgie Bell and Miles who are the best buddies and cheerleaders a gal could have. Andy Morewitz for his patience, support and friendship. My dude, Michael Fister, who always helps me see the bigger picture. Rebecca Green a great friend and one of the smartest and most loyal gals I know. Kim Dankner for her friendship and grammatical prowess. Mark Wood, the first person to read this novel and believe in it and in me. Shani Tuch and Dani Alpert for their unwavering support and for pushing me to take a chance and go for it. My gratitude gals Tiffany Zehnal, Johanna Whetstone, Janet Wood Suzy Shelton who pick me up when I'm down and continually fleece me when we play Bananagrams.

Laura Caldwell, Claire Cook, and Be Bettina Clairmont, for being the nicest, most supportive, informative authors out there and who graciously took me under their wings.

~Aimee

To my sister Julianne for the laughter, the fights, the late nights with wine, for our shared history, for being a great aunt to Riley, for sharing clothes but never guys and for being you. To George, you are my double negative and I am sure we were separated at birth. To Stina, we should never have been friends but we are. I promise to go camping with you if you never let me eat salted caramel in bed again. To Di, your probably sitting on my back patio right now and I never want it any other way, I love you all. And to Aimee, for making me write and making me laugh, you're simply an amazing lady.

~Melissa

Made in the USA
Lexington, KY
28 May 2015